THE LAST STOP

BEAR & MANDY LOGAN
BOOK 3

L.T. RYAN

with

K.M. ROUGHT

LIQUID MIND MEDIA

A Bear and Mandy Logan Mystery

L.T. Ryan
with K.M. Rought

❀ Created with Vellum

THE BEAR AND MANDY LOGAN SERIES

Close to Home

Under the Surface

The Last Stop

Over the Edge (Coming Soon)

1

RAYMOND FLICKED HIS LIGHTER AND HELD THE FLAME TO THE CIGARETTE dangling from his lips. When the tip burned cherry red, he took a deep drag and returned the lighter to his pocket. After holding the smoke for a few seconds, relishing the way his lungs burned, he exhaled toward the sky. His shoulders relaxed as the nicotine coursed through his veins.

It was two in the morning. The whisper of the wind through the cornfield sent shivers down his spine. Growing up here, you'd think he'd be used to it, but he'd seen too many horror movies in his youth to feel safe out here in *farm country*. Of course, he'd never admit that out loud, but he tried to avoid midnight strolls. Just in case.

Raymond forced his back to the crop, as though to prove to himself and anyone watching that he wasn't scared. A chill sped down his spine, and his stomach twisted in response. Pushing those feelings aside, he focused on the packed-dirt driveway instead, straining to see through the dark. They'd set up a couple of camping lanterns to load the truck full of packages, just enough light so they wouldn't trip over their own feet yet dim enough no one would be able to see them from the highway.

As Raymond stared into the night, something shifted in front of him. The darkness had coalesced into a figure now stalking toward him. He took an involuntary step backwards and stumbled over something, an ear of corn perhaps. His heart in his throat, he threw out his hands to regain his balance while focusing on the figure. This was why he didn't want to be out here in the middle of the night. You never knew what kind of psycho was out here.

"Ray," the figure snapped. The voice was low and gravelly. And familiar.

It was Luke Salazar.

Raymond let his shoulders relax. He took another deep drag of his cigarette, not letting his gaze wander from the other man until they were no more than a foot apart. In the meantime, he'd forced a bored look onto his face, though his heart was still pounding like he'd been stalked by a wild animal.

Luke looked Raymond up and down, spotting the cigarette in his hand and shaking his head. "Who said you could take a break?"

Raymond kept his cool. A hard thing to do around Luke, but the nicotine helped calm him. He took another puff and blew it into Luke's face. "What are you gonna do, fire me?"

Luke didn't flinch. "Get back to work."

Raymond held up the half-finished cigarette. "Give me a minute."

"Now." Luke used to be an easy-going guy, but lately he was on edge. Always ramped up to eleven. "We don't got time for this."

"It's not like he's here," Raymond said.

"He'll put a bullet in your brain. Or find an excuse to send you back to prison."

Raymond stiffened. "You told him about that?"

Luke shrugged. "Had to vet you." He paused a beat, seemingly waiting for further reaction from Raymond. "He don't care about it."

"Until he can use it against me."

"Until you give him a reason to use it against you." Luke snatched the cigarette from Raymond's hand, took a drag, then dropped it to the ground and scuffed it out with his boot.

It took every ounce of Raymond's willpower not to deck the other man. Luke had been the reason he'd gone to prison in the first place. They'd broken into that house together, but Luke had let Raymond take the fall. Acted like buying him a nice dinner after a year in a piss-stained jail cell made up for it. Raymond had chosen to be the bigger man, but he had Luke's number now. He knew better than to trust Luke.

Raymond chastised himself. If that were true, then he wouldn't be here right now. But he needed the money, and Luke knew that. The guy was good at what he did—convincing people to do what he wanted. And if Luke couldn't convince them, he'd blackmail them. Raymond was an open book, considering his arrest record was public knowledge. But Luke hadn't needed to do much convincing. All he'd done was promise Raymond a paycheck. But now, Raymond was wondering if it was worth the risk.

Luke eyed him, as if trying to read Raymond's thoughts.

Raymond brushed by the other man and walked back up the dirt road. He needed this job. And he needed to make sure he didn't end up back in prison. Not over something this petty. A few more months of loading boxes onto a truck in the middle of the night, and he'd be out of the hell that was Boonesville, Indiana.

2

BEAR TRIED AND FAILED TO IGNORE THE HEAT PRESSING DOWN ON HIM. HE had lost track of the hours he and Mandy had been on the bus. The air conditioner had given out about thirty minutes into their ride. At first, it had been nothing more than a slight inconvenience. But as the summer sun rose higher in the sky and knifed through the windows, he couldn't stop the sweat from beading along his brow.

Bear had mastered the art of shutting off part of his mind when needed. The part that harbored discomfort—heat, cold, pain, anxiety, all of it. Years of practice had taught him how to flip the switch and tune it all out. He normally saved it for life-and-death situations, but if he wanted to survive the next two hours, he'd have to tap into that part of himself. He was far too big for the seats, and while he'd been able to stick his left leg out in the aisle to relieve some of the pressure, his right leg hadn't been so lucky. Right now, it was jammed up against the back of the seat in front of him. Worse, the asshole sitting there had leaned all the way back. Pain shot down his leg, hip to ankle.

He'd considered waking the guy up to tell him to put his seat in the upright position, but the man had finally stopped yapping. Even his wife looked relieved to be listening to his obnoxious snoring rather than his every unfiltered thought. And Bear would bet money that everyone within a nine-seat radius felt the same way.

Instead, Bear did what he did best. He compartmentalized. Shut off the part of his brain that felt pain, then tuned out the noise around him. First, it was the whining engine of the bus, which had sounded like it'd seen better days. Then it was the constant murmur of voices, most of which were low enough to fall into the background, anyway. And the heavy metal screaming from someone's headphones. Last was Mandy, who had twisted around to kneel in her seat so she could talk to the woman behind them. Bear had seen the woman board, like he had everyone else on the bus. And like everyone else, she seemed ready to get to wherever they were going.

Join the club, lady.

Bear pulled a paper map from his pocket and unfolded it, snapping it open with a satisfaction that Mandy would never understand. She'd looked at him sideways when he'd bought it from the bus station, holding up her phone with a questioning look.

"Trust me," he'd said, "you'll be happy we have this." She'd rolled her eyes but had peered over his shoulder as he'd outlined their trip so far.

Leaving the Outer Banks behind had been easier than he'd thought. His childhood memories still pulled at him, but the more recent ones were reason enough to pack up his bags and take Mandy far away from the spit of sandy land. It wasn't like she was complaining. By the end, she'd been happier than him to leave.

Once spring hit and the weather cleared, Bear kept them on the move. Settling down had proven to be dangerous for his health, so they never stayed in one place for longer than a week. Mandy was happy not to be in school, but she was even happier when he took her to an amusement park for the first time. There wasn't a single roller coaster she couldn't survive, and even Bear was impressed with her iron-clad stomach. He couldn't always go with her—his height and weight made that difficult enough— but he was always there waiting for her when she got off, a wild grin on her face and excitement in her eyes.

In between theme parks, they'd snaked their way across the country. Bear couldn't remember the last time he'd traveled for fun, and he planned on taking advantage of every second Mandy was willing to spend with him. They'd seen the House of Mugs in North Carolina, the Salt and Pepper Shaker Museum in Tennessee, Dinosaur World in Kentucky, the American Sign Museum in Ohio, and the World's Largest Ball of Paint in Indiana. The latter had been less than impressive, but he and Mandy had made a game out of observing people and quizzing each other about them later. He won every time, but Mandy was getting better at taking in her surroundings and storing the information away, just in case.

Now they were in northern Indiana, traveling south toward St. Louis. Mandy was getting tired of the countryside, so Bear figured they could stop off somewhere with a few more people for a couple of days. St. Louis was a good bet. It'd be easier to blend into the crowd, even if there were a lot more cameras to dodge.

That voice in the back of his head telling him to keep moving was ever-present, and louder than it had been in weeks. Bear couldn't ignore it. It wasn't worth the risk of letting trouble find him with Mandy in tow.

Bear wasn't sure where that feeling was coming from. They'd been on the road for a couple of months, and nothing out of the ordinary had happened. Perhaps that was the problem. He was so used to dodging bullets and finding himself in the middle of some crazy conspiracy that he knew sooner or later the other shoe would drop.

Bear wondered what Mandy's life would've been like without him. What if he'd left her with someone better somewhere along the way? Would she be in school with lots of friends and getting good grades? He chuckled at the idea. Mandy threw him a confused look from her perch on the seat next to him. Mandy would still be Mandy, but she'd be in a stable home environment.

With Sasha gone and Jack Noble in the wind, all they had was each other. Maybe it was selfish, but Bear didn't know where he would go or who he would be without her at his side. And despite all the promises in the world, Bear didn't trust that she'd be safe with anyone but him. If someone kidnapped her and used her as leverage, there was no telling what he'd do to get her back.

His conscience wasn't appeased by much, but for the hundredth or thousandth time in the last couple of months, Bear had questioned and reaffirmed his decision. Mandy's childhood had been far from normal, but she was a good kid with a mind like a sponge. She could take care of herself, and it was Bear's job to make sure that never changed. As long as she wanted him around, he would be there for her. And he'd make sure she could take on anything life threw at her.

Bear turned and opened his mouth to ask her what she wanted for dinner in St. Louis when there was a loud grinding noise and the bus lurched to one side. A collective gasp went up from the passengers, followed by a scream when the bus lurched again. The driver slammed on his brakes. Bear couldn't stop his face from smashing into the seat in front of him. Mandy let out a strangled scream as she was thrown off-balance and tumbled to the floor in a less than graceful and unwilling backwards somersault.

Another bang, and the bus wobbled one last time before veering off the road and hitting a ditch beside the highway, tipping to one side and sending one woman straight out of her seat, across the aisle into someone else's lap.

So much for a peaceful drive through the Midwest.

3

BEAR HELPED THE BUS DRIVER UNLOAD ALL THE PASSENGERS ALONG THE SIDE of the road in front of a corn field on the other side of the ditch. The passengers looked panicked as they stepped off, perhaps concerned they'd be the one that caused the bus to tip. But the bus remained steady as they filed out, bags and all. The air whipped about, chilling Bear's sweaty brow. Assisting the other passengers gave him a sense of calm. Still, he couldn't help noticing the feeling of spiders creeping up the back of his neck. Sure, buses broke down all the time, but he hadn't gotten this far by believing in coincidences.

"Everything okay, Dad?" Mandy asked.

Bear still got a thrill whenever she called him that, even though he knew she did it for the sake of the woman who'd been seated behind them. He'd picked up on the subtle way the woman was listening in, seeing what he'd say.

Mandy tugged on his sleeve when he didn't answer right away. "What happened?"

"Not sure yet," Bear said, roughing up her hair a bit and dropping their bags at her feet. "Wait here."

Mandy grumbled and smoothed her hair down but didn't protest. Wandering over to the driver, who stood at the back of the bus with the rear-end cover open, Bear watched as black smoke billowed from the engine. The man waved a ragged cloth in the air in front of him, waiting for the fumes to disperse and trying not to choke in the process.

"I wouldn't get too close, son," the driver said. "That stuff is toxic." He was in his late sixties or early seventies, with a mop of thick white hair and a beard that made him look a bit like Santa Claus, though he was much too thin to pull it off. Bear had seen two young kids eyeing the man when they'd boarded the bus, whispering and standing up a little straighter as they passed.

"Any idea what went wrong?" Bear asked. He tried to peer closer, but the smoke was too thick. It burned his eyes, and he was forced to retreat and stand next to the driver.

"Won't know until the smoke clears, I'm afraid. Maybe not even then. I'm not a mechanic." The driver held out his hand for Bear to shake. "Thanks for helping me unload the other passengers. Appreciate it." Then he looked at Bear like he was seeing him for the first time. "Boy, you're a big one, ain't you? Must be something in the water around here."

Bear chuckled but didn't bother to correct him. "I'm good with my hands. Might be able to help you out."

The man shook his head. "Sorry, son, but I can't let you fiddle with it. Insurance and all that. Red tape. And if you got hurt? Well, they'd have my head. It'd make the papers." The man chuckled, but his eyes were serious. "I don't want to be one of those headline bus trips. Know what I mean?"

"Ah." Bear felt his heart sink. He looked left, then right. It was corn fields for as far as the eye could see. "So, we're stuck?"

"For now." With the smoke almost cleared, the old man stepped up to the engine and stuck his head as close as he dared. "Looks like one of the belts slipped free. Not sure how that could've happened. Must've been more than that, though, for it to smoke the way it did. I need to radio the shop back. They'll send someone out to fix it and haul the bus to the nearest station."

"What about us?" Bear asked.

"They'll send a new bus. But they don't have extras at the closest station. Might be a couple hours."

"A couple hours standing in a cornfield? We've got kids here. Older folks, too."

"I'm one of those older folks, you know." The bus driver gave him a pointed look. "It's the best we can do for now. Let's just pray we won't have to wait *too* long."

Bear nodded and headed back to Mandy. "Gonna be a while, kid."

Mandy groaned. "Seriously?" She pulled out her phone and started tapping away on it. "How long is 'a while'?"

"Couple hours, maybe more." Bear was already getting antsy. He spotted the man who'd been sitting in front of him talking the ear off of anyone who made eye contact. "We need to wait for the next bus. No clue where they're sending it from."

"I don't have any service." Mandy tipped her head back and groaned at the sky. "It's going to be a long couple of hours."

"And that's why I always carry a map with me," Bear said, fishing it out of his pocket. Mandy rolled her eyes, but then she leaned against him while he traced a finger along their route. "Caught the mile marker just before we broke down. We're about here."

Mandy sank a little. "There's literally nothing around us. How far away was the last town?"

"Maybe fifteen miles." Bear pointed to a little dot on the map west of them. "Boonesville is three miles in the direction we want to go. Wonder what the motel situation is there." He was tired of sleeping on the bus, and he could tell Mandy was too.

Before Bear could say anything else, the driver stepped out from behind the bus and used two fingers to whistle for their attention. "Listen up, everyone," he said, as they all crowded in close. "I've got good news and bad news. The bad news is our ride is busted. There's no way I can fix it out here. But the good news is we've got someone on the way to pick us up and take us to the closest station for the night. They'll be here in about two hours, so we need everyone to sit tight. The bus isn't going anywhere, so I'm going to open up all the windows and air it out. Once it's clear, you're welcome to return to your seats. Then, in the morning, I'll have a new bus, and we'll be back on our way to St. Louis."

"Why can't we just transfer to a new bus and go to St. Louis tonight?"

Bear asked. Sure, he'd rather spend the night in a hotel, but it'd be even better if that hotel was in the city they'd planned to be in.

"Because the driver picking us up is doing us a favor. He's been on the road all day, and by the time he gets to us, his shift will pretty much be up. We're not allowed on the road a minute past our allotted time. I know it's inconvenient, but it's the best we can do. Speaking of"—he continued, giving the crowd an apologetic look—"the motel that's agreed to let us stay the night doesn't have enough rooms for every single person. I'll need to know who here is traveling together, and which of you wouldn't mind sharing a room with one of your fellow passengers."

There was a grumble of disappointment from the people around them. "What about Boonesville?" Bear asked. "Are there more rooms there? It's only three miles down the road. Toward St. Louis."

The driver flashed him a very un-Santa Claus-like look of annoyance but managed to keep his voice even. "The bus won't be going to Boonesville. You're welcome to walk, if you like, and we can pick you up in the morning. But you'll have to be ready at seven sharp."

"We'll take our chances." Bear said, folding the map and swinging his bag over his shoulder. Mandy picked up her own bag, looking relieved. With their luck, they'd probably end up sharing a room with Chatty Charlie and his wife if they stuck around.

"If I don't see you at seven," the driver warned, "I'm hauling ass to St. Louis. We're already behind schedule. You won't be reimbursed, and they won't send another bus your way. You'll forfeit your ticket for leaving the group."

"Copy that," Bear said, turning around. Even at a moderate pace, it would only take them an hour to get to town. And after sitting on the bus for so long, it would be nice to stretch their legs.

They'd only made it about the length of a football field when a voice rang out behind them. Bear turned to see the woman Mandy had made friends with on the bus. She had corn-yellow hair, sky-blue eyes, and a bleached-white smile. Bear wondered if she'd been a gymnast in a previous life. While she was petite, her arms and legs looked strong, especially in her shorts and tank top. Her bag must've weighed at least thirty pounds, but she didn't struggle under its weight as she jogged up to them.

"Hey, Iris!" Mandy beamed. "You coming with us?"

The woman looked up at Bear. "As long as it's okay with your dad," she said. Then, more apologetically, "Sorry, but if I ended up rooming with that guy and his wife, I think I'd prefer to lay down in front of the bus instead of getting on it in the morning."

Bear hadn't thought anyone would be up for walking three miles to the next town, especially hauling their luggage, but he couldn't blame her for wanting to get as far away from Chatty Charlie as possible. Then again, he wasn't in the mood to make small talk with a complete stranger. Before he could say anything, Mandy tugged on his arm.

"Dad, please? Iris is cool. She was teaching me fun facts about Indiana before the bus broke down."

"You mean there's more than one?" Bear asked, grinning. He didn't want the company, but if she could entertain Mandy long enough for him to figure out their next move, he wasn't going to complain. "Yeah, sure," he said, not really feeling the truth behind the words. "The more the merrier."

4

THE WALK INTO TOWN WAS UNEVENTFUL. CARS PASSED THEM ON THE highway, but no one slowed down to ask if they needed help or a ride west. There was nothing but cornfields, and after a while, the scenery started to blur. Bear entertained himself with his own thoughts while Mandy and Iris kept up a steady stream of chatter. After the first fifteen minutes, he tuned them out, grunting in response whenever Iris lobbed a question his way. After the first two inquiries failed to garner any information, she stopped asking and focused on Mandy.

When they reached the small town of Boonesville, all three were sweaty and tired. It was the perfect early summer day—blue skies with fluffy white clouds, temperatures in the mid-seventies, and a slight breeze to cool them. Ideal for sitting on a riverbank, staring at the water with a beer in hand. Not for hiking along the highway to the middle of Nowhere, USA.

Technically, Nowhere was located in Oklahoma. Bear would have to remember to tell Mandy that later. For now, he needed a shower.

Badly.

Boonesville was what you'd expect from a small rural town in Indiana. Surrounded by farms, the main strip had all the necessities—a couple of restaurants, a post office, a hardware shop, and a place to get groceries.

There were a few other curiosities, like a small building filled with antiques and another loaded with used books, but it only took one glance to encompass the entire downtown.

Bear zeroed in on the bed-and-breakfast just off the highway. The tall, white house with maroon shutters and a navy-blue door looked ancient by most standards, but solid enough. Not that they had much of a choice. There was no motel, so it was either this or sleeping under the stars. And something told him Mandy wouldn't appreciate that experience as much as he would.

"Come on," Bear said, pulling open the front door. "Let's see what they've got available."

Mandy and Iris fell in line as they entered the establishment. The smell of coffee was so strong Bear's mouth watered. He could imagine the stack of pancakes he'd eat in the morning. He considered going to bed now, just so he could wake up early enough to get the first batch.

Everything about the B&B screamed *Grandma's house*. The front entrance was covered in rustic American décor. Hand-painted signs of the American flag. Farming tools hung on the wall like trophies. A slightly larger-than-average portrait of Jesus looked down on them. Doilies, potted plants and area rugs straight out of the fifties.

A few chairs were situated throughout the room, but a large desk in its center was the main attraction. Behind it, an older woman clicked away at a computer built in the nineties. Bear wondered if it was a stylistic choice given the rest of the décor. A sleek flat-screen monitor would've looked out of place amongst the rest of the furnishings.

Then again, they might not have needed or wanted anything more updated.

The woman looked up as they walked in. She had short curly hair, large round glasses, and a warm, easy smile. "Good morning! My name is Joyce. Lookin' to stay with us today?"

Bear walked up to the desk and returned her smile. "Yes, ma'am. Two bedrooms, please."

Joyce clicked her tongue and frowned. "I'm so sorry, but we only have one vacancy available." Her gaze flicked between Bear and Iris, probably wondering why they came in together with a kid if they didn't want to stay in the same room. "Is it just the three of you?"

"Two, actually," Bear said, putting a hand on Mandy's shoulder. "Me and my daughter. Is there anywhere else in town available for my friend?"

"I'm sorry, but I've got the only room within a fifteen-mile radius, give or take." Joyce sat a little straighter when she said it, and Bear got the impression she'd put her entire life into her business. Then she glanced at Iris. "There are some places I can recommend. If you go east, there's a town with a motel that should have some rooms available."

"I'm afraid that'd be a bit of a walk," Iris said. Then, when the woman pinched her brows in confusion, Iris continued. "We were on a bus heading to St. Louis when it broke down. The rest of the group went to check out that motel, but we decided to take our chances here. We had to walk a couple miles."

Joyce's eyes went wide. "Oh, dear. Well, the room does have a queen bed and a sleeper sofa. It's pretty comfortable. I've slept on it myself."

Mandy tugged on Bear's arm. "Dad, we can share, can't we? The bus is coming early tomorrow. We only need it for one night."

Bear didn't like the idea of sharing a room with a stranger, but he wasn't going to kick her to the curb, either. And he wasn't about to make Mandy go camping under the stars. Not without the proper equipment.

"It's up to you," Bear told Iris. "If you're comfortable, you're welcome to stay with us."

Iris looked like she was fighting with herself, but a few seconds later, she nodded her head. "Thank you. I appreciate that."

Bear nodded and turned back to Joyce. "We'll take the room."

Joyce was quick and efficient with the booking. "Breakfast is from six to nine every morning. It's made to order, but you'll eat it in the common area. Coffee is available all day. For lunch and dinner, I'd recommend the diner across the street. Order the French onion soup and thank me later." She spoke as if she'd said these lines a thousand times before. "The antique shop and the bookstore are open until eight. There's a bar one street over open until two. Since you're only staying the night, I won't weigh you down with too much information, but if you decide to stay longer, I've got a pamphlet of things to do around town and everyone's business cards."

"Appreciate it," Bear said, taking the room key when she offered it. "Which way to the elevators?"

Joyce smirked and pointed to her right. "Stairs are that way. You're on the top floor." She looked at Iris. "My grandson is in the kitchen if you need any help with your bags."

"I think I can manage," Iris said. "But thanks."

Bear led the way to the top floor and found their room. Every floorboard creaked and groaned under his weight. He inserted the skeleton key into the lock and twisted. The door swung open on well-oiled hinges. The three of them stepped through and took it all in.

"We landed in a florist shop," Bear said.

The walls, carpet, and curtains were various shades of green. The bedspread was covered in flowers, as was the tiny couch on the opposite wall. Vases of fake flowers sat on every surface, but the area rug tied everything together.

"Well," Mandy said. "This is something."

"That it is," Bear said. Turning to Iris, he pointed to the bed. "You can sleep there, if you like."

Iris looked at the couch, sized more like a love seat. The bed inside couldn't have been bigger than a double. "No offense, but I don't think you're gonna fit on that." When Bear opened his mouth to protest, she dropped her bag on the floor at the other end of the room. "It's for one night. I think I can manage."

"My back thanks you," Bear said.

"Oh no," called Mandy from the bathroom. She stuck her head back into the main room and gave them a pained look. "There are even more flowers in here."

Iris laughed and plopped down on the couch. "How did she even find a floral couch, anyway? It's hideous." Her eyes were bright. "I love it."

Mandy giggled. "Maybe at the antique shop. Or she got it flown in special just for this room." She turned to Bear. "Can we go to the bookstore?"

"I need a shower," Bear said. "And a moment to get my bearings."

Mandy nodded, knowing what he meant, but she couldn't hide the disappointment on her face.

"I'll go," Iris said, standing. She looked up at Bear. "As long as you don't mind?"

Mandy clasped her hands in front of her. "Please?"

Bear weighed his desire to keep Mandy in sight with his need to get his feet back under him. "Sure," he said. "But don't leave her side. Not even for a minute."

"I'll take good care of her," Iris said. "Might grab dinner, too. You can meet us at the diner if you want?" Then her eyes grew a little wider. "I don't think I ever got your name. I'm Iris. Iris Duvall."

"Riley" Bear shook her hand. "Thanks."

"No problem." She turned to Mandy. "You ready, kiddo?"

Mandy was already halfway out the door. "See you later, Bear!"

Bear shook his head and locked the door behind them. After his shower, he would debate the merits of eating or drinking first, even though he knew which would win out.

5

A BELL CHIMED AS MANDY PULLED OPEN THE DOOR TO ENCORE BOOKS. SHE stepped inside and took a deep breath. It smelled a little musty, but a hint of cinnamon in the air balanced it out. The shop was nice and cool, with plenty of little alcoves to explore.

It beat watching Bear break down his gun, clean it, and put it back together before checking every nook and cranny in the room for cameras or listening devices. Not that he would do that in front of Iris, but Mandy could tell he wanted to settle in, and every nerve in her body screamed that anything would be better than helping him do that. Including going to a bookstore.

A woman with curly brown hair popped up from behind the desk near the entrance, shifting a pile of books out of the way so she could peer at the newcomers. She was probably in her early thirties and wore a yellow and white floral dress. Mandy noted her characteristics in a single glance, just like Bear had taught her. Green eyes. Button nose. A beauty mark above her lip on the left side. She was short, just over five feet and wore silver jewelry and had painted her nails navy blue.

"Good afternoon!" Her smile was pure sunshine. "My name is Madge. If I can help you find anything, let me know. Thrillers are buy-two, get-one-free today. If there's anything you want that you don't see, let me know, and I might be able to get it for you."

"We won't be here long," Iris said. "Our bus broke down on the way to St. Louis, and we had to walk here to find a place to stay the night. Which way did you say the thrillers were?"

Mandy tried not to screw up her face in frustration. Iris was super nice, but she didn't mind giving away information about herself—or others—at the drop of a hat. Information was currency, and Bear had taught her to cling to it when she could. And she didn't think Bear would appreciate Iris telling everyone where they were heading next.

"You coming?" asked Iris, walking in the direction Madge had pointed her.

"Not a big fan of thrillers," Mandy said, turning in the other direction. "I'll be over here."

This was true. Mandy felt like her whole life had been a Ludlum novel, running from one place to the next, watching Bear fight off this bad guy or that in an attempt to find peace. She sometimes daydreamed about being a normal teenager—going to school and having sleepovers and maybe even a boyfriend. You know, something out of a Meg Cabot young adult book. But every time she tried to be normal, it backfired on her and those she tried to get close to. Like Jenny, back in the Outer Banks.

Shaking the memories from her mind, Mandy found the fantasy section and began perusing. She wasn't the strongest reader, but she liked escaping to different worlds full of elves and unicorns and dragons. It beat this reality, at least.

A pang of guilt stabbed her in the side. She didn't like being ungrateful for everything Bear had given her, and since leaving North Carolina, they'd had a whirlwind summer full of roller coasters and cheesy roadside attractions. She'd never admit it to him out loud, but she was the happiest she'd been in a long time. Maybe ever. It was easier to pretend she was on a road trip with her dad for the summer, rather than bouncing from place to place because it was too dangerous for them to settle down in one location. But they couldn't keep this pace forever, and she wondered where they'd end up next. Part of her wanted to go to California—Los Angeles or

San Francisco—and part of her wanted to hide out in the mountains of Colorado. Or maybe deep in the forests and deserts of Washington state.

"Find anything you like?" Iris asked from behind her, making Mandy gasp and spin around. Iris laughed. "Sorry, I didn't mean to sneak up on you like that."

Mandy drew her breath in long and steady, forcing her heart rate to slow as she took in the stack of books Iris held in her arms. All thrillers. "Looks like you did."

"Yeah, I eat this stuff up. It's so exciting." She frowned when she saw Mandy's hands were empty. "You didn't find anything? If you're worried about the price, I can pay for it. It's not a problem."

"I can afford a couple books," Mandy said, hating that it came out defensive. If only Iris knew how much money Bear had saved in the bank. Multiple banks, for that matter. She had the account numbers of seven committed to memory. "Just haven't found anything yet."

Iris must've realized how her question sounded because she set down her pile of books and started scanning the shelves. After a moment, she made a little sound of triumph, then pulled out one novel from all the others. "Here, try this one. I think you'll like it."

Mandy looked down at the cover. "*A Wrinkle in Time*," she read. "What's it about?"

"By Madeline L'Engle. A classic. It's about a young girl on a fantastical journey to find her missing father, who was working on a secret science project. And along the way, she fights through her insecurities to become a more confident version of herself. A leader."

Mandy didn't look up from the cover. Secret work? Out of all the books Iris could've pulled down, why did she choose this one? "Sounds interesting," Mandy said. And it did.

"You and your dad seem close," Iris prompted. "Did I hear you call him *Bear* earlier?"

Oops.

"Yeah. It's a nickname. Everyone calls him that."

"Even you?"

Mandy chewed the inside of her lip. *Information is currency.* Maybe if she gave a little, she'd get a little in return. "I'm adopted. Sometimes I call him Dad. Sometimes I call him Bear. He doesn't mind."

"I see."

"What about you?" Mandy asked, finally meeting Iris' gaze. "Are you close to your parents?"

"Not really," Iris admitted, no pain or regret in her voice. "My dad wasn't very nice. Not like yours. And my mom died when I was young."

Mandy didn't give her time to ask another question before asking her own. "Do you have any siblings?"

"Only child," Iris said, turning away to scan the shelves again. "What about you?"

"Same," she said. "Or at least I think I am. God, I hope I am."

"I always wanted a brother." Iris scooted down a few steps to look at a new bookshelf. "I thought it would be fun to be a big sister. But it wasn't in the cards." Running her fingers along the spines of several books, she asked, "Where are you guys from?"

"Here and there." It sounded a lot cooler when Bear said it. "What about you? Where did you grow up?"

"Florida." Iris made a face. "Too hot down there. Too humid. And a lot of weirdos."

"Bear says there's weirdos everywhere."

"He's not wrong." Iris picked up her books again. "Why are you guys heading to St. Louis?"

"We're just passing through." Mandy tried to sound nonchalant, but she didn't like all the questions Iris was asking. Then again, maybe Bear's paranoia was getting to her. Iris seemed normal enough, and after tomorrow morning, Mandy would never see her again. "Heading to the West Coast. My dad knows some people out there."

"I kind of like the Midwest, don't you?" Iris asked, looking wistful. "The simple life."

Mandy snorted. "More like the boring life."

"Boring isn't always bad." Iris's frown matched her tone.

Mandy couldn't argue. All she'd known was excitement for most of her life. It made normal seem boring and boring seem excruciating. Maybe she was an adrenaline junkie. Now that she'd experienced more than anyone else her age, she'd never be able to go back. She'd always be looking for the next thrill. The next hit.

"You about ready?" Iris asked. "We can grab dinner and then go back to our room. I don't want to keep you out too late. Your dad might think I kidnapped you." The corners of her mouth playfully twisted up.

Mandy gave Iris the chuckle she was looking for and followed her to the register, where Madge checked them out, humming in approval at their purchases. She even threw in a free bookmark for Mandy. *Reading is Magical*, it read.

Despite her reservations about spending the night in Boonesville, Indiana, Mandy was excited to dig into the novel and see how Meg saved her father from certain death.

6

BEAR HAD TAKEN A SHOWER, CLEANED HIS PISTOL, AND GIVEN THE ROOM A thorough once-over before feeling comfortable enough to leave. Even though they only planned on staying for a night, he liked to familiarize himself with his surroundings. Besides, he had time to kill, and it was better to do that outside of the room.

Boonesville was nothing special, though. The main strip held the most important buildings, and now that he was walking through town, he noticed that it did stretch out for a couple of blocks in each direction. There were plenty of small businesses and historic homes, with the occasional monument or fountain erected in the center of a garden. From the map in his back pocket, Bear knew there were a few hundred houses beyond the downtown area before giving way to farmland as far as the eye could see. In other words, more cornfields.

The town was quiet. Some families had ventured out of their houses for dinner at the diner. One young woman dropped a package off at the post office while a pair of teenagers stopped at the single-screen movie theatre to see what was playing. The building was so small, Bear wondered if they had any more than a dozen seats inside.

He didn't hate the small-town life, but it had its cons. The biggest being exposure. In a town this small, he felt as though a constant spotlight shone down on him and Mandy. Having been in this situation before, Bear figured the townsfolk would either leave him alone or get all up in his business. He preferred the former over the latter, but that didn't always get him what he wanted. Some people became more suspicious the longer he stayed and the more he kept out of their way.

The good thing about a place like this was the local food. Farm-to-table was the rage, and you couldn't get any closer to the farms than in this town. Fresh ingredients made for better meals. Same with the beer. That thought must have been what drove him forward, because when he found himself staring up at a sign for the Harvest Moon Tavern, his mouth was already watering thanks to the smell of seared meat and earthy hops.

Before he could take another step forward, a man stumbled out of the alleyway. Bear had just enough time to take in his ragged clothes and greasy hair before the man collided with him. Bear's reflexes took over, and he had the guy pinned against the wall while he reached for a gun that wasn't at his hip. He'd hid it in the room. Bear cursed and pressed his forearm across the man's throat, watching as his eyes bulged in response. The guy gurgled something, but it was just a string of meaningless sounds.

A second figure emerged from the bar, and Bear had to shift his focus to include both of them now. The other man was average height and stocky, wearing denim overalls and a plaid shirt with the sleeves rolled up. If Bear couldn't already guess he was a local farmer, the straw hat would've done the trick. The man looked to be in his sixties, with gray hair and a close-cropped beard. His eyes were dark blue and sharp as a tack.

"Whoa, whoa." The man said it without any alarm in his voice. He took a step forward but stopped when Bear angled his body as if to take on another threat. "Promise you whatever Carl here said or did, he didn't mean it, friend."

Bear didn't like the optics of the situation and let up on Carl's throat. The man gurgled again, but didn't move away, even when Bear took another step back.

"Name's Amos Wendell," the farmer said. "Don't think I recognize you."

"Just visiting," Bear said.

"Ah." Amos's eyes twinkled like he knew there was more to the story but understood not to ask. "That'll do it, then."

Bear looked back at Carl. "He okay?"

"Depends on your definition." Amos frowned and shook his head. "Man's had a tough life. Got into a rough spot a few years ago. Took to the bottle. And a few other things. Hasn't been the same since. He means well. Apologies if he stepped outta line. He don't mean anything by it."

"Just surprised me is all." Now that Bear had a better look at the man, he realized Carl wasn't close to being in his right mind. He sort of just stood there, swaying, his eyes blank. "Came out of the alley. Thought maybe he was gonna try to mug me."

"Do you realize how much bigger you are than the rest of us? He'd have a hard time of it, even if he wasn't in that condition." Amos chuckled. "You a big city guy?" When Bear shrugged, Amos nodded his understanding. "Not many muggings 'round here."

"S'pose not," Bear said. He looked Amos up and down one more time, then thrust his hand at him. "Name's Riley. Sorry about your friend."

"I wouldn't call Carl a friend. Still, seen the kid grow up. Hard not to feel for him."

"Kid?" Bear looked back at Carl. He appeared as though he were in his forties, at least. His eyes were bloodshot, and a string of drool seeped out of the corner of his mouth. As they stood there, he was slowly slipping down the wall. Soon, he'd be passed out on his ass, right there on the sidewalk.

"Drugs'll do that to ya." Amos nodded solemnly. "Lived here my whole life. Went to school with his mom. Saw him grow up. He was a good kid. Smart. Thought he'd go off to college and leave this place behind."

Bear couldn't help his curiosity. "What happened?"

Amos blew out a breath and shoved his hands deep into his overall pockets. "Guess he fell into the wrong crowd. Came and worked on my farm for a bit. His mom thought it'd be good for him. Build character." Amos shook his head. "Caught him stealin' from me. First time, I let him off with a warning. Second time, I sent him back home to his mom. I don't suffer fools."

"Can't say I blame you."

Amos scrubbed at his beard with a hand cleaner than Bear would expect from a farmer after doing a full day's work. "How long you in town for?"

Bear was back on guard. He liked Amos, but those kinds of questions weren't always followed with the best of reactions. "Just the night."

Amos tsked. "Too bad. Could use a big guy like you. Not as spry as I used to be." Carl tipped precariously, and Amos stepped forward to put an arm under the man's arm. "Guess I should get him someplace softer before he's down for the count."

"Need any help?" Bear didn't want to get involved, but it felt rude not to offer.

Amos smiled, like he knew where Bear's head was at. "Nah, you go have a drink. I'll get him where he needs to go. He'll be better by mornin'."

Bear stepped out of Amos's way and watched as the two of them walked down the sidewalk and turned a corner. Carl stumbled on occasion, but Amos was sure on his feet. Bear wondered how much the old farmer could carry and figured it was much more than the average sixty-year-old.

Shaking off the interaction, Bear entered the Harvest Moon Tavern, ready to wash this day down with an ice-cold beer.

7

DUSK WAS SETTLING IN. THE ESTABLISHMENT WAS BUSY, BUT NOT PACKED. There was a solitary man sitting at the other end of the bar, lost in his drink. By the slump of his shoulders, Bear could tell he was a regular. A couple of groups sat at tables on the other side of the room, laughing loudly and getting up occasionally to change the song on the jukebox. A woman sat nursing a beer at a table nearby and didn't look up when Bear entered. He assumed she wasn't waiting for anyone. Bear thought it might be funny if she and the guy at the other end got together and shared in their misery.

The bartender came out of the back as soon as Bear sat down, wiping the already-clean spot in front of him and tossing the rag over his shoulder. He was a burly man, closer to fifty than not, with a beard and a thick head of hair. His eyes were small and dark, which seemed out of place with the rest of him. Bear was still a head taller, but he wouldn't look forward to going up against the guy in a fight, regardless.

"New here?" the man grunted.

"What gave it away?" Bear asked.

"Your general lack of despair." The statement was accompanied by a wry smile. "What can I get you?"

"Whatever gets me closer to where that guy is." Bear pointed at the solitary man.

The bartender chuckled. "Roger that. Anything else?"

Bear checked his watch. He'd spent enough time walking around that he'd missed Mandy and Iris at the diner. "Cheeseburger. Bacon. Everything on it."

"Fries?"

Bear nodded. "Appreciate it."

"No problem." The man scanned the bar to make sure everything was in order before turning back to the kitchen doors. "Ten minutes."

No sooner had Bear taken a sip of his beer than the woman from the table slid in next to him, jostling his elbow and knocking over her own glass. It was empty now, but it clattered loudly and he heard a few of the people on the other side of the room react to it.

The woman leaned in close enough for Bear to smell the beer on her breath. "Hey, stranger."

He wanted to ignore her, but everything about her demeanor told him she wasn't going to pick up any subtle social cues. "Not really looking for conversation, lady." He wanted to enjoy his beer and burger, then get a good night's sleep.

"Me neither," she slurred.

She placed a hand on his arm, and it took everything in Bear not to jerk back. But when he looked down, there was a worn photo of a young boy, maybe twelve years old, clutched in her grip. She was staring down at him, rubbing his face with her thumb.

"My son," she said. After a moment, she tore her gaze away from the photo and looked at Bear. At one point in time, she'd been beautiful. Her brown hair was now mousey and dull. She wore makeup, but her lipstick was smeared, and her eyeshadow was too bright and bold. Dressed in a low top and tight jeans, her clothes looked like something that could've belonged to a teenager, not someone about his age. The lines on her face from a lifetime of worry had added ten years, minimum.

Before Bear could say anything, the woman spoke again. "Will you help me?"

Bear barely stopped the groan that escaped his mouth. What was it that made him look like a sucker? People used to be afraid to make prolonged eye contact with him. Now they asked him for his help at every turn. He should file a complaint.

"Look, I just want to enjoy my beer and—"

"He's fifteen now. Sixteen soon. Gonna start driving. I'm so scared." A sob escaped her mouth, but she didn't break eye contact. "Do you have a son?"

Bear's throat tightened. "A daughter."

The woman closed her eyes, as though envisioning what Mandy could look like. "She a good kid?"

"Yeah."

"Benji is, too." The woman opened her eyes, and they pleaded with him to believe her. "He is. But his friends are bad. Make him do things he doesn't want to do. Get him in trouble."

"Sounds like he shouldn't be hanging out with them, then." Bear stopped short of criticizing her parenting skills. He had no idea who this lady was or what she'd been through. Maybe she had an abusive husband. Maybe this Benji kid was a little shit, and she was too good of a mother to see past that.

"My husband died a few years ago." The slur in her speech had calmed down a bit. "Drugs. Always drugs. Too many needles. Cared more about that than us. He died, and I was so mad. I was furious." The tears she blinked back now had nothing to do with sadness. "But I thought maybe it would be easier without him. I could focus on us, me and Benji. Get our lives back on track. But then he met those friends, and he's doing the same things his dad did. Selling drugs. Getting into trouble."

Bear could picture it. All told, it wasn't a unique story. He'd heard hundreds of variations of it. Still, he felt bad for the woman. No one deserved to go through that. Bear wasn't sure what he would do if Mandy ever ended up in that situation. Maybe he'd be at the local bar spilling his guts to a random stranger too. But more likely, he'd hunt down anyone who tried to hurt his little girl.

The woman pressed the photo into Bear's hand. "Will you talk to him? Please? I don't know what else to do. Where to go. No one will help me."

Bear tried to give the photo back. "Have you gone to the police?"

She was already shaking her head. "They won't help. No one will.

You're the only one."

"You don't even know me. I'm here for the night, and then I'm gone."

"Please." The tears were back, and this time it was from utter devastation at the sheer thought of losing her son. She folded Bear's fingers over the photo. "You're big. You can talk to him. Scare him straight. Please."

The bartender chose that moment to come back with Bear's burger, placing the steaming plate in front of him. He looked at the woman to Bear's right and shook his head. "Cindy, I told you. You can't be bothering people."

Cindy patted Bear's hand where it was closed over the photograph. "He's gonna help me, Locke. With Benji."

The bartender looked at Bear with a knowing, apologetic look in his eyes. "I'm sorry—"

"It's fine." The last thing Bear wanted to do was cause this woman more pain.

Cindy slipped from her stool, stumbling for a moment before finding her footing and shuffling out the door without another word or backward glance. Bear watched her go, then turned back to the photo in his hand. Benji looked young and happy. Carefree. Like all kids should be at his age. The smile was so wide on his face that it was hard to imagine him as anything but. He looked a lot like his mom—or, at least, what she would've looked like when her life held more promise than tragedy.

"Want me to toss that for you?" Locke asked, holding out his hand.

Bear hesitated. "Is it true?"

"Which part? I'm guessing she told you about her husband? I don't like talking ill about the dead, but they're both better off without him."

"And Benji? He really selling drugs?"

The man shrugged. "I try to keep my nose out of other people's business. Hard not to hear the rumors, though. He's gotten into trouble a few times. Not sure about the drugs." He still had his hand outstretched. "Want me to take that?"

Bear slipped the photo into his pocket. "Nah. I'll hold on to it for now."

The bartender gave him a look like he'd seen this play out plenty of times before. Then he shrugged and walked to the other end of the bar. "Suit yourself."

8

BEAR HAD JUST TAKEN THE FIRST BITE OF HIS BURGER WHEN SOMEONE ELSE slid into the seat next to him. Was he wearing a neon sign that drew the desperate in like flies? There were half a dozen chairs open between him and the man at the other end of the bar, so Bear knew they were there to talk to him.

"Can't a guy eat in peace?" he asked.

"Sorry." It was Iris. "Just happy to see a friendly face. I can go sit somewhere else if you want?"

Bear grimaced. "No, it's fine. Sorry. I just had a weird conversation with one of the locals."

"That woman?" Iris looked over her shoulder at the door, where Cindy had disappeared. "Who was she?"

"No one I know."

"What'd she want?" Locke came over and looked at her expectantly. "Tequila pineapple, please. And a shot." Then she looked back at Bear, waiting.

Bear bit into his burger and chewed. He didn't want to have a conversation with Iris, especially about what had just transpired, but he didn't want to be rude. Considering they had to spend a night in the same room, it was just bad for business. He swallowed his mouthful of food. "Where's Mandy?"

"Back at the room." Iris laid some bills on the counter when Locke came back with her drinks. Taking the shot without wincing, she turned back to Bear. "You had the only key, by the way. We had to get Joyce to give us a spare. Mandy wanted to read. I was feeling antsy. Figured I'd come here for a drink. I doubt she'll get into too much trouble."

Bear snorted. She clearly didn't know Mandy very well. Then her words finally caught up with his brain. "She wanted to read?"

Iris took a sip of her drink, smacking her lips at the end. "*A Wrinkle in Time*. Did you ever read it?"

"Of course I've read it," Bear said, puffing up his chest. "It's a classic."

"After I told her what it was about, she seemed pretty interested." Iris' lips were quirked up at the corners. Her eyes were sly. "Why is that, I wonder?"

"Because kids like stories about magic and becoming heroes?"

"True." She bobbed her head, waiting for Bear to continue. When he didn't, a laugh escaped her mouth. "Or maybe she likes the idea of keeping her dad safe. Instead of the other way around."

"All dads are protective of their kids."

"Not all dads."

Bear had to give her that one. "All good dads."

After a beat of silence, Iris turned in her seat to face him. "Mandy thinks the world of you, you know. I wish I had a dad like you when I was a kid."

Bear grunted in response and took another bite of the burger. Washing it down with his beer, he nodded at Locke for another.

"You don't talk much, do you?" Iris asked.

"Only when I have something to say."

"You seemed to be talking to that woman quite a lot."

"She was worried about her kid. Guess I could relate."

"Oh, no." Iris' face pinched up in concern. "What's wrong with her kid?"

Bear sighed. This woman was relentless. "Drugs. Following in his father's footsteps. I didn't ask too many questions."

"Drugs, huh?" Iris had a lost look in her eyes. "Why you?"

"Because I'm big and scary," Bear said, tossing back half of his fresh beer. "She wanted me to talk to her kid."

Iris' laugh was low and delicate. "I don't think you're that scary. More like a big teddy bear." Her eyes grew wide. "Is that why Mandy calls you Bear?"

"All my friends call me Bear." He grinned, and he couldn't help giving it a sharp edge. "And it's not because I'm cuddly."

Iris was unfazed. "Well, I'll keep that in mind." She sighed. "Where are you from, Bear?"

He shrugged. "Here and there."

Iris snorted. Loud. "That's what Mandy said, too. You've got her trained well. You know, I don't mean to be nosy." Playing with her glass, she rolled it between her hands and watched the liquid slosh side to side. "I'm just a chatty person, and I like to know things. I'm from Florida, by the way."

"Too hot. Too humid."

"Too many weirdos."

"There are weirdos everywhere."

Iris cut a glance at him, her eyes dancing with laughter. Bear didn't know what it meant, and he didn't bother asking. He drained his drink instead.

"Excited to get to St. Louis tomorrow?" she asked.

"Is anyone excited to get to St. Louis?"

Iris shrugged.

"We're just passing through."

"So I've heard." Iris finished her drink, too.

Bear threw some bills on the counter and waved the bartender off when he went to get change. Under the guise of stretching, Bear surveyed the room and saw a few more people had come in while he'd been eating. But it was a far cry from overcrowded. Bear wondered how well the Harvest Moon did on a good day. They had great food. That'd help.

He was through the door by the time he felt Iris at his back. When he turned to look at her, she held up her hands in surrender. "Not following you, I promise. I'm gonna take a walk."

"At this time of night?" It wasn't late, but the sun had dropped below the horizon. "You want some company?"

"Nah." She smiled when he frowned. "See? This is why you have a reputation as a teddy bear."

Bear grumbled. He still didn't like the idea of her being by herself in a strange town. "You sure?"

"Oh, yeah." Her smile brightened. "I can take care of myself."

Bear watched her disappear down the sidewalk before turning back to the bed-and-breakfast, ready for a good night's sleep. Tomorrow, they'd be in St. Louis and away from everyone else's problems.

9

WHEN BEAR WOKE UP THE NEXT MORNING, IRIS WAS ALREADY GONE. HE wasn't sure how she'd managed to sneak out with all her belongings without waking him, but it didn't matter. Once they arrived in St. Louis, they'd be going their separate ways, regardless.

Mandy had stayed up far too late reading her book and was a nightmare to get moving that morning. Bear had dragged her from the bed by one foot and plopped her down on the floor, bedding and all. She'd grumbled with indignation but had hauled herself up and into the shower without much protest while Bear had gone downstairs to drink two strong cups of coffee and eat that stack of pancakes he'd been dreaming about.

He'd half expected Iris to be down there eating breakfast. She wasn't. Perhaps she'd gone across the street to the diner instead. Bear thought about asking Joyce or her grandson if they'd seen her, then decided he didn't care. They'd either see her at the bus stop, or they wouldn't.

Boonesville didn't have an actual bus stop. Bear hadn't wanted to take any chances, so once Mandy was ready and had eaten her own weight in pancakes, they marched out to the off-ramp with fifteen minutes to spare. The old man had told them seven sharp, and Bear wasn't going to risk getting stranded out here with their next destination within reach. Standing by the off-ramp ensured the bus driver would see them. And there was no way they'd miss the bus when it went by.

Mandy checked her watch at five of the hour, then tilted her face to look up at Bear. "Iris is going to miss it if she isn't here soon."

"She'll be here," Bear assured her. Iris had wanted to get out of town as much as he did.

Mandy frowned. "What if she doesn't make it?"

"Then she doesn't make it." When Mandy scowled at him, Bear adjusted his tone. "She knew the deal. Seven o'clock sharp. She was packed up before we were. Maybe she caught an earlier ride out of town."

"From who?" Mandy looked up and down the highway, which was shockingly empty. The only thing they heard was early morning birdsong. "What if something is wrong?"

"Not our problem," Bear grumbled.

It had just turned seven, and the bus driver had yet to show. The flat land around the highway offered clear visibility in any direction. Bear could tell the bus wasn't headed their way yet. Maybe the old man hadn't been as serious about the time as he'd appeared.

Five minutes went by. Then ten. By the time a half hour had elapsed, Bear knew something was wrong. No Iris, and no bus.

He ran through possible scenarios, if for no other reason than to pass more time. Either the bus had come by early or it was late. If it had come early, he should've been notified. The driver had known which town they had been staying in, and Joyce had stated she had the only accommodations in the vicinity. The driver could've called to tell them to be ready.

Or maybe he had. And that was why Iris wasn't with them. Perhaps she'd gotten the phone call and then left Bear and Mandy behind. But why? Iris had liked Mandy. Bear and the woman had a somewhat pleasant talk over a drink. It seemed too malicious to go out of her way to sneak out of the room and leave them to their own devices. It's not like they didn't already have a seat on the bus. Iris had nothing to gain here.

But the fact of the matter was that Iris had walked off on her own last night, then returned and retrieved her belongings without waking Bear or Mandy. It felt pretty damn deliberate.

Bear shook the thoughts from his mind. If the bus was late, their best bet was to wait for it here, in case it came by. It was a bit of a walk back to the bed-and-breakfast. If they tried to go back now, there was a better chance they'd get stuck in town.

Even if that was the case, that didn't solve the problem with Iris. Where was she, and why hadn't she shown up on time? Why had she taken her stuff and left? Bear should've checked the diner on his way out, just in case. Maybe she'd lost track of time.

Mandy looked up from her book, as though she could sense Bear's thoughts. "What now?"

Bear checked his watch. They'd been waiting for forty-five minutes. Something told him the old man wasn't coming, no matter how long they waited. "You hear anything last night? Iris coming back and getting her stuff? Her leaving this morning?"

Mandy shook her head. "Why wouldn't she have woken us up?"

"Don't know," Bear said, "but I'd like to find out."

Bear gave it another fifteen minutes, but it had become obvious that the bus wasn't coming for them. Without another option, he and Mandy headed back into town. When they walked through the front door of Joyce's Bed and Breakfast, the owner looked up at them in surprise.

"Didn't think I'd be seeing you two again," she said. "What happened?"

"Bus never showed," Bear said. "You don't have any messages from the driver, do you? About it coming early or late?"

Joyce looked down at a memo pad sitting at the corner of her desk and flipped through the top few pages. "Nothing here. I haven't been at my desk all morning, but I can usually hear the phone ring even from the kitchen. No one left a voicemail."

Bear bit down on a curse. "What about Iris? You see her at all this morning?"

Joyce shook her head. "I was up at five. Didn't see anyone coming or going at that hour." Her eyebrows pinched together. "She's not with you?"

Bear ignored the question. "Any chance I can use your phone? I'd like to call the bus company."

Joyce pushed the phone closer to him and sat back in her chair, expectant. Bear wondered if this was the most excitement she'd seen all month.

Was there a group of little old ladies in town who sat around in a circle and traded gossip? Maybe he and Mandy would be front page news.

Bear pulled out his ticket stub, dialed the phone number for the bus company, and sat on hold for close to ten minutes before someone answered. It took another ten for them to find the bus information. A woman with a strong Southern accent and a forced cheery disposition was on the other end of the line.

When the hold music clicked off, Bear stood a little straighter.

"Thank you for holding, Mr. Logan. We appreciate your time." The woman clicked her tongue in exaggerated disappointment. "Looks like your bus hit the road at six thirty-five this morning, according to our logs. It's on its way to St. Louis right now."

"On its way to St. Louis?" Bear did some quick mental math. "It was supposed to stop at Boonesville at seven to pick up three passengers. Why didn't it do that?"

"Hmm." The woman paused for a moment. "It seems there's a note here indicating those three passengers declined the pickup, so the bus passed through on its way to St. Louis."

Bear roared into the phone. "What do you mean declined the pickup? We didn't decline anything."

"I'm sorry, sir, but that's what the log indicates." The woman's tone was still sugary-sweet. "Is there anything else I can help you with today?"

"Yeah, you can send us another bus to take us to St. Louis."

"I apologize, sir, but that won't be possible." The woman didn't give Bear time to roar again. "We won't have a bus out that way for another two weeks. By declining the pickup, you forfeited your ticket. Would you like to book a new trip to St. Louis?"

Bear fumed. "Was it a woman?"

"I'm sorry, sir. I don't understand your question."

"Was it a woman?" Bear ground out. "Who declined the pickup?"

"The log doesn't indicate who declined the pickup, sir. Would you like me to book a new ticket for you?"

Bear hung up the phone instead of answering her. He looked down at Mandy and pocketed his anger for now.

"Well, kid, looks like we're spending another night."

Mandy looked at him, then at the woman behind the desk. "I wanted more pancakes, anyway."

10

BEAR BOOKED THEIR ROOM FOR ANOTHER NIGHT AT JOYCE'S BED AND Breakfast, much to the delight of the owner. Bear had asked Joyce for every possible way to get to St. Louis. There were no car rentals out here. No taxi services. The best she could do was a cousin with a truck who made weekly runs to the city. It'd be another few days before he left again, but it was the quickest way out of Boonesville. Joyce wrote the man's name and address down on a piece of paper, folded it up, and handed it to Bear. He didn't even look at it before shoving it into his pocket. Maybe they'd get lucky and find a way out before then.

After dropping their bags off, they made their way across the street to the diner. They'd both already eaten breakfast, but it beat sitting in the room stewing. Maybe a miracle would fall into their laps and someone would walk in with their ticket out of there. If anything, the coffee would fuel them for whatever came their way that day.

Sal's Diner was a relic of the 1950s. The building itself was a tin can, fitted out with light green siding and chrome accents. Inside, the tables and chairs looked to be original, if the scuff marks and broken vinyl were any indication.

And it smelled like heaven. Coffee blended with bacon and maple syrup. When they walked in, Bear took a deep breath and let it out with a smile, his mouth beginning to water. He looked down at Mandy, whose eyes were wide as she took in the place.

A woman approached them. Red hair pinned back in a smooth bun, and a frilly apron over a dress that matched the diner's exterior. She even wore low pumps and a pearl necklace. The look fit her so well, Bear couldn't decide if this was her everyday image or if she only dressed this way when she was on the clock.

"Welcome to Sal's Diner. Two?"

"Yes, ma'am." Bear pointed to the corner booth. "Can we take that one?"

"You sure can." The woman grabbed a pair of menus and led them to their seat. As they settled in, she pulled out a notepad and smiled down at them. "My name's Bette, and I'll be taking care of you today. What can I start you off with?"

"Coffee. Black." Bear looked at Mandy.

"Juice," Mandy said. Then her eyebrow twitched up. "Orange."

"Good choice. It's fresh-squeezed every day." Bette beamed. "I'll give you a minute to check over the menu. Let me know if you have any questions."

Bear looked at Mandy instead of the menu. As soon as Bette moved out of earshot, he gave her a subtle nod. "Pop quiz. Go."

Mandy rolled her eyes, but she sat up a little straighter. "Eight people. Six men, two women. First pair is a married couple in their sixties. He's wearing a white dress shirt and blue slacks with brown shoes. Long over-coat on the back of the bench." Mandy's eyes never left his. "She's wearing a blue and white floral dress with pearl earrings. Both have gray hair."

"What did they order?" Bear asked.

Mandy skimmed the menu. "He got Sal's special, with sausage instead of bacon. She ordered an omelet. Looked vegetarian, with peppers and mushrooms."

"Good. Next?"

"Younger couple, thirties. Not married. He's wearing khaki shorts and a blue t-shirt. She's wearing a black skirt and a white top. She ordered a breakfast sandwich with sausage. He ordered a stack of pancakes with bacon on the side. They're sharing it."

"Next?"

Mandy sighed and closed her eyes. "Old man at the bar, drinking coffee and reading the newspaper. Black pants, gray shirt. Two younger guys at another booth. They haven't ordered yet. Both in black shorts. One has a red shirt and the other—the one with the earring—is in orange. Last man is in his forties. Dressed like he just came in from a run. In black and green. Eating egg whites and bacon. Orange juice and water."

"Good. Which one has a tattoo?" Bear asked.

Mandy's eyes popped open. She looked like she was fighting the urge to turn around and scan the crowd. "Um." She hesitated, looking disappointed in herself. "I didn't notice a tattoo."

"Me neither." Bear chuckled when she scowled at him. "Just wanted to test you."

"Did I pass?" Mandy asked.

"You got an A. Good job."

"What did I miss?"

Bear's eyes never left Mandy's. "The young woman's top is pale yellow, not white. And the guy in the athletic wear didn't just come in from a run. His shoes are brand new, without a spec of dirt. And he left the tag on his shirt. Might've been on accident, but I doubt it. He's trying to impress people."

Mandy turned around and scanned the diner again. When she turned back, her mouth was twisted in disappointment. "Damn," she whispered.

"You did a good job," Bear said. "Takes practice."

Bette chose that moment to come back and get their orders. Bear couldn't stop himself from ordering French toast and bacon for them to share. The food was out in less than ten minutes, all piping hot and delicious. They dug in, and for a few minutes, they didn't speak.

The chatter in the diner was low, but Bear could tell Mandy was keeping her ears open while she ate. Just like he'd taught her. A surge of pride flooded his body, and he had to work to keep the smile from his face. The kid was stubborn as hell, and talking back was hardwired into her psyche, but those were good traits to have out in the real world. Meant people wouldn't push her around. He felt more at ease, knowing she could give as much as she got.

She was fifteen now, though he couldn't look at her without seeing that little girl he'd met all those years ago. They'd been through so much together, and it had changed Mandy, for better and for worse. But she was still just a kid. Innocent and naïve. Maybe not as much as her peers, but much more than Bear, who was older and had seen and experienced the worst parts of humanity.

He didn't wish that upon Mandy, but he hated the fear that clawed its way up his throat whenever he thought about her striking off on her own. In three years, she'd be a legal adult. If she wanted to leave, he couldn't stop her. And part of him didn't want to. Mandy deserved to see the world, to experience it on her own. But he'd be lying to himself if he denied that the bigger part of him wanted to keep her close and safe for as long as she would allow him.

"You're staring," Mandy said, not looking up from her plate.

Bear opened his mouth to respond, but movement from the corner of his eye caught his attention. Out the window, a group of three boys were walking down the middle of the street, laughing and yelling and seeing how far they could throw rocks. Bear couldn't tell if the aim of the game was to hit something or not. They all looked to be about Mandy's age, though there was one trailing behind on a bike that looked a year or two younger. He wondered if the kid was someone's little brother.

One of the boys looked familiar, and it took a second for Bear to realize it was Cindy's son, Benji, the one who had gotten caught up with a bad group of friends and was selling drugs, just like his dad had been. The kid was taller than the others, but he wasn't the leader. He was posturing. Even from a distance, the look in his eyes told Bear the boy was afraid.

"Can I get y'all anything else?" Bette asked, appearing by the table and dragging Bear's attention away from the window.

"I think we're all set, thanks."

"No problem. I'll bring the check right out."

Bear looked back at Mandy. If she had gotten mixed up with a group like that, he would've done anything to make sure she came home safely. Cindy wasn't handling it well, but Bear had no idea what the woman had been through. What kind of husband had the boy's father been? She'd turned to alcohol as a coping mechanism. That had torn plenty of families apart, but dealing drugs was another ballgame.

He thought about the man he'd seen outside the bar. After everything else that had happened in the last twenty-four hours, Bear had almost forgotten. That guy had been strung out on something, and he couldn't help but wonder if Cindy's son was mixed up with the same thing.

Not to mention Iris was still missing.

Bear shook himself. He didn't know that for sure. She wasn't at the bed-and-breakfast and she hadn't gotten on the bus, but she'd also collected her belongings and left without detection. Possibly called the bus company to decline their pickup. That indicated intent, though not necessarily a nefarious one, even if Bear's stomach twisted in discomfort.

"Listen," Bear began, and Mandy looked up at the sound of his voice, "I've got something to do. You okay hanging out in the room for a while?"

Mandy groaned. "What could you possibly have to do here?"

"Something I want to look into. Would rather not have you along, just in case. You still got your book?"

"I'm almost done with it. Then I'll be super bored." She smiled wickedly. "Then who knows what kind of trouble I might get up to."

Bette set the bill on the table in front of Bear. "Our dishwasher is out of town for a few days. Could use another one." She looked down at Mandy with a sparkle in her eye. "It's not great money, but enough to put some change in your pocket."

When Mandy looked like she was waffling, Bear chimed in. "I'll double it."

Mandy's eyes lit up. "Deal."

Bear handed a wad of cash to Bette. "Keep the change." He stood and gave Mandy a stern look. "I'll be back for you later. Don't leave. And listen to Bette, okay? Don't cause any trouble."

Mandy blinked up at him with her all-too-innocent eyes.

"Me?" she said. "Never."

11

MANDY WASN'T SURE HOW SHE FELT ABOUT DOING MANUAL LABOR WHILE Bear went after those boys walking down the street.

She wasn't sure why he'd been so interested in them. As soon as they'd strolled into view, he'd been laser-focused on the group. At first, she thought he'd spring another pop quiz on her, so she studied them without drawing attention to herself. There were three boys walking—one with sandy-blond hair, one with jet-black hair, and one with light brown hair— and one on a bike, also with black hair. Probably brothers. They all wore shorts and t-shirts, and three of them had ratty sneakers on their feet. One wore a pair of brand-new basketball shoes. They were stark white against the black pavement.

Bear had looked lost in thought while he stared after them, and when Bette had interrupted his train of thought, he was resolute. Mandy knew that face. No matter how much she begged and pleaded, she wouldn't change his mind. But she wouldn't stop herself from trying.

"Come on, kiddo," Bette said. "Let's get you set up."

"Mandy," she said. The last thing she wanted was to be called kiddo all day. What was it about that word? She was fifteen, after all. "My name is Mandy."

"Mandy," Bette said, by way of greeting. "Nice to meet you. This is an easy job, but a boring one. When I used to do dishes, I tried to make a game of it."

"You used to be a dishwasher?" Mandy asked. She wondered how long it took Bette to become a waitress. At least she got tips now.

"When I was about your age," Bette confirmed.

"And you've worked here the entire time?" Mandy tried to keep any judgment from her voice. Bette looked to be in her early forties. That was a long time at the same dead-end job.

"Not the whole time." Bette sounded wistful. "I moved to California for a couple years. Tried to be an actress. It didn't work out."

"Why not?"

Bette shrugged, and for the first time, she looked a little sad. "Expensive. Not my kind of town. Can you believe I missed this place? Los Angeles was too busy. Too dirty. I like to smell the clean air and see all the stars in the sky."

Mandy thought it smelled too much like manure but kept that to herself. She liked the same things too. Could she live in a town like Boonesville? They were stuck here for another night, maybe longer, and she was already going stir crazy and counting down the hours until they were back on the road.

The doors of the kitchen swung open at Bette's touch, and the waitress led Mandy over to the sink. Despite her full stomach, the smells emanating from the stovetop made Mandy drool. Maybe she'd work up an appetite again, and Bette would give her a free lunch.

Bette pointed to the man making pancakes on the griddle. Now that Mandy had a better look at him, she realized the guy had to be in his seventies. He looked strong, and the way he handled his knife and spatula told her he was quick, too. "That's Sal. He's owned this place for sixty years. He doesn't talk much. Try to stay out of his way, and you'll get along fine. Just stick to the dishes, okay?"

Mandy nodded and turned toward the sink. The soapy water already looked dirty, and there was still a huge pile on the counter.

"I assume you know how to wash dishes?" Bette asked, one eyebrow quirked up.

"Yes ma'am." Bear made her do the dishes since he cooked.

"Good. Pretty standard, then. Try not to get the floor too wet. It can be slippery."

"What happens if I get them all done?" Mandy asked.

Bette's eyes twinkled. "There's always something else to clean." She pointed to a garbage can against the wall. "And you can take that out back when it gets full. New bags are on the shelf over there."

Mandy heard the door chime as someone new entered the restaurant. The stovetop was situated in front of a window facing the dining room, so Mandy could keep an eye on everyone coming and going. That reminded her.

"Bette?" she asked, just as the woman was about to pass through the kitchen door. "Did you see a woman come in earlier this morning? Blonde hair and blue eyes. Her name was Iris. She probably had her bags with her."

"Don't think so, honey." Her eyebrows pinched together. "She a friend of yours?"

"Kind of. We came in on the bus together. I just wanted to say bye before we left."

"I'll keep an eye out." Bette winked and went to greet the newcomers.

Mandy fell into an easy routine after that. The diner was busy enough that she always had something to do, but not so busy that she couldn't let her mind wander. Sal liked to play Big Band music on the little radio sitting on the counter next to him, and Mandy liked that there were no lyrics. It let her think without too much distraction.

Every time someone new entered the restaurant, Mandy made a mental note of what they looked like and how they behaved. She separated them into categories like *morning person* and *disgustingly in love* and *definitely fighting about something*. To her annoyance, the *suspicious* category was empty, but she still found a way to entertain herself. Even though she couldn't hear anyone speaking from the dining room, she managed to read some lips and get the gist of everyone's conversations. As far as she could tell, no one was talking about her or Bear, the newcomers.

In between washing dishes, when she couldn't find anything else to clean, Mandy opened her book and read a page or two. *A Wrinkle in Time* was so different from all the other books she'd been forced to read in school. Maybe because she'd picked it up voluntarily.

It wasn't just that Meg was relatable, but the world itself. Or worlds, rather. Mandy had traveled all over the world, but she'd never seen anything like the places in this book. Maybe by the time she was older, they'll have figured out how to travel to different planets or realities. She vowed to be the first person on that spacecraft.

Mandy had finished one more chapter, disappointed that the book was going so fast. She went to place it on a shelf out of the way of the water and missed. The book tumbled through the air, and she had to swat it out of the way of a puddle she'd created from splashing around too much. But when the novel hit the floor, it bounced, and a piece of paper fluttered out of the binding.

Sal turned at the noise, and Mandy mumbled an apology. Confirming nothing had broken and Mandy wasn't injured, Sal returned to the vegetables he was chopping. As soon as he had, Mandy snatched up the book and tucked it under her arm, then retrieved the note, which was now a little wet around the edges. It was from Iris.

Mandy,

Don't show this to your dad, okay? And don't worry about me. I can take care of myself. Hope you enjoy St. Louis. Eat some toasted ravioli for me, will you? Stay safe. I'm sorry I didn't say goodbye.

Iris

She read the letter three times before it registered. Iris had left on purpose, but she'd wanted Mandy to know she was safe. She had wanted to say goodbye but didn't. Or couldn't. And she didn't want Bear to know any of this.

Why?

Mandy debated on throwing the note away but decided to tuck it back into her book. She didn't want to betray Iris' request, but Mandy didn't like keeping things from Bear. Not when they felt this important, anyway. What if there was some clue in the letter that Mandy had missed, and Bear would be able to see?

She needed some air. The trash wasn't overflowing, still she hauled it out of the garbage can anyway and tied the top shut before slinging it over her back. It probably weighed half as much as she did, and she was proud her legs didn't give out under its bulk.

Tossing it above her head and into the dumpster out back proved to be more difficult, and it took her two tries before getting it on her third attempt. Letting loose with a little cheer of victory, she faced the mouth of the alley and let the breeze cool the sweat on her brow.

All thoughts of the letter were wiped from her mind as she turned toward the street just in time to see a kid with jet-black hair whiz by on his bike.

12

BEAR STROLLED AWAY FROM THE DINER. HE IGNORED THE URGE TO LOOK over his shoulder and check on Mandy through the front windows. Plenty of people were in there, and Bette would take care of her if needed. He'd been surprised when Mandy agreed to the job, but he knew all too well that earning your own money was one of the best incentives out there. Especially for a teenager.

The boys he'd spotted from the window were about a block and a half ahead now. They weren't quiet, so it wasn't hard for Bear to follow. He didn't have to be right on their heels to keep an eye on them. The kid on the bike seemed more nervous than the others. Bear caught him looking over his shoulder a few times. The kid never alerted the others to Bear's presence.

Bear took his next right turn and cut down a parallel street, kicking up his pace until he could hear the group just ahead of him and off to the left. All his old habits fell into place. The way he kept a subtle eye on his surroundings by looking at the reflections in shop windows. How he would stare up at the sky or a large tree as though appreciating nature's beauty. He stopped short of pulling out his phone and pretending to take a call, however. These were just a group of kids, after all, and there was no indication they were up to no good. Yet.

Even if he managed to scare the boy straight today, he doubted the kid would change his attitude overnight. Once Bear left town, the threat would be gone. No one would stop him from going back to his friends.

Bear had decided to turn around and not waste his time when he heard tires squeal and an angry honk, followed by hoots of laughter. He turned back toward the main road just in time to see the driver of the car —a young woman, maybe seventeen—flip off the boys and tear away. Maybe they knew her from school, or maybe she'd been the unfortunate victim of a prank.

Either way, the kids crossed the street and headed down an alley, turning right at the far end. The kid on the bike stopped and threw a look over his shoulder, checking to see if the coast was clear. Bear slipped behind a tree, certain the kid hadn't seen him, and waited for him to follow his friends. Once he did, Bear picked up the pace and shadowed them across the road, pausing at the corner of the alleyway.

Halfway down the block, the three kids were standing against the brick façade of a building. The sandy-haired boy lit a cigarette while the other two shuffled away from him. He rolled his eyes and blew smoke in their direction.

"Come on, man," one dark-haired kid said, waving it away. "My mom will kill me if she smells that on my clothes."

"Tell someone who cares, Brent." The sandy-haired kid took another puff, this time blowing up into the sky and away from the others. "When's this guy gonna show up?"

Benji checked his watch. "Any minute now."

"Better have all our money this time, or I'm gonna be pissed." The sandy-haired boy's face turned dark. "We can't show up short again."

"You mean *you* can't," Brent said. "You really thought they weren't going to notice?"

The other kid took a final puff of his cigarette and flicked it at Brent, who cried out in surprise.

"The hell, Jake?" Brent said. "What's your problem, man?"

"You." Jake pushed off the wall and got in the other kid's face. "You're here because I let you be here. I know how much your family needs the money," He sneered, allowing time for the words to sink in. "So why don't you shut up and mind your own business?"

Benji stepped between the two of them when it looked like Brent was going to swing on the other kid. "Shut up." He glowered at both of them. "He's here."

A man emerged from the shadows across the street, stumbling towards the boys, who stood together despite their bickering. Jake took a step forward. He was tall for his age, but skinny. The guy approaching them was slim too, but he was in his twenties and had a lot more muscle. If he hadn't looked half out of his mind, Bear would've been worried for the boys. As it was, the newcomer didn't look like he could swing on a toddler without falling over.

Jake crossed his arms and tilted his head up so he was looking down his nose at the man. "You got the money?"

The other guy sniffed, looking the kid up and down. "You got the stuff?"

"We're good for it." Jake slipped something out of his pocket and held it up. "Are you?"

The man snatched at the bag, but Jake was too quick. At the same time, the other two boys stepped up and blocked the man from getting any closer. They were just kids, but they still outnumbered him. And they were a lot more coherent.

After digging around in his pockets for a few seconds, the man emerged with a fistful of money and smacked it into Brent's outstretched hand. Brent counted through it twice before giving Jake a curt nod. Jake tossed the baggie at the guy, but it sailed past his outstretched hand and fell to the ground. The man scrambled to pick it up, then dumped out a portion of whatever was inside and threw it straight into his mouth. A shiver of relief visibly ran through him.

Bear had seen enough. He stepped out into the open, not bothering to conceal his approach. He wanted to see how the boys would react to a newcomer, and he was not disappointed. The first to spot him was the man, who ran away as fast as he could. That alerted the others to his presence.

The moment the three of them spotted him, Jake's eyes grew hard, but Brent's widened and he took a step back, like he wanted to run. Jake grabbed a fistful of his shirt and kept him in place. For his part, Cindy's son stood his ground too, but he looked more wary than his leader.

The kid on the bike, though, didn't hesitate. The moment he saw Bear approach, he kicked off and sped down the street, away from all of them.

"This is a private meeting, old man," Jake called. "I'd turn around if I were you."

Bear scowled at being called an old man. Kids were too bold these days. "Good thing you're not me, then." He looked them each in the face. "What did you sell him?"

"We're not telling you shit," Jake said. His voice was even. Tough. But as Bear got closer, he looked less sure of himself. Maybe he hadn't been able to tell how big Bear was from halfway down the block.

"I suggest you reconsider." Bear looked at Benji. "Your mom's worried about you."

The kid scowled, and Jake's face split into a wide grin. He shoved Benji's shoulder. "Seriously, dude? Your mom's so lame."

"Hey." The low growl of Bear's voice had all three snapping to attention now. "I suggest you boys straighten up before we have a problem."

Jake rolled his eyes. "Listen, man, we're not afraid of you. Why don't you mind your own business before you do something you regret."

Bear reached out and grabbed a fistful of Jake's shirt, yanking him closer, almost lifting the kid from the ground. Jake cried out as his shirt began to rip, but Bear didn't let go. He brought the kid within inches of his face, so there was no chance in hell the kid didn't hear every word Bear had to say.

"Listen up, you little prick. There's always going to be someone bigger and badder than you. Today, you're lucky it was me." Bear grinned maniacally. "I'm a good guy." He let the smile drop. "The next person you piss off might not be."

"Please don't hurt him." Benji was trying to tug Jake out of Bear's grip, almost in tears. "Let him go. Please."

Bear shoved the kid to the ground. "Go home. All three of you. And I better not catch you selling again. You got me?"

The boys didn't say a word as they helped Jake to his feet and then dashed off down the road. It was answer enough for Bear.

13

Luke's basement. The last place on Earth Raymond wanted to be, yet here he was.

It was organized chaos. Half the shit was the guy's grandmother's old furniture or family keepsakes. The old lady had died a few years back, and Raymond had helped Luke sell off as much as he could. They made a couple thousand dollars from selling her furniture to the antique store in town. The rest of it had gone to a yard sale. Not all of it had sold, so Luke had shoved the remains down here. He'd given Raymond half the cash for helping. It was right after Raymond had gotten out of prison, and it was enough to get his feet under him. But that money hadn't lasted long.

The rest of the basement held Luke's paraphernalia. The gaming area comprised a new TV and recliner, an older sofa—which Raymond sat on now—and a floor lamp held together by duct tape. No one would accuse Luke of being rich, but Raymond knew how much that television had cost. It was the first thing Luke had bought with his grandmother's money.

Beyond the gaming area were stacks of boxes and equipment to set up Luke's operation. Not all of it was here. Some remained at a couple friends' houses. Luke was looking to expand. Until he found a better place, most of it had to stay in his basement where he could keep an eye on it. Especially since he was trying to hide it from more people than just the cops.

Raymond leaned forward and put his head in his hands. Why was he here, getting mixed up with Luke Salazar again? They'd been best friends when they were kids, but that relationship had died the minute Raymond had gone to prison for the guy. Luke had tried to make up for it, letting him crash here for a while, giving him that cash to get started, and giving him a job when no one else would hire him. But if Raymond got caught with any of Luke's products, it'd be a fast track back to a jail cell. No friendship was worth that.

Making up his mind, Raymond stood and crossed the basement. He had one foot on the bottom step when he heard voices above him. Luke had invited Raymond over to ask him something, but the guy always had to bullshit for twenty minutes before getting around to the point. With a beer in hand, it usually didn't bother Raymond, but he was too on edge. And he was trying not to drink like he used to. That's what had led to his stint in jail the first time.

But before Luke had had a chance to ask Raymond for whatever favor, someone rang the doorbell upstairs. Luke had told him to hold on, going up to see who it was. Raymond hadn't been able to make out any words, but the voice sounded like it belonged to a kid. Maybe it was Luke's brother Jake, who seemed to be following in his brother's footsteps. Raymond had thought about talking to the kid and trying to set him straight, but it wasn't worth the fight. Luke had this crazy idea that he was setting up an empire, and Jake would take it over someday. Except he treated his little brother worse than anyone else.

At the bottom of the stairs Raymond could hear what they were saying. It wasn't Jake, but he still recognized the voice. One of Jake's friends' little brothers, he thought. Bobby, maybe? The kid was only ten and way too young to be hanging out with Jake and the others. Then again, Raymond couldn't talk. He'd gotten up to much worse at that age.

"—came out of nowhere." The kid was out of breath and huffing between every other word. "Ran as soon as I saw him."

"What'd he look like?"

"Big. Brown hair and a beard. Didn't recognize him."

"Any tattoos? Scars?" There was a tinge of anger in Luke's voice, but Raymond couldn't tell if it was directed at the kid or this mysterious stranger. "Was he with anyone else?"

"He was alone." Bobby's voice came out a little steadier now, but he still sounded afraid. "Didn't see any tattoos or scars, but he was wearing a jacket. I'm sorry—"

"Where's Jake?"

"I left him behind. I can—"

"Go find him. Tell him to come back here. No stops on the way." Luke paused, and Raymond tried to envision the look on his face but couldn't. "And tell him to leave his punk ass friends at home."

Bobby didn't answer, and Raymond envisioned him hopping back on that bike of his and speeding away as quickly as he could. Sure enough, he could hear the dirt and stones kicking up from the tires. A second later, the door slammed shut, and Luke's footsteps stomped above. Raymond had just enough time to make it back to the couch before Luke came back down.

Even if Raymond hadn't been eavesdropping, he would've noticed Luke's mood shift.

"Everything okay?" Raymond asked, trying to sound nonchalant. "What was that about?"

"You see a new guy in town? Big motherfucker with a beard? Sticking his nose where it don't belong?"

Raymond shook his head. "Why? Who is he?"

"Don't know. But I'm about to find out." Luke sat in his recliner and kicked his feet up. "We got another problem."

Raymond had a feeling that even if it wasn't his problem, Luke was about to make it his. "What is it?"

"Lily."

That was the last name Raymond expected to hear. Lily was Luke's on-again-off-again girlfriend and had been a pain in his ass for years. Luke had a lot of vices in his life, but Lily was the worst one. They'd fight one day, then be all over each other the next. No matter how many times she dumped him, he always chased after her. Always won her back.

"Look man, I'm not really good at dating advice," Raymond started.

Luke shook his head. "It's not like that. She's become a problem."

"*Become* a problem?" Raymond laughed, ignoring the sharp look from Luke. "Dude, she's *been* a problem."

"She's been *my* problem," Luke said. "Now she's *our* problem."

"How do you figure?"

"She gave me an ultimatum." Luke hesitated, and it was so out of character, Raymond's stomach tightened in response. "I either give up the operation, or she goes to the cops. She thinks I'm in over my head."

For once, Raymond had to agree with her. This operation of his was dangerous. Luke had suppliers, but his job was to manage the driver who distributed the fentanyl to the closest cities. His boss was paying him well too, and Luke didn't even have to be out getting his hands dirty. He had his own guys for that. But Luke couldn't stop there. He had started a side hustle to get some extra cash. Cutting other stuff with the fentanyl. It was working for now, but it was only a matter of time before he got caught. And Raymond had no intention of being around when he did.

"Maybe she's got a point." Raymond kept his voice neutral. He wasn't about to get into it with Luke over this, but it needed to be said. "You'll get caught, and it won't end well for you."

"It won't end well for you either," Luke said, matching Raymond's tone. "She knows about you, man. If she goes to the cops, you think they're going to let you off with a warning?"

Raymond stood up so fast, his vision darkened around the edges. When his head cleared, he glared down at Luke. "Why does she know I'm involved? Why'd you tell her?"

Luke shrugged and spread his hands like it wasn't a big deal. "It just slipped out."

"Slipped out?" Raymond grabbed at his hair and pulled. "What the hell, man? I'm not going back to prison."

"Then I suggest you do something about it." Luke was still sitting, but his voice held an authority that towered over Raymond. "I'm sick of dealing with her bullshit."

"Then why don't you handle it yourself?"

"If anything happens to her, I'm the prime suspect. I gotta have an alibi."

"If anything happens to her?" Raymond let Luke's words sink in. When he caught the other man's meaning, he stumbled back to his seat, desperate to light a cigarette right about now. "You can't be serious."

It was Luke's turn to stand. "Look, I ain't giving this up. Not for her or anybody else. She wants to threaten me? She's gonna have to live with the consequences. It's been over for a long time. She wants me to choose? Then I'm choosing."

"And you want me to—" Raymond broke off. His stomach was in his shoes now. "I can't. If I get caught—"

"Don't get caught." Luke turned and walked back over to the stairs. He paused on the first step and met Raymond's gaze. "You do this for me, and I'll set you up for good. Get you away from here. One last favor. I promise you that."

Like an idiot, Raymond believed him.

14

BEAR WAITED UNTIL THE KIDS WERE OUT OF SIGHT BEFORE MOVING. THEY didn't even look over their shoulders as they ran down the street and turned the corner. He had no idea if what he'd said to Benji would wake him up, but he hoped it gave the kid something to think about. Jake was the ringleader, which meant it might not matter what Bear said to the others. That kid knew his friends well and would find a way under their skin if he wanted them back on his team. But Bear felt a little better having done something.

Bear walked back the way he'd come. He shoved his hands deep into his pockets and rediscovered the note Joyce had given him earlier that day. He had hoped another way to escape the small Indiana town would've come to him in the last hour or so, but it seemed like the woman's cousin might be his only chance to get to the city within the next two weeks.

With an air of defeat, Bear pulled the note out of his pocket and opened it, coming to a stop as he digested the name and address. With a chuckle, he emerged from the alley, back onto the main street, and walked in the opposite direction from the diner. Mandy would be safe and occupied for the next few hours, enough time for him to make his introductions.

Or re-introductions, as it were.

Twenty minutes later, Bear walked up a gravel driveway in plain view of a two-story farmhouse surrounded by cornfields on one side and pastures full of a dozen cows on the other. This was the kind of home Bear had envisioned Amos living in, and he wasn't disappointed. The house was white with brown shutters, and though it looked its age, an obvious addition to one side gave it a modern appeal.

A rusty old truck sat in the driveway next to a much newer black Ford F150. Bear had ditched his own Ford a while back, relying on buses and trains to move him and Mandy across the country. He could pay cash that way. And that helped them to remain anonymous. But he'd kill for his own ride right about now.

Bear stepped up onto the freshly painted porch and knocked on the front door. The creak of a floorboard was not caused by anyone walking to the door, but rather the house settling. Only silence ensued. After a minute, he knocked again. When he raised his fist for a third time, there was a bark behind him, and he turned to see a blue heeler sitting at the bottom of the steps. Its brown eyes were sharp, set against a patchwork of gray and black fur.

"Well, hello there." Bear stepped off the porch, and the dog stood, turned around, and took a few steps before looking over its shoulder at him. "You want me to follow you?" When the dog barked and took off toward the barn, Bear chuckled and trailed after it.

The air out here was clean and crisp, and he liked the sound the breeze made as it wound its way through the fields, rattling husks and leaves. There were a few clouds in the sky today, but they were white and fluffy and scattered and moving quickly. As they passed in front of the sun, he felt some respite from the heat.

Ahead, the dog slipped between the barn doors, then barked twice. Bear heard a man's voice answer but couldn't make out what was said. As Bear approached, he was careful to make his presence known. The last thing he wanted was to be greeted by a shotgun to the face.

Poking his head inside, Bear caught a whiff of manure and hay before spotting Amos with a pitchfork, removing old feed and throwing it in a wheelbarrow. The farmer was dressed much like he had been when Bear met him, though his clothes were dirtier than they had been outside the bar the night before. Two sets of matching overalls, perhaps. One for work, the other for dress. His hands reflected the work he'd already done that day.

Amos looked up when Bear's silhouette blocked out part of the daylight filtering through the barn doors. "Well, I'll be." With a grin stretching across his face, Amos stopped what he was doing and leaned on his shovel, pushing his straw hat up to reveal a sweaty brow. The dog waited at his feet for further command. "Didn't expect to see you again. Thought you were just in town for the night."

"So did I. The universe had other plans."

"God works in mysterious ways." Amos's eyes twinkled, and Bear couldn't decide if it was with hidden knowledge or something more mischievous. "Maybe you're meant to be here."

"I am still looking to leave." Bear didn't like asking for favors, but the pressure to get him and Mandy out of town was mounting. The urge that kept him on the move—the one that had kept him alive for so long—was getting harder to ignore. And with St. Louis a good five hours away in one direction, he knew it wouldn't be easy asking someone to drop everything to take them there. "I heard you might be able to help with that."

Amos took off his hat and scratched at his head, then replaced it and started shoveling again. "Who told you that?"

"Joyce." Bear leaned up against one of the wooden supports for the barn. "Said you make a trip to the city once a week."

"Won't be for another few days," Amos said, stopping again to lean on his shovel. "I'll have to make room for you. Won't be a free ride."

"Prefer it that way." Against his better judgment, Bear could feel his hopes getting up. "Happy to pay my way, either in cash or labor."

"Would prefer the labor." Amos kicked the side of the wheelbarrow, overflowing with feed. "I got an opening right now if you can start today."

Bear thought of Mandy back at the diner. She wouldn't expect him for another few hours. Coming back smelling like manure was less than ideal, but they had a room with a shower, and he had a few changes of clothes.

He could do laundry before they left. The biggest annoyance would be the trek back and forth between town and Amos's farm, but he could do it for a few days.

Bear stepped forward and reached out a hand. "Got yourself a deal."

Amos shook Bear's hand, and his dog barked its agreement. Chuckling, the old farmer gestured to his friend. "This is Daisy. Had her from a pup. Smartest dog I've ever been blessed to know. Swear she used to be human."

"Must get lonely out here." Bear grabbed the wheelbarrow and followed Amos out behind the barn to his compost pile. "You live by yourself?"

"For a few years now." Amos looked back at the farmhouse, his expression turning somber. "Wife died five years ago in January. Had a baby girl together, though she's not a baby anymore. Got a kid of her own. My granddaughter." He pulled out a photo of a girl who looked to be about Mandy's age. "She's older than this now. In college. Send 'em money when I can, but farmin' ain't for those lookin' to get rich."

Bear thought of the addition on the house and the new truck in the driveway. "Seem to be doing okay for yourself."

"Yeah, I get by. Lotta people in town bring me their old furniture to fix. That helps." The man tucked the photo back into his wallet and led Bear over to a four-wheeler with a cart hooked up on the back. "Got a fence that needs repairin'. Might as well do it while I got two extra hands. You up for it?"

Bear looked at the little four-wheeler, which had seen better days. "Not sure it'll hold my weight."

"How you feel about walkin'?" Amos asked.

"Better than trying to fit into that cart. I'll make it."

Amos pointed to the top of a hill. "I'll meet you up there." He turned to the dog. "Daisy, you keep him company, all right? Make sure he doesn't wander off."

Daisy barked once and looked up at Bear, her tongue lolling out the side of her mouth. He chuckled and scratched behind her ear, and she didn't even flinch when Amos started up the ATV. The toolbox and pile of wood in the back rattled as he made his way across the field, but everything stayed put.

Bear looked down at the dog. "Come on, girl. We're burning daylight. Time to get to work."

15

FOR THE REST OF THE DAY, MANDY'S THOUGHTS WERE PREOCCUPIED BY THE letter from Iris she'd found in her copy of *A Wrinkle in Time*.

When had Iris slipped it between the pages? Mandy had had the book on her since she'd bought it, so the only opportunity Iris had was while they had been sleeping. Bear hadn't heard Iris come back for her stuff and leave again, and neither had Mandy. Goosebumps traveled down Mandy's spine as she imagined Iris sneaking in and out that night, and never feeling the woman's presence.

That led to another question. Who was Iris Duvall?

Mandy hadn't thought she was anyone special. Sure, she was pretty and smart and funny. Iris liked to talk a lot, and she was kind of nosey, but Mandy hadn't thought that was suspicious. Some people were just friendly, and Iris had appeared painfully ordinary. Even Bear hadn't seemed too concerned by her presence, not even when he'd decided they could all stay in the same room together. If he'd had any doubts, he would've come up with an excuse to stay somewhere else.

But why had she slipped the note into Mandy's book? Iris must've known leaving in the middle of the night would look strange, otherwise she wouldn't have told Mandy she could take care of herself.

Don't worry about me. Mandy wasn't familiar with the woman's handwriting, but there was nothing suspicious about the note. It didn't seem rushed or like it'd been written under duress. In fact, it was nice and neat, like Iris had written it in good lighting, on a flat surface, like a desk. Had she written it after she and Bear had parted ways outside the bar? Or had she written it much earlier?

And then there was *that* part of the letter. The part where Iris had told Mandy not to tell Bear about the note. Did Iris think Bear would be concerned and look for her, anyway? If she didn't want to be found, why not just say goodbye? Or just say nothing at all. No note. No, nothing. It seemed more and more likely that she'd been the one to cancel their bus ride to St. Louis, even though the note ended with a wish for them to have fun in St. Louis. All that did was ensure Bear stuck around town even longer.

Frustrated, Mandy stuck her hands into the sink's warm, soapy water. After a few seconds, she came up with the last plate and scrubbed it clean. The diner was a little slow at this point in the afternoon—too late for lunch and too early for dinner. She'd already taken out the garbage, wiped down the counters, and asked Sal if he needed her to do anything else. All he did was grunt and shake his head.

Drying her hands, Mandy closed her eyes and tried to put the puzzle pieces together. Iris had left voluntarily, presumably, and didn't want anyone looking for her. Did that mean she was on the run from something, or someone? Did she have a plan? One that she couldn't let Bear get involved in? Mandy was flattered that Iris had decided to write her a letter to say goodbye, but she almost wished the woman hadn't. At least Mandy would've had fewer questions.

Opening her eyes, Mandy looked through the order window and out into the empty diner. Bear would probably be gone until dinnertime, so she had another couple of hours to kill. Tossing her apron on the counter, Mandy pushed through the swinging doors and caught Bette fiddling on her phone in one of the booths.

Bette looked up at her with a smile when she approached. "Hey, kiddo. What's up?"

Mandy tried to hide her dismay at being called 'kiddo' again. "Not much. Anything you need done out here?"

"Don't think so. I've already filled all the shakers and made sure all the ketchup bottles were full." Bette looked around like something might jump out at her. "Dinner rush should be coming in an hour or two. There'll be more to do then."

"Am I allowed to take a break?" Mandy asked. She'd been thinking about maybe stopping back at the bookstore. She was almost done with *A Wrinkle in Time*, and she wanted to see if there were any other books like it. "To walk around the block or something like that?"

"Of course." Bette checked her watch. "How's fifteen minutes? If no one else comes in while you're gone, maybe we can reorganize the pantry. It's been needing an overhaul for a while, but it's too much for one person to do on their own."

Mandy didn't think that sounded like fun, but it beat standing around asking herself the same questions about Iris. "Sure. I'll be back in fifteen. I just want to go to the—"

A woman outside entered her field of vision, and Mandy's next words stuck in her throat. There was no mistaking that corn-yellow hair walking down the opposite side of the street. Mandy didn't remember Iris having a green jacket like that, but maybe she'd bought it from somewhere around town.

"Something wrong, honey?" Bette asked, following Mandy's gaze out the front window.

"I think I see my friend," Mandy said, in a daze. Before she knew it, Mandy was running through the doors and across the street, ignoring Bette's shouting behind her, and chasing down a woman she never thought she'd see again.

16

IT HAD BEEN A WHILE SINCE BEAR HAD DONE SO MUCH MANUAL LABOR, AND despite staying active, he knew muscles he hadn't used in some time would be sore tomorrow. Nothing beat honest work with good company, and Bear had had a full day of both.

Amos had lived in that farmhouse his whole life. It had been his parents' before him, when the town was much smaller and the price of corn much lower. They had died when he was young, and he was forced to take over the family business halfway through high school. But he never looked back. It had provided him with honest work for close to fifty years. It's where he had married his wife. Where he'd raised their child. It held all his memories, good and bad. His whole life was tied to the farm.

Bear had been happy to help. Not just in exchange for the ride to the city, but because the outside world ceased to exist when you were working hard. Other than thoughts of Mandy, Bear didn't think about much besides the task in front of him. It was refreshing to put all his anxiety out of his head. For once, he wasn't worried about what could happen a week from now. All that mattered was the next hour.

Walking back to town allowed him to immerse himself back into the real world, like a free diver coming back to the surface. He needed time to adjust to the pressure that existed outside Amos's home. It was an uncomfortable feeling, but it came back to him without much effort.

The unanswered questions bouncing around inside his brain bothered him—not because he was worried, but because they presented an unknown.

First and foremost, Bear wanted to know where Iris had gone and whether she was okay. Part of him worried about her safety. She'd disappeared in the middle of the night, after all. But another part was curious about where she had gone and how she'd managed to sneak in and out without waking him. Then, of course, there was the fact she was presumably the one who canceled their bus ride to St. Louis.

But there was a second layer of mystery to the situation: this town. Those kids were far too young to be selling drugs to grown men, like the one he'd seen earlier. Bear wasn't naïve—he knew kids did that in school —but why were they the ones out in town, selling to the locals? Why wasn't it someone older, with more power and edge?

Bear tried not to think of the fear and pain in Cindy's eyes, but he kept coming back to it. *What if it was Mandy?* The last thing he wanted was to get involved in small town drama, but that train had left the station the second he'd decided to follow those kids down the street. Now it was only a matter of time before the consequences of his actions caught up to him. What form would they take this time?

Some of the tension left his shoulders as he closed the distance to Sal's Diner. He didn't like letting Mandy out of his sight, but she was fifteen now. She wanted, and deserved, more freedom. There would be plenty of time for her to be afraid of the world. For now, he wanted to stoke the fire of her curiosity. As much as it pained him to think about it, she'd want to strike out on her own someday. And he'd be damned if he didn't prepare her for that.

Getting a job and taking care of herself for a few hours a day was a good start. He'd already ramped up her training in anticipation of this. First, they had worked on her observation skills, making sure she knew her surroundings well enough to predict and anticipate problems. That started with people-watching and ended with making the call of whether to remove herself from a situation. For now, that was her only exit strategy. In the future, it might not be an option.

Mandy was ready for more—hand-to-hand combat and various weapons training had already started. He knew she could handle it, but part of him wanted her to retain her innocence. It wouldn't last forever, and he wanted to nurture it for as long as possible. But soon enough, the world would come knocking, and he'd have to make sure she was ready for it.

The smell of Sal's cooking permeated the air a block from the diner. Bear's mouth watered, followed by his stomach growling. Amos had made him lunch, but that had been hours ago. He was already gauging how much he could eat, and whether he could get Mandy to pay for it with her newfound cash.

Chuckling to himself at the thought of her rolling her eyes at the idea, Bear pulled open the door to the restaurant and heard the comforting ring of chimes as he did so. The dining area was less busy than he'd thought it'd be, but Amos had let him go just before the dinner rush.

Bette stood from one of the booths and joined him at the door. "You just missed her." Bette paused, looking thoughtful. "You know, I don't think I ever got your name."

"Riley," Bear said, still processing what Bette had said. "What do you mean, I missed her? She was supposed to stay here."

"I think she's coming right back." Bette's face fell when she saw the seriousness of Bear's. "She said she saw a friend out the window. Wanted to say bye to her."

"Friend?" Bear's stomach tightened. "What friend?"

"I don't know her name. But I saw her out the window. Looked older than Mandy. Not her age, you know?"

"Blonde hair?" Bear asked. He was already halfway out the door.

"Yeah. Is she okay?" Bette frowned, and there was real concern there. "Is she in trouble?"

Bear didn't answer. He had too many competing thoughts and his stomach sunk. Why was Iris still in town? And why had she reemerged the minute Bear had left Mandy on her own? What was going on here?

17

MANDY KNEW SOMETHING WAS WRONG WITH IRIS THE SECOND SHE'D started following the woman. Mandy called out, but Iris hadn't turned around or even indicated she'd heard Mandy. At this point, she was just out of shouting range, and Mandy's shorter legs meant she was falling behind. She could run to catch up, but she didn't want to spook Iris or bring any attention to them.

Besides, she wanted to watch from afar and see where Iris would go.

Heart pounding, Mandy followed her target, just like Bear had taught her. Stay out of their direct line of sight. Don't look too interested. Hang back and keep your eye out for trees to slip behind or alleys to dart into. The biggest tip Bear had instilled in her was to anticipate her target's next move, but that required knowing her surroundings, and she wasn't familiar enough with Boonesville, Indiana. Bear probably already had the town memorized, but Mandy had spent her time with her nose in a book. She was kicking herself over it now.

Iris had taken a right down one of the side streets, and Mandy hurried to cross the road to keep the woman in view. Traffic was starting to pick up now that it was closer to dinnertime, and Mandy felt torn about it. On the one hand, it meant more people seeing her and watching her every move. On the other, more people to help if something went wrong.

A pang of worry lit up Mandy's entire nervous system like a control panel with a short circuit. Bear wouldn't be happy that she left the restaurant, even if only for a few minutes. Then again, knowing why Iris left and why she'd canceled their bus ride might be worth the trouble. As angry as Bear would be, she knew he'd want those answers, too.

And that was only if Bear found out. Maybe she'd get back to the restaurant before he knew she was gone.

Sticking close to the sides of the buildings, Mandy noticed a man emerge from the shadows with a cigarette in his hand. Mandy considered calling out to warn Iris, but the guy wasn't subtle. He shouted something Mandy couldn't hear, and Iris turned around to see who it was. Mandy ducked behind a tree before either could spot her, then counted to ten before sticking her head back out. The pair of them were walking side by side now, and Mandy had to hurry to catch up.

Even from a distance, she could tell the two were arguing. There was something familiar between them. Strange, considering Iris hadn't seemed like she'd known anyone in town. Hadn't she ended up here by accident too?

Rounding the corner, Mandy was surprised to see the buildings give way to a field across the road. Like everywhere else in this stupid town, it was a cornfield. Seriously, did they eat anything else? Was it all corn on the cob and cornbread and corn pudding and corn pie? She wasn't sure that last one was a thing but knowing how much the people of Boonesville apparently loved corn, she wouldn't be surprised.

Darting from one tree to another, Mandy moved closer to Iris and the man, who had stopped on the side of the road. They were still arguing, but she still wasn't close enough to hear what it was about. As their voices got louder, she could hear their tone.

Mandy took in the man's appearance for the first time, now that she had a better vantage point. He had dark hair and a tanned face. Tall and lanky, but still muscular. His clothes were baggy and seemed old and worn. There were a few tattoos on his arms, but there was no way she'd be able to see what they were from this distance. She might not be able to identify him later.

Something didn't sit right with Mandy about the guy, and she patted the little knife she kept tucked into her boot. It wasn't big, but it was sharp, and Bear had taught her the best places to strike, just in case. The last thing she wanted to do was hurt someone—or worse—but she wasn't the type of person who could sit idly by, either.

It was a risk, but Mandy sprinted forward to another tree, about twenty feet away. She stopped behind it, breathing hard, and listened for any shouts of surprise or approaching footsteps. Hearing none, she peeked her head around the trunk and took in the scene before her. In only a few seconds, it had changed wildly.

The man flicked his cigarette and lunged to wrap his arms around Iris' biceps, gripping them tight enough that she cried out in pain. He was shaking her violently, and her knees were collapsing beneath her. All of a sudden, she was on the ground, and he was on top of her. Something flashed in his hands that could only be a knife, and that's all the incentive Mandy needed.

She darted out from the tree and ran. Bear would yell at her for this later, but she didn't care. Instinct had taken over. Instead of running away from the situation, she ran straight for it. Pulling out her own blade, she prayed she'd be able to get to her friend in time.

18

BEAR WAS FRANTIC WHEN HE EMERGED FROM THE DINER ONTO THE STREET. He hadn't thought to ask which direction Mandy had gone in, but Bette had followed him out of the diner and pointed down the road.

"She went that way, then turned onto the street down there. Do you want me to call the cops?"

"No." That was the last thing they needed. "I'm sure she's fine. Just wanted to make sure she's not getting into any trouble. You know how kids are."

Except Mandy wasn't most kids.

She'd gotten herself into trouble plenty of times, like when she saw fit to sneak out of the house and spend the night in a submersible that ended up getting washed out to sea in a rainstorm. But Bear was more concerned about what kind of trouble might find her out here. Boonesville wasn't exactly a hub for criminal activity, but even that group of kids could hurt her if they wanted to.

Walking at a brisk pace, Bear racked his brain for any reason Iris would still be in town. She'd disappeared in the middle of the night with her belongings and left him and Mandy stranded. Why would she come back? Why even show her face at all? Was it to lure Mandy away from Bear? He couldn't imagine she'd do something like that, but Mandy was just about the only way to get to Bear. He would do anything to keep her safe.

No one is after you, he reminded himself. No one knew he was here, and even if they did, why would they want him? His records were wiped clean. A free man, he was tied to nothing and no one, except his daughter. But just because there wasn't a paper trail didn't mean people forgot what Bear had done. Plenty of people out there would still love to put a bullet in his brain. And that wasn't even considering what Jack Noble had been up to these past few months. It was reasonable to consider that someone would go through Bear and Mandy to get to him instead.

Quickening his pace, Bear rounded a corner and heard a scream—half fear, half rage—and sprinted toward it. Without a doubt in his mind, he knew it was Mandy. Was she hurt? Would he be too late? His thoughts turned to instinct as he charged forward, his gaze landing on a small group of people across the road. On the edge of a cornfield, a few of the stalks were bent like they had been fighting, or someone had tried to drag one of them out of view.

As Bear approached, he could make out the scene. A man lay on his back, a knife stuck in his throat. Blood pooled from the wound, but even from a distance, Bear recognized the handle of Mandy's knife. Quick and decisive, she had pierced the artery, right where Bear had instructed her. The man wasn't moving. Now or ever again.

To the right were two more bodies. A woman lay on the ground, one leg at a strange angle. A smaller person—Mandy, Bear realized—held the woman's head in her lap. Bent over the woman, her body shook with sobs. When Bear got close, Mandy's head snapped up, and Bear could see the panic in her eyes before it was replaced with momentary relief and then anguish.

"Bear," she choked out. The sobs were coming harder now. "I didn't know what to do. He was hurting her. I tried to stop him." She looked down at the woman. "I thought it was—I tried to stop him. But he hit me. And I was scared. And I just reacted. I'm sorry—"

Bear was there now, taking his little girl by the shoulders and hugging her tightly, trying to protect her from everything that had already happened. Mandy refused to let go of the woman, refused to let her be alone. It took Bear a few seconds, but he realized it wasn't Iris, though they looked strikingly similar. The same blonde hair, the same blue eyes, though these were staring up at the sky, lifeless.

Mandy's words had turned incoherent, and her shaking sobs sent vibrations throughout Bear's entire body. It shook him to his core, and something angry and distraught settled into his stomach. His little girl had killed someone—in self-defense, sure, but it would haunt her for the rest of her days. She'd always question whether it was the right move. Would never forget what she'd done.

Bear pulled Mandy away from the dead woman and sat her down a foot or two away. He could already hear sirens and wondered if Bette had called the cops. Or had someone seen it all unfold? Even if there was footage, Mandy's DNA was everywhere. Her knife. Her fingerprints. Bette had seen the direction she'd gone in, had seen Bear follow in her footsteps. It wouldn't be hard to put two and two together.

But that didn't mean Bear had to make it easy for them.

As he started to stand up, Mandy cried out, gripping his arm tighter. His heart squeezed in protest, but as the sirens approached, he knew he only had a few seconds. Forcing her chin up, he made her look him in the eyes.

"I need to do something real quick. I'm not leaving you. I'll be right back." Dropping his voice, he put an edge of command into it he knew she'd respond to. "Do you understand?"

Unable to speak, she nodded her head, tears still flowing down her cheeks. Bear stood, this time without protest from Mandy, and walked over to the woman. There was a purse on the ground beside her, and Bear pulled her wallet from the bag and threw it as far as he could into the cornfield. Maybe the cops would find it, maybe they wouldn't. But it'd slow them down. Distract them.

Next, he walked over to the man. He thought about taking the knife from the man's throat, but what difference would it make? Mandy was covered in blood, beside herself with regret and grief. They'd figure out what happened sooner rather than later. Instead, he pulled a wallet from the man's pants and threw it in the same direction as the woman's. It'd take forever to find them again, but it was a risk he was willing to take.

The cops sure as hell weren't going to give him that information, so he'd take it himself.

Bear returned to Mandy a few seconds before two police cars screeched around the corner and pulled to a stop a dozen feet away from them. Four cops got out of their cruisers, raising their guns and yelling at him to step away from Mandy and put his hands in the air.

"Everything is going to be fine," Bear whispered to her, ignoring their commands for the moment. "Don't tell them anything. You give them nothing, you understand?" Mandy's eyes were wide as she took in the scene before her, nodding subtly enough that the cops couldn't see. "You don't say anything to them without me in the room."

"Hands up! Face down on the ground! Now!"

Bear spent one more precious second taking in every inch of Mandy's distraught face before complying with the orders. The second he landed on the ground, two of the officers rushed forward and placed him in handcuffs. Another approached Mandy, noting the blood on her clothes and face. With only a second's hesitation, that officer took out her handcuffs and wrapped them around Mandy's wrists.

Bear's heart broke into a million pieces.

19

BEAR TUNED OUT THE OFFICER'S WORDS AS HIS MIND WENT INTO OVERDRIVE. He'd been placed in handcuffs before. He knew the drill. Nothing they said would be a surprise. As long as he didn't put up any resistance, he'd be able to make it out of this okay.

The two were escorted in separate cars back to the police station. Two of the officers stayed behind to secure the scene, and Bear was grateful the woman was the one to drive Mandy to the station. Bear had seen the nondescript building on the other end of town a few times since arriving but hadn't paid any attention to it. The parking lot was out back, so if it weren't for a small sign in front, he wouldn't have known it was the jail at all.

Bear had stayed silent the entire ride. Not that the officer in the front of the car had tried to ask him any questions. The man kept his eyes forward, on the road, while Bear craned his neck around, trying to keep Mandy's car in sight. He couldn't see her through the tinted windows and knew she couldn't see him either.

The minute they arrived, Bear allowed himself to be pulled out of the police car, only to dig his heels in until Mandy emerged from her own vehicle. He waited to lock eyes with her before relenting to the officer's demands. With a single look, he tried to express all his love and care for her, but her eyes were glazed over, and she only stared at her own feet as she allowed the female cop to guide her through the doors. He had never seen her eyes so vacant, and if his heart wasn't already shattered, seeing her falling into shock finished the job.

Bear didn't put up any resistance after that. He didn't want to give them any excuse to keep them longer than necessary. The fact of the matter was they had no motive for either him or Mandy, and it wouldn't be hard for any attorney to argue that what had happened was in self-defense. But the entire process would still be traumatizing for Mandy.

Another officer joined them at the door and led the group to a separate room for booking. With two officers guarding him—and the third looking on warily—Bear's handcuffs were removed briefly before being secured around a metal bar in front of a stool on the other side of a desk. He'd been through this process before, and he could count on one hand the number of times he'd been given the courtesy of removing his own belongings from his pocket. The officers at the scene had already confiscated his wallet and searched him for weapons, finding none, but they did a second pat down, anyway.

Mandy's handcuffs were removed, and the female officer explained everything she was doing before searching her. Unlike Bear, Mandy was allowed to remove her own jewelry and shoes before sitting down on the stool next to him. The officer elected not to restrain Mandy again, and though Bear was grateful, he had to shake his head at their lapse in judgment. Sure, she was young, but he could all but guarantee Mandy would be able to get the upper hand to escape if given the chance. Not that she was in any mindset to do such a thing.

"Mr. Logan? I need you to answer some questions."

One of the officers had walked around the other side of the desk, behind a plastic barrier, and sat behind a computer. The other towered over Bear, looking down his nose and monitoring every hair follicle on Bear's body. He had the urge to scratch his nose with his middle finger but resisted. The smoother he made this process, the sooner they'd be out of it.

The officer behind the desk asked him basic questions, like his name, age, and address. He left the more interesting questions—like what he was doing in Boonesville and why he'd been next to two corpses and a bloody girl—for the investigating officer. Next to him, the female officer asked Mandy the same questions. Following Bear's lead, Mandy answered, not giving away any additional information or emotions.

At one point, the female officer led Mandy away to take her bloody clothing. Bear could hardly concentrate on the questions being posed to him. It took about ten minutes, and the officer behind the desk seemed more irritated. Maybe it wasn't smart, but Bear couldn't stop himself from watching the door, awaiting Mandy's return.

Finally, his daughter shuffled back into the room wearing a pair of light sweatpants and an oversized t-shirt. She kept her eyes on the ground, her face still shiny with tears, but Bear was relieved to have her back.

When the questions were done, the officers led Bear and Mandy down a short hallway. The floor was cool beneath his stocking feet, and he could hear Mandy's teeth chattering behind him. The AC was cranked up to its max to combat the heat of the day, but something told Bear she was shaking for a different reason.

They led Bear to a room at the end of the hallway. At the threshold, he stopped and turned back to look at Mandy. The female officer had her hand on Mandy's arm as she guided her into the room next door. When Mandy realized they were being separated, she looked up at Bear with panic in her eyes. Despite the lump of fear and anger rising in his throat, he arranged his features until he was sure he was radiating a confident calmness. It wouldn't stop Mandy from panicking, but he still wanted his face to be the last thing she saw. He tried to look strong, confident. He'd be damned if he let himself appear as scared as he felt at that moment.

Bear was no stranger to fear. He'd experienced it his whole life, and he knew the differences between what was real and imagined. Take flying, for example. He knew he was safe in the air, but he had no way of convincing his body it wasn't in immediate danger. The fear of getting a bullet to the brain had kept him alive in countless circumstances. The terror was real, but he had learned to use it to his advantage.

This was different.

When it came to Mandy, Bear had a harder time checking his emotions at the door. He couldn't flip the switch that let him think clearly.

Logically, he knew that as long as they told the truth and didn't cause any problems, they'd be able to walk away from this. But he couldn't ignore the growing panic in his chest. It told him to tear this entire place apart, kill every person inside, and get Mandy as far away from here as possible.

A voice in the back of his head screamed at him that wouldn't be the best course of action for Mandy, and so it was only through sheer force of will that he was able to watch the officer guide her into her own interrogation room before being shoved into his.

With a less than gentle touch, the officer who had been towering over him had unhooked his handcuffs long enough to secure him to the table. Bear felt his eye twitch and knew he wouldn't be able to keep his mouth shut.

"What's on the menu tonight, officer? I could go for some fish and chips. You got any back there?"

The angrier officer whipped his head around, but the other one—younger and thinner—put his arm out to stop him. "Mr. Logan, I recommend you take this situation seriously."

Bear let his flippant demeanor drop. "I just saw you put my daughter in handcuffs. You better believe I'm taking this seriously." Then, to the other officer, "I'll have a glass of water if you're all out of fish. With lemon."

The younger officer shuffled the other out of the room, and Bear sat with some satisfaction as the door slammed shut behind them. He had no idea how long it would take for someone to question him—had a feeling they'd let him sit for a while—so he settled into a more comfortable position, closed his eyes, and prepared himself for every possible scenario that might come next.

20

MANDY SAT DOWN IN THE CHAIR THE OFFICER HAD PULLED OUT FOR HER AND looked around the interrogation room while the officer observed her. She'd had enough conversations with Bear—and had seen enough movies —that she wasn't surprised by what she saw. It was plain, painted white, with a single table in the center of the room, a chair on each side. There was a place to handcuff her hands in front of her, but the officer who had booked her hadn't bothered to replace them.

Mandy wondered what would happen if she gave the cops the slip. She was small enough at five-foot-one that if she were to ask to go to the bathroom and then disappear when someone's back was turned, she'd probably be able to hide long enough to escape the building. After that, she'd be more than capable of stealing supplies and living in a cornfield for a few days until she could meet up with Bear again.

But if she ran away, what would happen to him? Would he get into even more trouble? And how would that make her look? Guilty, that's for sure.

You are guilty.

A shiver went down her spine, and the goosebumps that had been marching up and down her arms seemed to grow in strength and size. She couldn't stop her teeth from chattering, and though her fingers were numb from cold, she didn't think it had all that much to do with the artificial chill in the air.

She'd murdered someone. From this day on, that would never change.

Mandy ignored the intrusive thought and continued her investigation of the room. There wasn't much more to look at, though. Just a one-way mirror and a camera in the corner of the room. To distract herself, she started counting the ceiling tiles. That had always been a comfort to her. When she got done with that, she counted the floor tiles. The numbers didn't match up.

That bothered her.

She tapped the fingers of her left hand to match the ceiling. The fingers of her right hand to match the floor. Repeating this until the numbers evened out.

"How are you feeling right now, Mandy?" the female officer asked, standing off to the side. She had a small notebook in her hands that Mandy hadn't noticed before. "Is there anything I can get you?"

Mandy thought of several answers to the woman's first question, but none of them seemed appropriate. Or productive. So she answered the second one instead. "A glass of water?" She hated how small and scared she sounded. "And maybe a sweatshirt?"

The woman nodded and left the room. Mandy resorted to counting ceiling tiles again, this time categorizing them—white, off white, discolored, damaged. The floor tiles had gold speckles on them, and she counted how many resided in each square and figured out the average number. It was fifty-two. Bear would be proud of her for noticing such a minute detail.

Before she knew it, the female officer came back with a zip-up gray hoodie and a glass of water. Then she sat down in the chair opposite and folded her hands in front of her, leaving them on the table in plain view. "My name is Officer Judy. I'll be asking you a few questions today. Is that okay with you?"

Mandy slipped on the hoodie, zipped it all the way up to her chin, and took a sip of water before she answered. It gave her time to think. She was surprised Officer Judy was questioning her—she didn't look like an investigator. Maybe that's what made her a good one. Bear had told Mandy not to answer any questions, especially without him in the room with her, but how was she supposed to say no? Wouldn't she get in trouble? Would Bear get into more trouble if she didn't cooperate?

Instead of speaking and giving away her thoughts, Mandy nodded her head, forcing herself not to look down at the floor and start counting again. Staring at the front of Officer Judy's uniform, she memorized her badge number and noted every wrinkle in the fabric.

"Good. Thank you." Officer Judy took a deep breath and leaned forward, whispering. "I'm a little nervous because I don't normally do this sort of thing, but I'm the only female officer, so sometimes I question the women who come in here."

When Mandy didn't react in any way, Officer Judy leaned back and cleared her throat. "Mandy, what did you do this morning, before coming here? Did you go for a walk with your dad? Did you visit anyone?"

Mandy blinked. She thought the woman would've started questioning her about the incident right away. These questions didn't seem so bad. "We woke up early to catch our bus out of town, but it never came. Then we went to the diner for breakfast, even though we already ate. I think my dad just wanted to figure out how we'd get to St. Louis. Then Bette—the waitress at the diner—said she needed some help with the dishes. She'd pay me to work there for the day. Dad said he'd double it." She almost said, so it'd keep her out of trouble, but that sounded too incriminating. "That's where I was all day."

"What about your dad?" Officer Judy asked. She kept eye contact with Mandy, not looking down at her notepad once. "Where was he after you had breakfast at the diner?"

Mandy didn't want to answer this question. If she told them Bear had left once he saw those boys outside the diner window, would that make him look more suspicious? But she couldn't lie either. Bette and the other diners would tell the officers that Bear hadn't been there the whole time. "He left," she said. "I don't know where he went."

"Do you like working at the diner?" Officer Judy asked.

Mandy blinked at her. Why didn't she seem more concerned about Bear leaving? "Um, I guess." Shrugging, she did her best to keep her attention on the officer and not look down at the floor. That might make her look more suspicious. "It's kind of boring, but having my own money is nice. I like Bette. She's friendly."

"Bette's the best." Officer Judy grinned. "She always gives me extra whipped cream and fruit on my pancakes. And it's the good stuff, too. Homemade. Can't beat it. Have you had the pancakes yet?" When Mandy shook her head, Officer Judy clicked her tongue. "You'll have to try them soon. They're the best you'll ever have, trust me."

Mandy didn't know what else to do, so she just nodded and said, "Okay."

"Do you have a start time or an end time at the diner?"

"We didn't talk about that. I figured I'd ask Bette what time she wanted me to come in tomorrow when she sent me home for the night."

"But you left the diner around four, is that right?"

Heat crept up Mandy's neck. The sweater was doing its job, but this was something else. They were getting closer to talking about the incident now. "Yes."

"Was your shift over?"

"No."

Officer Judy tilted her head to one side. "Why'd you leave?"

"It was my break. I asked Bette. She said I could go for a walk."

"Any particular reason you went for a walk?"

Mandy hesitated. She could've just said it was to stretch her legs, but she knew someone would question Bette sooner or later, corroborating Mandy's story. If she lied now, she'd get into more trouble. Not for the first time since all this started, Mandy wondered if she should just keep her mouth shut. Sure, she might look like she was hiding something, but she technically didn't need to talk at all. Especially without her guardian present. She knew that much.

Officer Judy must've understood her thoughts from the expression on her face. "I know you're scared, but I want to help you, Mandy. Whatever happened, we'll figure it out. But I need to know the truth. You can trust me."

It took everything in Mandy not to scoff at the statement. She had seen enough injustices in the world to know that there were very few people you could trust. Sure, there were good cops out there, and Officer

Judy genuinely seemed to be one of them, but she also had a job to do. She wanted the truth more than she wanted to help Mandy.

Mandy drained her glass, then tugged her sweatshirt around her shoulders. "I thought I saw a friend of mine." She pushed the empty glass across the table. "Could I have some more water, please?"

Officer Judy hesitated, warring between wanting the answers now and keeping Mandy comfortable. The woman rose from her chair and took the empty glass from the room. It gave Mandy a few minutes to herself to figure out how much she'd tell before shutting down. The last thing she wanted to do was relive what had just happened, but it'd be so much worse for both of them if she refused to explain what she had been doing there—especially if she had done nothing wrong.

Mandy started counting the specs on the floor again when the officer didn't return within a few minutes. When fifteen more went by, Mandy started to worry. She didn't like feeling trapped in this room, and even though she could stand up and walk around, something told her that wasn't allowed. She settled for jiggling her leg up and down and counting the beats to pass the time.

She'd do anything to keep from thinking about what had happened earlier that day.

When the door finally opened, Officer Judy entered. In one hand, she had Mandy's glass of water. In the other, she had her book, *A Wrinkle in Time*. Mandy frowned at it. The last time she'd seen it, she'd left it behind at the diner because she thought she'd be back after a few minutes. How had Officer Judy gotten her hands on it? Had someone gone to the diner, or had Bette come to the station with it?

"This friend of yours," Officer Judy began, setting the glass of water down out of Mandy's reach, "was it a woman named Iris?" When Mandy didn't answer, the woman opened the book and took Iris' note from the pages. Officer Judy's eyes were harder than they had been, like she had come to some sort of unsavory conclusion and was just waiting for Mandy to confirm her findings. "Why wouldn't she want you to tell your dad about the fact that she was leaving? Was she afraid of him?" Officer Judy leaned closer. "If he's hurt you, we can protect you. Find you a good place to stay until we can locate the rest of your family."

"He would never hurt me," Mandy snapped. Just the idea of this woman insinuating that was enough for anger to course through her body. "And I don't have any other family. He's all I've got."

Officer Judy pressed harder. "Why was Iris afraid of him? Why didn't she want him to know that she had left?"

But Mandy was done answering questions. If Officer Judy thought Mandy would say anything bad about her dad, the woman had another think coming. Mandy would sit in silence for the rest of her life if that's what it took to protect Bear. They were a family, and she would go to the ends of the universe to make sure no one would tear them apart.

21

BEAR SAT IN SILENCE FOR AT LEAST A HALF HOUR. HE'D LOST COUNT. THE room offered no way for him to know, so he gave into the stale air and monotonous silence and stilled himself.

He wasn't sure if they let him wait because he'd talked back to Officer Stick-Up-His-Ass, or if they'd always planned on letting him sit with his thoughts. But if they thought it would bother him, they had another think coming. They had no idea who he was. They'd be on the phone with the Feds right now if they did.

A cold shiver of dread snaked its way down his spine and settled in his gut. They had his real name and ID. Sure, the address was bullshit and wouldn't lead to anything, but it'd be enough for someone clever. What if they *were* on the phone with the authorities, calling in backup to haul him off to some dark site to question him? His records had been wiped, but he had no idea what Jack Noble was up to these days. If Jack had gotten himself in trouble, there were plenty of people who still knew about their partnership. And those people would want to talk to Bear—or worse, get the upper hand with Jack through Bear and Mandy.

He shook the thought from his mind and worked to ease the tension in his gut. This was exactly what they wanted from him—to psych himself out before they ever stepped into the room. It made their job a lot easier.

To hell with that.

He retreated into a meditative state. He noted the white walls, the one-way mirror, the camera, and the steel desk. The ceiling tiles were off white and pockmarked. The floor tiles were flecked with gold. He let this information enter his mind and settle somewhere in the back to recall it later.

The handcuffs were cool against his wrists, and his legs were going numb from the pressure on his sciatica. The air was cool enough that a few goosebumps had erupted across his arms. But he didn't let any of this bother him.

Acceptance was bliss.

There weren't many sounds in the room, given that it was barren, and the door was soundproof. He could hear the air moving through the vents, and that strange buzzing from the florescent lights. Otherwise, he sat in relative silence.

The opening of the door broke the silence, and Bear's trance. A lone figure walked in with the confidence of someone who held power and expected to be obeyed. Bear surmised this was the sheriff, the big gun. Was it due to the severity of the crime, or because the sheriff was the only one willing to sit across from him?

"Mr. Logan, my name is Sheriff Woodard. I'm here to speak to you about the incident on Pine Road this afternoon."

As the sheriff proceeded through Bear's rights and why they'd detained him, Bear studied the man. Sheriff Woodard was in his fifties, a little over-weight, with a thick salt-and-pepper beard and thin hair to match. You could count the tiny sprouts popping up through dying follicles in his widow's peak. Woodard's eyes were deep brown, and his thick eyebrows made them look darker and more intense. Evil, in a way. His uniform was crisp and clean, and he held himself like someone who had seen just about everything over the years. Bear had an inkling the man had been in this profession for a long time.

Bear couldn't help but respect the man right away. This wasn't just some small-town sheriff looking to have a dick-measuring contest. Woodard had a job to do, and he would do it well. Bear was innocent. That *could* work in his favor. But he knew Woodard would do everything within his power to make sure someone was brought to justice for the crime committed today. Didn't matter if that person was guilty or not. If they confessed, they were done.

"Do you understand your rights?" Woodard leaned back in his chair and waited for a response. The game had begun.

"Yeah."

"What are you doing in Boonesville, Mr. Logan?"

"Passing through."

"Got any family here? Friends?"

"Nope."

"Why are you passing through? We're not the biggest dot on the map. Nothing to see or do here." He scratched at the hair on his chin. "I assume you can understand my confusion as to why you are here."

"Our bus broke down. Decided to stay here for the night."

"You and your daughter, you mean. Mandy?" When Bear nodded, Woodard continued. "You arrived with someone else though, didn't you?"

Bear didn't give away any of his thoughts when he answered. "Someone else who was on the bus tagged along with us."

"Iris Duvall. Did you know her?"

"Like I said, we met on the bus. She decided to accompany us here. We were meant to get a bus out to St. Louis this morning."

"But that didn't happen?"

"We liked the pancakes so much we caught another ride back to town." Bear winced the moment the words left his mouth. The man was just doing his job. Being an asshole would only make things worse for Mandy. "We missed the bus. Or, rather, it missed us."

Woodard appeared unfazed by the sarcastic reply. "Can you walk me through what you did today, Mr. Logan? From the moment you woke up to the moment you found yourself here?"

"Woke up, had some breakfast. Got my daughter to the bus stop. Waited there for a while, and when the bus didn't show, we headed back to town." Bear knew Woodard was looking for more information on Iris, and though he didn't want to tie himself to her, he figured it best to be upfront about it. "Iris was staying with us for the night, since there was only one room available in town. She wasn't there when we woke up, and she didn't meet us at the bus stop. When we went back to the bed-and-breakfast, I called the bus company, and they said someone had canceled our pickup. I assumed it was her."

"Why do you think she did that?" Woodard was taking notes now.

"No idea." Bear decided to move on from that sooner rather than later. "After that, we went to the diner across the street. A waitress there, Bette, gave Mandy a job washing dishes. I went for a walk, and then I went to Amos's house."

Woodard looked up, surprised. "Amos Wendell's house?"

"Yup."

"Why there?"

"The owner of the bed-and-breakfast gave me his name and address. Said he could get us to St. Louis before another bus made it through town."

"Another bus isn't gonna make it through town."

"Right. That's why I went over to his place to talk to him about a ride."

"He can corroborate your story?"

"He can. Will he? You probably know him better than I do." Bear worried for a moment that maybe Amos would lie about him being at the farm. After all, two locals were dead, and Bear was at the crime scene. But Bear had spent an entire afternoon with the man, had gotten a sense of the man's character. Amos wouldn't go out of his way to lie to the police. "Spent the rest of the day with him, helping to repair a fence and get some other chores done. Told him I'd work in exchange for him driving us to the city this weekend."

Sheriff Woodard pivoted again. "What's your relationship like with your daughter?"

Bear's jaw tightened. He could sit in this seat all day and not break a sweat, but when it came to Mandy and any threats against her life, he became twitchy. "Not sure what kind of question that is, Sheriff. She's my daughter."

"Are you close? Spend a lot of time together?"

"Yes." His teeth clenched.

Woodard studied him for a moment, waiting for him to elaborate. When he didn't, the sheriff sighed and shuffled some papers together while he gathered his thoughts. "How would you describe her? Friendly? Outgoing?"

"When she wants to be." Bear chose his words carefully. There was no way they wouldn't be used against Mandy later. "She's quiet. Had a tough childhood. But she's a good kid. Knows right from wrong. Always tries to do the right thing."

Woodard folded his arms across his chest. On anyone else, it could've looked defensive or even apathetic, but Bear could feel the other man sizing him up, trying to draw conclusions from what was in front of him. "Gotta admit, the evidence is pretty straight forward here. The young woman was stabbed in the chest. My guys tell me the height and angle of the wound is a pretty clear indicator that Mandy couldn't have done it. I imagine she saw what was happening and went to intervene, trying to do the right thing, as you said. She's got some bruises on her arm. He must've tried throwing her off, but she stuck him in the neck with a knife instead."

"Self-defense." Bear's voice was flat and unemotional, even though all he wanted to do was throw Woodard to the floor and break through that door. Gather Mandy up in his arms and make her forget any of this happened. "Like you said, the evidence is straight forward."

"Be that as it may, Mr. Logan," Woodard said, leaning forward on the desk now, "there are a few aspects of this situation that don't sit right with me."

Bear remained silent, not wanting to give Woodard the satisfaction of revealing that he was burning with curiosity. He didn't want to come off as too interested. He wanted to know all the facts, but Woodard could misconstrue it as something else.

"Neither victim had identification." He studied Bear closely. "Both of their wallets were missing."

Bear said nothing.

"Know anything about that?"

Bear shrugged. "I can't tell you why either one of them would leave the house without their wallets. I didn't know them."

Woodard made a non-committal sound. Then he pulled a piece of paper from his notebook and read it out loud. "Don't show this to your dad, okay? And don't worry about me. I can take care of myself. Hope you enjoy St. Louis. Eat some toasted ravioli for me, will you? Stay safe. I'm sorry I didn't say goodbye." Woodard looked up and made direct eye contact with Bear now. "Iris."

Bear couldn't stop his brows from furrowing. How long had Mandy had this letter? Why hadn't she shown him? Sure, Iris had told her not to, but this pretty much proved that Iris had skipped out on them with a purpose.

"Do you have any idea why Ms. Duvall wouldn't want you to know about this letter?"

"No, I don't," Bear said. "She'd spent more time with my daughter than I had that day, but we seemed friendly enough. The only reason why she might not want me to know is because she's the one who canceled our bus ride."

"Would that have made you angry?"

Bear stilled. Something wasn't adding up here. "Why are we talking about Iris? Is she hurt? Did something happen to her?"

"We're just gathering relevant information at this point. Are you going to answer the question?"

"Would it have made me angry? Yeah, sure. We were looking to go to St. Louis. We had a ride. For her to call and cancel the pickup because she was staying behind was inconsiderate. Not to mention, it doesn't make sense."

"Would you have confronted her about it?"

"If I'd have known where she was, sure. But something like that isn't worth getting into a screaming match over."

"Why do you think she was scared of you?"

Bear leveled him with a look. "Scared? Look, pal, lotta people are scared of me. I'm aware of what I look like, my size. But I never gave Iris any reason to be afraid. Sounds to me like she was hiding something."

"Like what?"

"Hell, if I know." Bear sat back in his chair. He wished he could've crossed his arms over his chest, but they were still cuffed to the table. "Look, you said it yourself, this situation is pretty straightforward. My kid is only fifteen. She shouldn't be questioned without a guardian or lawyer present. She's traumatized, and I want to make sure she's okay. If you've got nothing on me, I suggest you let me go. Now."

"Is that a threat, Mr. Logan?"

Bear scoffed. "I'm tired. Hungry. I'm worried about my kid. I've got nothing more to say to you. I did nothing wrong. And neither did Mandy."

Woodard's next words were interrupted by a sharp, quick knock on the door. The sheriff got up and opened it, but Bear couldn't see who was on the other side. They kept their voices low, but Bear could read the tension in Woodard's shoulders. A minute later, he turned back to the room and walked over to Bear. After a second's hesitation, he pulled out a key and unlocked Bear's handcuffs.

"You're free to go."

Bear didn't want to look a gift horse in the mouth, but he couldn't help questioning the sheriff's motives. "Why?"

Woodard looked like he didn't want to answer. "Because I'm not in the habit of keeping innocent men locked up." He gathered his belongings and indicated Bear lead the way out of the room. "And because someone I trust just vouched for you."

22

MANDY WAS STANDING WITH AMOS AT THE FRONT ENTRANCE TO THE POLICE station, dressed in baggy sweatpants and a sweatshirt. The moment she saw Bear, she launched herself into his arms and snuggled her face into his chest. He could feel tears through his shirt, but she didn't make a sound. Didn't shake or cry out or complain. Just hung onto him for dear life.

Bear made eye contact with Amos. "What are you doing here?"

"Bailing you out."

"Why?"

Amos smiled like he'd expected that question, but still didn't have an answer for it. "Come on."

Bear hesitated. The last thing he wanted to do was stick around here, but he didn't like owing anyone favors. Why would the old farmer go out on a limb for him? A piece of the picture was missing. Bear was at war with himself, debating between figuring out what the hell was going on around this supposed sleepy Midwestern town, and getting the hell out of Dodge.

Amos waited with the door open, looking at Bear expectantly. Mandy still clung to Bear. Whatever happened next had to be the best move for her. Part of that decision was making sure he explored all his options. He needed to know what Amos had to say, if he had any relevant information. If he didn't, then Bear would cut his losses, and they'd find another way out of town.

At the truck, Bear turned to the old man. "Mind giving us a minute? I haven't talked to her since we got here."

Amos's eyes were sad as he nodded and leaned against the hood of his truck, tipping his head back to look up at the stars. Bear opened the back door of the F150 and placed Mandy inside. He had flashbacks to when she was smaller and couldn't climb up into the seat by herself. She used to get so mad and frustrated that she'd needed his help. Now, she was compliant and silent.

"Hey," Bear said, waiting for her to look in his direction. She didn't make eye contact. "Are you hurt? Do you want to go to the hospital?"

Mandy shook her head. When it was obvious Bear was waiting for a verbal answer, Mandy cleared the emotion from her throat and choked out, "I'm okay. Probably a couple bruises. Nothing bad."

"Good." Bear's voice was quiet and even. "You can change your mind about that any time. Just say the word, we'll get you checked out."

"Okay."

"Mandy. I need you to look at me."

It was clear she didn't want to, but she forced her eyes to meet Bear's. He wasn't prepared for the depth of pain and emotion there. It broke his heart, but he didn't let it show on his face. "I need you to listen to me. Are you listening?"

Mandy nodded. Then added, "Yes."

"Good." Bear made sure he had her full attention. "You did nothing wrong; you hear me? Nothing. You remembered everything I taught you to stay safe, and your instincts took over. You did a good job, kid."

Mandy's eyes filled with tears. "I killed him." The tears fell down her face, but her voice remained even. "And I couldn't save her."

Bear wiped away what he could, but the tears kept falling. He felt his own eyes water in response. "Yes...I know. But you tried. You did the right thing. We can't save everyone." He thought of Sasha and Pierre and everyone else he'd lost over the years. "But you're still here. That's important."

Mandy nodded, her eyes still the size of saucers. "What's going to happen now? Are we in trouble?"

"Not sure." Not wanting to lie to her, that would just make it worse in the end. "We need to figure out why Amos is helping us, and then come up with a plan. They know this was self-defense, otherwise they wouldn't have let us go. But that doesn't mean they're gonna let us leave town. We gotta play it smart."

Mandy nodded, but after another moment, the tears started spilling from her eyes again. "I'm sorry, Bear. I didn't mean to cause any trouble—"

"Hey." Bear's voice was quiet but firm. He held her face in his hands until she looked at him. "I'm proud of you." He kissed the top of her head. "You tried to save her life. Most people aren't that brave. You have nothing to apologize for. Got it?"

Mandy nodded, though she was still sniffling. "Thank you."

Bear shut the truck door, causing Amos to turn toward him. If he'd heard any of their conversation, he didn't indicate it. The man climbed into the front seat and started the engine. Bear got in after him.

"Suppose you have a few questions for me," Amos began.

"Why'd you vouch for us?"

Amos sighed as he pulled out of the parking lot. "Spent the day working alongside you. Get to know a man that way. Heard the way you talk about your daughter. Felt like I should speak up for you. Let Sheriff Woodard know my opinion."

"You two know each other well?" Bear asked.

"Small town. We go way back. Been friends for a long time. He knows I don't stick my neck out for nobody."

"Lucky me, I guess." Bear let Amos have a chuckle at that before asking, "How'd you hear about this, anyway?"

"My cousin is a bit of a gossip," he said, rolling his eyes and keeping the truck moving forward. "Joyce called to tell me what was going on. Described you pretty well. Not hard to figure out who it was. Figured you didn't leave the farm after a hard day's work just to go commit murder. Ran into Bette on the way there. She'd been called over because you two had been in the diner that morning. Got part of the story from her. She'd brought over Mandy's book from Sal's."

Mandy groaned from the back. "They still have it, too. Now I'll never get to finish it."

Bear wanted to ask her about the letter, but he didn't want to push her right now. "And then you decided to go out on a limb for me?"

"It's a little more complicated than that, but yeah."

Amos turned the truck down a side street, and Bear looked over at him. "Thought we were going back to the bed-and-breakfast?" Not that he had any interest in facing the town gossip. She'd probably have a million questions for him.

"Figured you two could use a good meal after the day you had."

"Appreciate that," Bear said, "but I think we're going to turn in early."

"Thing is," Amos said, pulling into his gravel driveway, "your release came with the condition that I keep an eye on you. At least until the police gather some more information. I've got a couple empty rooms and plenty of food in the house. You can make yourself at home." He glanced at Bear after putting the truck in park next to the old Ford. "I know it's not ideal, but it beats sitting in a cell."

Bear appreciated the kindness, but that didn't mean he liked being forced into this situation. The cops would keep an eye on them, whether or not they were at Amos's house. But the old man had a point. Sheriff Woodard would feel more comfortable with Amos on the job, which meant Bear had a little more room to stretch his legs.

Besides, it was obvious Amos knew more than he was letting on, and Bear was ready to get to the bottom of this.

Amos jumped down from the truck with a groan, and Bear and Mandy followed him up the steps of the front porch. Putting the key in the door, he didn't turn it. He looked over his shoulder at Bear. "Last thing I want to do is spring anything else on you, but you have to understand that you're far from being in the clear right now."

"They wouldn't have let us go if they thought we'd done anything."

"I'm not talking about the cops."

With that, Amos turned the key and opened the door. Daisy greeted him, tail wagging and nose sniffing the air. Going over to Mandy, she started inspecting her shoes like they were the most interesting items she'd ever come across.

Amos flipped the light on. A large kitchen appeared with a wooden table in the center. It was well-used, but clean and big enough to hold a large family for dinner. Bear could just imagine what Thanksgiving or Christmas would have been like in this house. How good the food would have tasted. The love and laughter these walls had witnessed.

But the mood turned sour when he realized someone was hovering in the doorway at the opposite end of the room, cloaked in shadow, unmoving. He hadn't realized he'd taken a step toward them until Amos put a hand to his chest to stop him.

"No use hiding anymore," he said to the shadow. "You can come out now."

A woman emerged. Blonde hair, blue eyes, and a scowl on her face. Mandy's gasp told Bear that she'd put two and two together faster than he had, but the name on her lips confirmed what he was seeing.

"Iris?"

23

IRIS LOOKED DIFFERENT FROM THE LAST TIME BEAR HAD SEEN HER, THE WAY she carried herself. Where she'd once looked like a ray of sunshine, she now appeared a rain cloud. Or rather, a thunderstorm with a hint of the hurricane to follow. The scowl on her face was directed at Bear, but for the life of him, he couldn't figure out why *she* was pissed at *him*. If anything, it should be the other way around.

But when she looked over at Mandy, the scowl dissipated, replaced by a hesitant and guilty smile. "Hey, Mandy. You doing okay?"

Mandy's mouth was still open in silent shock, and when it didn't look like she'd be able to respond, Bear stepped to the plate. The anger he'd felt at missing the bus and getting involved in whatever was going on in this godforsaken town had risen to his limit, and he couldn't stop himself from directing it at the source.

"Who are you?" he demanded. "Is your name really Iris Duvall?"

Iris flipped a golden lock of hair over her shoulder and eyed him coolly. "Yes."

"Did you cancel the bus pick up this morning?"

Guilt flickered across her face again, replaced with a guarded look a second later. "Yes."

"Why?" Bear threw his hands up, and he saw Iris subtly shift into combat-ready mode. Was she really that afraid of him?

"I needed to stick around town a while longer."

"Why'd you have to get us involved?"

Iris looked back down at Mandy, who had closed her mouth and was now looking at the woman with her own mixture of anger and hurt, and directed her apology at her rather than Bear. "I'm sorry. I didn't want you to get mixed up in all of this. Really, I didn't. But I needed an excuse to be stranded here. Couldn't look like I'd done it by choice. You were collateral damage."

Mandy scoffed and crossed her arms over her chest. "Gee, thanks. That makes me feel so much better."

"And the letter?" Bear asked. Mandy looked up sharply, but he ignored the surprised look on her face. "You made it look like you were afraid of me. You disappeared, and I became suspect number one."

"Unintentional," Iris replied. "I just wanted to say goodbye. I didn't think the police would ever get their hands on it."

"We've known you for twenty-four hours, and you've already upended our lives." Bear fought to keep the growl out of his voice and failed. "Who are you?"

"I've upended your life?" Iris took a step forward, and if Bear thought she might've been readying herself for a fight before, there was no doubt in his mind now. Her fists were clenched at her sides, all her muscles were taut, and she steadied her feet as she planted them beneath her. "Who am I? Who are *you*? You're not just some guy traveling around the country with his daughter. Who are you really?"

Bear narrowed his eyes at her. "That's none of your business."

"You made it my business the minute you ended up at a crime scene."

"What are you, a cop?" he asked. That would explain some things. "A Fed?"

"People are *dead*." Iris didn't seem to notice that a sob escaped Mandy's throat at her words. "Why were you there? Did you do that to her? To them?"

"Mandy thought it was you." Bear aimed a loaded finger at her. "She thought she saw you outside the diner, so she followed the woman out to the road. What did you expect to happen? You left us stranded here. You left her a cryptic note."

Iris narrowed her eyes at him. "This isn't my fault."

"Isn't it?" Bear threw his arms out to his sides. "Then whose is it? Whatever mess you're in, leave us out of it."

Amos stepped forward, trying to break the tension between the two of them. "It's a little too late for that."

Iris ignored the old man. "You're already involved. You're a witness. I want to know what happened."

Another sob escaped Mandy's throat, and she bent over in an attempt to put her head between her legs. Her body shook with the effort of keeping silent, but Bear could see the tears dripping from her face onto the linoleum floor.

Bear stepped closer to Mandy and put a comforting arm around her shoulder, then looked up at Iris. "Not now."

"But—"

"*Not now,*" he said, daring Iris to question him again.

Iris took a deep breath, held it for a few seconds, and let it out slowly. The change in her demeanor was immediate. She was either an incredible actress or an expert in compartmentalizing. Maybe both. Bear realized that whatever information he thought he'd gathered from their earlier interactions was false, so he threw it out the window. He had no idea who she really was, and that bothered him. He wasn't used to getting false readings on people.

"Let's take a break from this," Amos suggested. "Not used to having so many hands around. Y'all can help me with dinner. Lots to do."

Iris and Bear glared at each other, but neither objected. Bear had to admit he was starving after today. Mandy needed a distraction too, and there was something calming about completing minute tasks, combining ingredients, and smelling the results come together into a meal.

Bear broke first, nodding at the old man, and Iris retreated a step, shaking out her hands and looking around the kitchen. "What's on the menu?"

"Got a roast ready to go in the oven," Amos said, cutting across the kitchen and opening the fridge. It was well-stocked. "Potatoes and carrots need chopping. Plus, everything for the salad. Someone can work on putting the pie together, too."

"You were planning on eating all this yourself?" Bear asked, eyebrow raised.

"Old habits," he said, with a wave of his hand. "If I can't eat all the leftovers, I take them to some of the elderly folks around town. They always appreciate a good meal, and I usually get a nice conversation out of it."

Bear rolled up the sleeves of his shirt and walked over to the kitchen sink, scrubbing his hands as clean as he could get them. After drying them on a towel, he turned back to the farmer. "What do you want me to do first?"

"You seem like a meat and potatoes kind of guy," Amos suggested. "Peeler's in that drawer to your right." He turned to Mandy, still wiping tears from her eyes. "You, dear, can help me with the pie, since you're so sweet. You okay with that?"

Mandy nodded, wiping the last of her tears from her face. "Sure."

"That puts me on salad duty," Iris said. "Fun."

Amos shot her a look as he guided Mandy over to one of the counters to start preparing the blueberries. "Yes, I thought you could reflect a little on how all those different vegetables work together to create something delicious. One bitter radish can ruin the whole mix."

"Let me guess," Iris said, hands on her hips. "I'm the bitter radish?"

"If the shoe fits," Amos said.

Bear hid his snort behind a cough and got to work.

24

WHEN THEY LAID THE SPREAD ON THE TABLE, IT WAS SOMETHING TO BEHOLD. If Bear hadn't already been starving, just looking at all that food would've made his mouth water. Even Mandy looked a little livelier now that they had stopped talking about the dead woman and moved on to a more congenial topic—dinner.

Amos sat at the head and said grace. Bear bowed his head and saw Mandy do the same, but he could still feel Iris' eyes on him. She'd become less hostile over the last hour, but now her gaze took on a wary quality. Ironic, considering that, between the two of them, she had proven herself the least trustworthy. But some people just don't spend enough time looking at their own reflection.

After grace, the four of them piled their plates high with food. Roast beef with potatoes and carrots, asparagus and salad. Bear didn't bother trying to leave room for the pie. He'd make room sooner or later. Maybe it was the long day of labor or the thought of being stuck in a cell or fear of their immediate future, but food had never tasted so good. Maybe it was that everything was fresh and homemade. Can't beat a farm-to-table kind of meal.

With a mouthful of roast beef, Bear looked over at Amos, who did him the favor of not avoiding eye contact. "What did you mean when you said we're far from being in the clear?" Bear asked. "You said you weren't talking about the cops."

Amos sighed and put his fork down. He glanced at Iris, but she was busying herself with her salad. There was something calculating in her eyes that resembled a predator lying in wait to make their strike, but Bear couldn't tell if he was the prey.

"There's a lot more going on around this town than you realize," Amos started. "A lot more. And somehow you stuck your foot in the hornet's nest."

"Sounds about right," Bear said, and Mandy gave a weak chuckle. "Promise you I can handle it. But not if I don't know what's going on."

Amos took a moment to gather his thoughts. Then, without saying anything, he stood and walked into the other room. When he returned, he had a finger of whiskey for each of them. Bear accepted it and tipped it down his throat. Warmth worked its way into his stomach and settled there like a mother's embrace.

"Good stuff," he told the old man.

Amos smiled. "Thank you."

Bear quirked an eyebrow. "You made this?" When Amos nodded, Bear grunted in appreciation. "There anything you can't do?"

"Protect my friends and family, it seems." Amos sat back down in his chair, cut another hunk of meat off his roast, and speared it with his fork, but he didn't bring it to his mouth. "Boonesville might look like an idyllic Midwestern town, but we have some of the same problems the big cities have."

"Drugs?" Bear ventured. "Murder?"

"Wasn't always like this, of course. Been here my whole life. This is the kind of town you'd see in some Hallmark movie. The kind of town you'd want to raise your family in."

"When did it change?"

"Not sure. Over the years, I suppose. As the surrounding cities grew, so did we. Families expanded and kids stayed behind to take over their parents' businesses or start their own. But in the last few years, things have gotten rough. Lot more crime. Sheriff Woodard had to expand his department just to handle it."

Bear wanted to ask Amos how long he'd known Woodard and why the sheriff trusted the old farmer so much, but he didn't want to distract. "Is there any one person behind it?" Bear asked. "The increase in crime, I mean."

"Yes and no." Amos finally stuck the piece of meat on the end of his fork into his mouth and chewed thoughtfully. After he swallowed, he said, "That gentleman you met outside of the bar, Carl, was the start of it for me. My awareness, I mean. When he was workin' on the farm, he'd come in hungover. Then he'd come in drunk. Not smart when you're workin' around machinery. I was patient with him. Like I said, he'd had a tough life. But then he showed up on something different. Caught him stealin' money from me. Not like I have a whole lot to go around, but I get by. Especially now that the house is empty, and it's just me. Everyone's got to have a rainy-day fund. Though, I suppose mine was actually my granddaughter's college fund. Guess Carl thought he was entitled to it."

"You fired him," Bear said, remembering their first conversation.

"That I did." Amos didn't look proud of that fact. "But I got a bug up my ass about it. I was close to his mom. Cared about the kid, you know? Didn't want to see anyone throwin' their life away. So I did a little investigatin' on my own. Found out who he was buyin' from. Then found out who was supplying."

"You get a name?" Bear asked.

Amos hesitated, like he knew this information had to come out, but wasn't quite ready to let it go. With a deep breath, he said, "Luke Salazar."

"Haven't heard the name," Bear said.

"He doesn't have many friends, and the ones he has, well, they don't talk about him, if you catch my drift."

Bear did. "So he's got an operation here, supplying the town. Good for pocket change, but any dealer I've met wants to make more money. He probably sends people out to the cities, doesn't he?" Bear watched as Amos hung his head, and it clicked into place. "That's your job, isn't it, driving his supply to St. Louis? That's why you go out there once a week. Not just for your crops."

"This is nothin' I wanted to get involved in," Amos said. "But he didn't give me much of a choice."

"You the only one?" Bear asked. "Or does he have other people working for him against their will?"

"He's got a few."

"More than a few," Iris interjected. "I know you don't like talking about it, but this is bigger than you want to admit, Amos. We have to do something about it sooner rather than later. Before more people get killed."

Amos shot her a look, and as much as Bear wanted to ask what she meant by this being bigger than even the old man was aware of, it didn't seem like the time or the place. Especially when Amos turned back to Bear with more vulnerability than he'd seen.

"My main concern is the people in this town. My friends. My family." His voice broke, and it took a few seconds for him to regain his composure. "Whatever else is going on, the rot is focused here, in my hometown. We have to take care of that first."

There was too much pain in Amos's voice for Bear to ignore. He was a good man. A proud one. Someone who made his living by working hard and being kind to people. It was difficult to believe he'd done Luke's bidding without good reason. Bear made sure his words were gentle before he asked the main question on his mind. "What do they have on you?"

Amos opened his mouth, but before he could answer, there was a sharp knock on the door.

25

LUKE SAT IN THE DARK OF HIS BASEMENT. HIS HANDS CURLED AROUND THE outside of the armrests of his chair. He'd been in the same position earlier that day, sitting across from Raymond. They hadn't been close in years, but Luke owed him one. His friend had taken the fall for him and hadn't complained once. After Raymond got out, he wasn't quite the same, but Luke had been trying to help the guy.

And now Raymond was dead.

He'd been prepared to deal with Lily's death. When Luke sent Raymond after her, he'd all but told him to kill her. She was about to snitch on them, and Luke couldn't have that. Having poured everything into his business, he wasn't going to let some junkie, get in the way of that. He'd already come to terms with her permanent absence from his life, but when he'd heard about Ray, it'd felt like a knife to the gut.

Anger surged through Luke's body, and he squeezed the armrests in the chair until his fingernails screamed. He couldn't remember the last time he'd cried, but a tear slipped from his eye, and he swiped it away angrily. Rage propelled him to his feet, then dragged him around the room at a relentless pace, wearing a track in the carpet and barely avoiding the precious equipment around the room.

Not one to doubt himself but building his operation from the ground up had been more dangerous and difficult than he'd anticipated. The job he'd been hired to do was a no-brainer—receive the shipments in bulk, bag them up to sell, and pass them off to his contacts who'd sell them to their willing customers. Taking a little off the top and flipping it for profit should've been just as easy. It's not like the guy sending the shipments would drive out to Loserville, Indiana to check every ounce. As long as the money was right, they didn't care.

But it had been harder than he'd thought to keep everything under wraps, and now with this big guy in town, Luke had to make a decision. Did he kill the guy now and make it look like a suicide? Like the guy felt guilty for killing Raymond and Lily? Or would he get the guy thrown in jail? The former was Luke's preferred option, but if he was caught, it'd all be over. And he'd already sacrificed more than he'd ever wanted to.

Then there was the kid. Luke didn't know her name, but from what his men had gathered, she was the big guy's kid. They'd told him that she'd been there too. Had been involved. It's not like he had a man inside the police department, so this was all conjecture. Still, it provided an opportunity. What if Luke threatened the kid? Would that make the man leave, or would it bring even more hellfire down on Luke?

If she was about Jake's age, maybe he could give his little brother an assignment.

As soon as the thought occurred to him, Luke batted it away. Jake wasn't ready for that, and he couldn't deal with his little brother messing this up. They'd have one shot to do it right, and Luke wasn't sure he'd ever forgive Jake if he dropped the ball. Or died in the process.

A shrill sound emanating from the chair made Luke whirl around. Heart pounding and eyes wide and probing, it took him a moment to realize his cell was ringing. Stalking over to the chair, he snatched it up, expecting for a moment that it'd be Raymond with some good news, only to have reality hit him in the gut again.

The name on the screen had him holding his breath, and he took a few precious seconds to catch his breath and slow his heart rate down. When he knew his voice would be steady, he swiped the screen and held the device to his ear. "Salazar."

The man on the other end of the line had a deep voice that oozed power and confidence. He was a man used to getting what he wanted without having to ask twice. The slow, methodical way he spoke had its intended effect. His voice commanded attention.

"Mr. Salazar," the man said. "How are you today?"

"Mr. Reagan." Luke controlled his voice even though the last thing he wanted to do right now was to be polite. "Everything's on schedule. What can I do for you?"

"I didn't ask about the shipment," Reagan said, chastising him. "I asked how you are today."

Luke's eyebrows knit together. Mr. Reagan wasn't known for his friendliness. Politeness, sure. But that was to throw his enemies off-guard. He never pretended to be friends with his subordinates. This was wildly out of character. "Sir?"

"Your friend died, did he not?" There was a hint of amusement in his voice. "Or, he was killed. I'm sorry for your loss."

Luke had to bite back the snap in his voice. "Thank you."

"I've heard some unpleasant rumors lately, Mr. Salazar. I was hoping you could clear some things up for me."

A layer of sweat coated Luke's forehead. "What kind of rumors?"

Reagan's voice was no longer congenial. "You tell me."

Luke knew it was a trap. Would he admit to something Reagan wasn't even aware of yet? Would he incriminate himself in the process, or dodge responsibility? This guy wasn't like other men Luke had dealt with in the past. He wasn't someone you could punch in the face and share a beer with an hour later, all your hard feelings forgotten. No, Mr. Reagan would much rather put a bullet in your brain and make your replacement clean up your body, so they knew exactly how high the stakes were.

"There's a new player in town," Luke admitted. "I'm taking care of it."

"A new player?" Reagan didn't sound all that surprised. "Who?"

"Not sure yet. Big son of a bitch. Keeps sticking his nose where it doesn't belong. Thinks he's the vigilante type." Luke wondered if he sounded as anxious as he felt. "Like I said, I'm taking care of it."

"See that you do. I was displeased with your latest return. You're the only one of my distributors who came in short. I don't want to see that happen twice in a row."

Luke stood up a little straighter. "It won't," he began. "I promise, I'll—"

"You know what," Reagan said in a quiet voice that still made Luke swallow his next words, "I think I'll send some of my guys your way."

"That's not necessary. I can handle one guy."

"Clearly, you can't." The bite in Reagan's voice sent a chill through Luke. "Otherwise, I wouldn't have heard about it in the first place. My men are already in place. They'll be paying you a visit soon enough. Make sure you have your affairs in order, Mr. Salazar. Don't let me catch you slipping."

Reagan hung up the phone.

Luke stood in shock for several seconds before hurling his phone at the wall and watching it erupt into a million pieces.

26

Amos stared in the direction of the front door for a solid ten seconds before pushing his chair back. After a long look at Iris, he walked over to the door to find out who was interrupting his dinner. Bear didn't wait for him to report back. He wanted to see and hear firsthand who it was, whether it was Luke Salazar, the police, or someone new.

Amos shot a look at all three of them hovering over his shoulder, but he didn't tell them to go away. On the other side stood a short, stocky woman with flyaway curly hair as wild as her eyes. She wore dirty overalls and muddy boots, but the detail that drew Bear's attention was the blossoming bruise under her right eye, visible even against her ruddy cheeks. It looked like she'd had a bloody nose too and hadn't gotten it all off her face.

"Rhonda?" Amos stepped aside, allowing the woman to enter the house. "What the hell happened?"

Rhonda glanced at the onlookers. First, she looked at Bear and took in his bulk. Then her gaze shifted to Iris, shock and then confusion settling over her face. Mandy only got a brief glance before Rhonda looked back to Amos. "Who are these folks?"

"Friends," Amos said, giving her a nod that told her she could trust them. "Are you okay? Tell me what happened?"

"I went over to Garrett's to pick up some stuff." She glanced at Bear, and he inferred that the *stuff* in question was likely drugs. "He wasn't there, but these two guys were. They asked me some questions, and when I wouldn't tell them, they shoved me around. I kicked one in the crotch, and the other punched me in the face so hard, he knocked me out. When I came to, they were already walking away." Rhonda was on the verge of tears, and she had to take a deep breath to calm herself. "I stayed down until they left. I was so afraid."

"Do you know who they were?" Bear asked. "Did you recognize the men?"

Rhonda looked between him and Amos, her lips pressed so tightly together that they turned white. Bear wasn't sure if she was trying to hold back her sobs or if she simply didn't trust him enough to answer his question.

Amos placed a gentle hand on her shoulder. "You can trust him."

Rhonda didn't look convinced, but with four sets of eyes on her, she didn't have much of a choice. "I didn't recognize them. They sounded like they were from out of town. Didn't really fit in here, you know?"

Bear heard the unspoken words. *Kind of like you.* "What'd they look like? How'd they dress?"

"Tall. Broad. One was bald. The other had light brown hair. They were both dressed in suits without the jackets. That's what caught my attention. Not much use for a suit out on a farm."

"Is that where Garrett lives?" Bear asked. "Out on a farm?" When Rhonda nodded, he added, "What's out there? What kind of stuff were you picking up?"

Rhonda looked at Amos again. "How do you know you can trust him? How do you know he isn't working for Luke?"

"I didn't even know Luke's name half an hour ago."

The woman looked around the group. "I don't know any of you from Adam, so how do I know you're not lying?"

Iris stepped forward. "We're walking in circles here. We can't help each other if we don't know what's going on."

"Help?" Rhonda shook her head so hard, she hit Amos in the face with her frizzy hair. "No one can help us. Look what happened today. Could be us next."

Amos still had a hand on Rhonda's shoulder, and he used it to turn her back to him. "Not if we stick together. Luke might have a few guys on his side, but we've got the numbers. We can't be afraid."

"Speak for yourself." Rhonda pointed a finger at her eye. "Look what they did to me. For no reason. I'm lucky it wasn't worse." Rhonda shook her head again, this time in dejection. "I don't think they worked for Luke. Not his style."

"Rhonda, please." Amos sounded desperate, the look in his eyes held a touch of panic. "We're glad you came. We need to figure out who these new guys are and what they're doing here. Maybe it'll help us stand up to Luke."

"Yeah," Rhonda said, forcing a smile. It didn't reach her eyes. "Sure." After a second's pause, she cleared her throat and put a hand on the door-knob. "Thanks for listening. Sorry if I interrupted your dinner."

"You want a plate?" Amos asked. Then, with a soft smile, "Bag of frozen peas for your eye?"

Rhonda just shook her head again. "I've got stuff at home. See you, Amos." She glanced at Bear, then back at the old farmer. "Be careful."

Bear gave it a few seconds after Rhonda shut the door before speaking. "She doesn't seem to like me much."

"We're all wary of newcomers," Amos said. "Especially ones that look like you."

"You didn't seem too worried when we first met," Bear said.

Amos shrugged and headed back into the kitchen. "Looks can be deceiving."

"Is she gonna be a problem?" Bear asked.

"I don't think so. She's scared, but she's on our side."

Bear looked at Iris, who didn't seem as convinced. "How many people do you have on your side at the moment?"

Iris snorted. "Depends on how you define that." She sat down to pick at the rest of her dinner, but mostly just pushed her food around her plate. "No one we know actually wants to work for Luke, so they're willing to listen to us. But he's got enough dirt on all of them. And after what happened today?" Iris had to pause for a moment to regain her composure. "He'll use it to his advantage, and they'll be even less willing to step out of line."

Bear had so many questions for both of them. What did Luke have on Amos, and why was Iris involved if she wasn't from around here? What's more, how did Luke set up this whole operation of people willing to put their reputations on the line for him? Amos was a good man. He wouldn't go against his morals for just any old reason. It had to be a big one. That had to be the case for the rest of the town, too.

But Bear knew that no matter how many times he asked the question, Amos and Iris wouldn't give him any answers until he proved he could be trusted. He could imagine only two ways of doing that—either by gathering valuable information or taking Luke Salazar out of the picture. While the second option was more efficient, it was also more dangerous, both for him and Mandy, as well as everyone else in town. Bear didn't know enough about the guy to determine whether he was a credible threat. Who knew what sort of resources he had at his fingertips? And considering he had this much dirt on this many people, Bear figured it was better to err on the side of caution.

But something about the way they all avoided talking about Garrett's farm told Bear there was something more going on here.

"You'll get them back on your side," Bear said, and Iris raised an eyebrow against his unwavering confidence. "You just need to tip the scales in your favor."

"And how do you propose we do that?" she asked.

"Not sure yet." Bear yawned. "That's a problem for tomorrow."

27

BEAR HARDLY SLEPT THAT NIGHT, THANKS TO HIS BRAIN WORKING THROUGH the events of the last twenty-four hours. But he'd thought through every possible scenario and had come up with a game plan for the day.

Although, getting up wasn't quite as easy when his whole body hurt. He might not go to the gym regularly, but Bear kept in shape. It was nothing compared to what Amos had put him through the day before, however, and Bear was sore from the tip of his toes to the top of his head. It took him a good twenty minutes of stretching before he felt his muscles loosen up.

Amos was already up and out at the barn by the time Bear made it downstairs, but the old farmer had made a fresh pot of coffee, and Bear figured that was his way of saying good morning. The liquid was hot and strong, rejuvenating him in a way nothing else on the planet could. It woke up his muscles and sent his brain into overdrive.

Amos had promised to keep Bear overnight to ensure someone had an eye on him, but the night was over, and Bear was free to go. The cops wouldn't like it, but if they were going to arrest him, he wished they would hurry up and do it. No point in skulking about and shooting him dirty looks. It's not like it would be hard to keep an eye on him in a town this small, anyway. Even if they couldn't see where he was going, someone would be sure to remember him. There wasn't anyone in town —except maybe Amos—who was loyal to Bear and willing to stick their neck out.

Which was fine by him. The feeling was mutual.

Bear shook his head. Amos hadn't asked Bear for help, and Bear hadn't volunteered it. But he couldn't help being curious about everything, given he'd found himself in the middle of it. Bear owed the old man a debt for vouching for him in front of the police, and he'd find a way to pay that off. He just hoped it didn't involve getting shot at.

Amos had left the old truck's keys on the kitchen table, and Bear figured that was invitation enough to head over to the bed-and-breakfast to get their stuff. The old man had offered him and Mandy their own rooms and food on the table in exchange for their help, and as much as Bear had tried not to get involved, he had admitted he was as entangled in this as the rest of them. Maybe more so with the police considering him a murder suspect.

No sooner had he picked up the keys than Mandy appeared around the corner, dressed in Amos's granddaughter's clothes and rubbing the sleep out of her eyes.

"Where are you going?" she asked.

"To pick up our stuff at the B&B. Be back soon."

"Can I go with you?"

Bear kept his face neutral. "You stay here. Keep an eye on Iris."

"Why?"

"I don't trust her."

"You're gonna go do something and you don't want me along."

Bear shrugged. She was a smart kid. "The two aren't mutually exclusive."

Mandy rolled her eyes, crossed her arms, and leaned against the door-jamb. "You're not going to cause any more trouble, are you?"

"Only if they cause it first." Bear winked, and his heart swelled at the smile that bloomed on Mandy's face. "Sit tight. I'll be back soon. Keep an eye on Iris."

"That sounds boring."

"Not all missions are exciting," Bear said, turning toward the door and swinging it open. "But that doesn't mean they're not necessary. I'll be back."

He could've sworn Mandy mumbled something under her breath as he was closing the door, but he ignored it. She wouldn't be happy, but at least he hadn't lied to her. Iris was keeping something from them, and he wanted to know what it was. But first he had more pressing matters.

As Bear pulled out of the driveway, he spotted a police cruiser parked along the road. The guy wasn't trying to hide, not that there was much coverage out here.

Bear didn't have to worry about dealing with the officer because the kid—twenty or twenty-two—was passed out in his front seat. He'd probably been on overnight duty. It was still early enough that the next shift hadn't relieved him. Bear drove right by the cop without waking him up, despite the clunking of the truck.

What he wouldn't give to sleep like that.

No one else followed him to Joyce's establishment. Bear was relieved to have the spotlight off him for a couple of hours. Now he just needed to get through this next part without drawing any undue attention.

When Bear walked through the front door, Joyce was sitting behind her desk, a cup of coffee in one hand and her glasses perched on the end of her nose. She looked up when he entered, a smile already on her lips, but it dropped away when she saw who it was.

"Mr. Logan," Joyce said, her lips pursed in disapproval, but it couldn't hide the excitement in her eyes. "There are some nasty rumors going around town about you."

Bear was grateful to get this part out of the way quickly. "Do you believe them?"

Joyce thought for a moment, taking a long sip of her coffee before setting it down and leaning back in her chair. "No. I talked to Amos. I believe what my cousin has to say about you."

"He's a good man. Thanks for putting me in touch with him. He's been good to us."

"You're welcome." Joyce stood up. "He tells me you'll be staying with him now. You're not going to cause him any grief, are you?"

"Not my intention."

"It never is." The woman looked at him with a piercing gaze. "Amos has been through a lot the last couple of years. He deserves a break."

"Can't imagine he'll get much of one on the farm. Keeps him busy." Bear rearranged his expression into something curious and innocent. Joyce seemed to be one of the town's gossips, and he needed information. "Amos told me his wife died a few years back."

Joyce nodded. "Not just that, though. His daughter married a real piece of work. Although he never hit her, he was quite the sociopath. She finally left him, but it didn't make the situation much easier. He's been fighting for custody of their daughter and trying to prove she's an unfit mother." Joyce laughed but sobered. "If you knew her, you'd know that's a ridiculous claim."

"If she's anything like Amos, I can believe it."

"Her daughter is off to college now. A real good school, too. She wants to be a lawyer. I think the situation with her father inspired her. But it's expensive. Jenna is a single mom, and her own lawyer bills almost bankrupted her. Amos doesn't get too much from the farm. He does what he can, but they struggle. We're all struggling." She gestured to the house around her. "It's not easy living all the way out here and maintaining a small business."

This hadn't been the information Bear was looking for, but it proved useful. If Amos was being blackmailed, there was a good chance it had to do with his daughter and the court case. Maybe Luke had found the woman's ex-husband and threatened to give him information proving she was an unfit mother. All it took was a few planted drugs.

Bear wasn't sure how much Joyce knew about Luke Salazar, and he didn't want to throw Amos under the bus. Especially if she decided to ask around for more information. Might draw the wrong kind of attention, either to Luke or the mystery men Rhonda had run into.

"I'd really like to do something nice for Amos," Bear said. "As a thank you. I'm helping on the farm, but I think he'd appreciate some of his friends getting together. Give him a little break from the monotony, you know?"

Joyce's eyes lit up. "That's a great idea. He's always bringing everyone dinner or doing handiwork for them when he can. I think he'd appreciate if someone cooked him a meal for once."

"Who are some of his closest friends?"

"He's pretty friendly with Locke, who runs the bar down the road. And him and Sal go way back. Bette, too. Then there's Rhonda. Amos helped her get her farm off the ground. Jerry—"

"What about Garrett?" Bear asked. If he wasn't direct, she'd be listing names for the next hour. He was only interested in one.

"Garrett Cohen?" Joyce tapped a finger to her lips. "Well, I don't know if I'd call them friends."

"Amos was talking about him yesterday. Maybe they've gotten closer recently." Bear didn't give her time to think about that too hard. "Do you have his address? I think I'll start there."

"Yes, of course." Joyce dug around in her desk and pulled out her address book, copying down the information onto a sticky note and handing it to him. "Maybe we could get Sal to cook for us. We could decorate the diner and have a party there."

"Sounds like a great idea." Bear was already heading toward the stairs to get their belongings. "I'll talk to Garrett and Locke and see what we can come up with."

Joyce looked overjoyed by the idea, and by the time he came downstairs with his stuff, she was already on the phone with someone. Bear gave her a little wave and snuck out the front before she could stop him with more ideas. Maybe if they figured out their situation with Luke, they really could throw a party to celebrate.

Bear's relief at having escaped Joyce was erased by the image that met him as soon as the door shut behind him.

28

Sheriff Woodard leaned against the hood of Amos's truck, hand resting on his sidearm, a look of disapproval on his face. Bear ignored the man until he threw his and Mandy's belongings into the truck. He stopped short of hopping inside and driving away with the guy still leaning against the hood, but only because that would cause more problems than it was worth.

Would've been hilarious, though.

"Can I help you, Sheriff?"

Woodard didn't bother beating around the bush. "Why aren't you with Amos? You were supposed to stay there."

"You can't keep me prisoner, Woodard. Not legally."

"I could throw you in a jail cell," Woodard said. There was no passion in his voice. No arrogance. He wasn't the kind of guy who would do it just to prove he could.

"You could," Bear agreed. "But you haven't." Bear gave the other man a moment to explain, but when the sheriff stayed silent, he continued. "Without charges, there's not much you can do. Look, I'm not gonna skip town. I've given my word to Amos."

"That don't mean much to me," Woodard said.

Bear nodded. He understood. "But you trust Amos." When Woodard's face pinched in annoyance, Bear knew he had him right where he wanted him. "And Amos trusts me. I'm helping him on the farm for a few days. My plan was always to hitch a ride to St. Louis by the weekend."

"Tell that to the officer at Amos's house."

Bear scoffed. "If he hadn't been sleeping on the job, he would've seen me leave. Might want to invest in a couple more officers. Or a bigger pot of coffee."

Woodard was scowling now, and Bear had a feeling that officer would get an earful when he returned to the office.

That wasn't Bear's problem. "We good here?"

"No, we're not good." But Woodard pushed off the hood, anyway. "I'm choosing to trust Amos. But that doesn't mean I trust you, Mr. Logan. I'll be checking in."

"You do that." Bear flashed the man a wide smile, then hopped into the truck and backed out into the street. He rolled down the window and gave the other man a salute. "Nice talking to you, Sheriff. Have a good day."

In his rearview mirror, Bear could see Woodard watching him while he drove down the main street. It was only as Bear turned the corner that the other man made his way over to his cruiser. Bear didn't think Woodard would follow him, but he made a few random turns and traveled up and down just about every side road in town to make sure no one was tailing him. When he was satisfied, he pulled out the slip of paper Joyce had given him with Garrett's address on it. Pulling into someone's driveway first, Bear turned around and headed in the opposite direction, away from town and toward the man's property.

Bear didn't know what to expect when he pulled onto the farm, but it didn't look much different than Amos'. There was a sizeable farmhouse off to the right, set back away from the road, and plenty of fields surrounding the man's home. One was filled with corn, but the rest were open, and Bear could see some animals off in the distance, grazing and enjoying the sunny morning. There was still a chill in the air, but it was quickly warming up. It would be a scorcher later.

The main difference between Garrett's and Amos's properties was the barn. Amos's was a decent size, though it was about enough for his animals and a little bit of storage.

Garrett's, on the other hand, had to be four times as big. The paint looked fresh, and there were still scraps of unused wood and buckets of paint along one side, like Garrett had just finished construction a few days ago. Based on what Bear could see from his vantage point, the barn was much too big for the number of animals and crops the man had. So if it wasn't being used for farming equipment and food, what was all that space for?

Bear pulled up and around the side so he could keep the truck out of view of the house, though it didn't look like anyone was home. All the windows were dark, and there was no vehicle in the driveway. Of course, that didn't mean much, and Bear decided if Garrett or someone else came out to investigate, he'd tell them Amos sent him to pick something up. Might get him in the door enough to look around, at least.

Stepping out of the truck, Bear took a minute to take in his surroundings. It was quiet out here, with just a breeze rustling through the corn and a few birds singing from the trees. There were no sounds of tractors or four-wheelers, and he couldn't even hear the town traffic from out here. It would've been peaceful if he wasn't on high alert. It could be a death sentence to be caught off guard. The types who lived out here were usually the shoot-first ask-questions-later kind of people.

Bear let the door to the truck close as quietly as possible, then took a few steps toward the barn. He had picked up his gun from the bed-and-breakfast and now had it tucked into the waistband of his jeans. The weight was a comfort, though it'd be a last resort. He didn't need to bring any more trouble onto himself.

Besides, he *was* trespassing. Was it smart to be creeping up on someone else's property while he was under investigation, let alone carrying a firearm? No. But this mystery with Garrett and why none of the others wanted to talk about him made the back of Bear's neck itch. There was a reason everyone was keeping it under wraps, and Bear wanted to find out what it was. Amos might not have told him what was going on, but he'd left Bear his keys. The old man wanted Bear to figure it out without anything leading back to him. Inconvenient for Bear, maybe, but good survival skills for Amos.

When no one jumped out from behind the barn, Bear walked closer and noticed the door was latched by a heavy piece of wood. Maybe there was nothing special inside. Bear almost turned around and saved himself the trouble, but his gut told him to keep digging.

Bear pulled the door open enough to stick his head inside and take a quick glance around. Much to his disappointment, the barn looked normal. There were stacks of hay to one side, and a work bench to the other. Tools lay scattered here and there—Garrett was not as orderly as Amos. The whole thing smelled of manure and hay.

Bear considered going up to the house and knocking on the door. He could introduce himself as a friend of Amos, and maybe whoever was home would allow him to step inside. Then he could excuse himself to the bathroom and have a look around for a few moments, unencumbered by curious eyes.

But there was something off about this barn. Bear stepped inside and let his eyes adjust to the darkness around him. More details came to light, and he realized the inside was much smaller than the outside. Maybe Garrett had built a hidden room. It could be for extra storage, but why not just put a door in the wall? And what was so secret about needing some extra room to store your equipment?

Bear figured he was on the right track, even if he didn't know what it would lead to yet. If Garrett was in the same business as Amos, it was likely he could use the storeroom for the drug supply. Amos didn't have as much room at his house, so maybe the surplus went here. Amos had a good relationship with Sheriff Woodard, so the cops wouldn't be busting down his door looking for anything suspicious. Maybe Garrett wasn't as well-liked as his counterpart, so he had to put in extra precautions to make sure he wasn't caught.

Sticking to the outside wall, Bear made his way around the barn, looking closely for anything that seemed to work as a door handle or lever. He had to keep stepping over shovels and hoes and bits of detritus. Whoever this guy was, Bear wasn't sure he took much pride in his line of work. You'd think he'd at least keep his walkways clear.

When Bear got to a part of the barn that was clear of debris, he knew he'd found what he was looking for. This area was walkable. He'd let the rest of the barn go by the wayside because he was hardly dealing in that business anymore. Whatever was in this storeroom had turned into Garrett's number-one priority.

The wall in front of him looked normal until he peered closer. Along one side was a chain that fed from the upstairs area. There was no hook on the end, and it didn't appear to go to anything. What's more, it was high enough off the ground that most people wouldn't be able to reach it. If Garrett was as tall as Bear, he'd have no trouble grabbing hold of the bottom two inches and pulling it down.

So that's what Bear did.

He heard a gear turn, and the wall popped open, revealing another room. Bear slipped inside, greeted by the stench of ammonia. It was so strong, it made his eyes water. He could no longer smell the excrement from the other room. That had been a good cover while out in the main portion of the barn, but now the smell was overwhelming.

But Bear pushed forward, blinking away the stinging in his eyes and taking shallow breaths until he got used to the stench. Even before he'd walked into the hidden room, Bear knew what he was going to find. There were a lot of different reasons why he'd be smelling ammonia like this, but only one made sense when he considered what Luke was up to, and why Amos hadn't wanted to tell Bear about Garrett.

The room looked like a makeshift chemistry lab—and that's exactly what it was. Tools hung from the wall while bottles lined just about every shelf and surface. In contrast to the rest of the barn, this room was organized, if not clean. And it wasn't hard to figure out what Garrett got up to in his spare time.

Whatever Luke was up to, it involved a meth lab tucked away in Garrett Cohen's barn.

29

MANDY BENT OVER AND PLACED HER HANDS ON HER KNEES AS SHE TRIED TO catch her breath. Her lungs burned, mucus built in the back of her throat, and her legs were almost numb. She wasn't out of shape, but it'd been a while since she'd gone on a run at a six-minute-mile pace, and her body had forgotten how to regulate her heartbeat and breathing.

Panic set in as Mandy felt like she couldn't catch her breath. Tunnel vision made her dizzy, as did the lack of oxygen, and she wobbled before crouching down on the sidewalk and pretending like she was tying her shoe. She wanted to lay flat and open up her lungs as much as possible, but she didn't want to attract any attention. Besides, she was almost all the way to the center of town. Someone would worry if they saw a girl lying down in the middle of the sidewalk.

After Bear had left, Mandy went back upstairs and changed into a different outfit. Amos still had a few of his granddaughter's things from when she'd stayed during the summer, and since the clothes were a few years old, they fit Mandy perfectly. The floral patterns weren't her style, but it was better than whatever the officers had given her. Besides, Bear would be back soon enough with her clothes, and she could feel like herself again.

Bear had told her to stay put and keep an eye on Iris. It was obvious

Iris wasn't telling them the whole truth, so it's not like Mandy disagreed with that decision. She just didn't want to be the one to do it. Part of her was still mad at the woman for abandoning them and making them think she was missing. If Iris hadn't called to cancel their bus, Mandy never would've hurt that man, and they would've already been to St. Louis and beyond.

Thinking of what she'd done didn't make the panic go away. In fact, Mandy felt her chest tighten in anger and fear and frustration. Her breaths became shallower, and the dizziness only got worse. Mandy knew that she hadn't done anything wrong—the man had attacked the woman, and she had come to the stranger's defense. But it didn't make it any easier knowing she'd ended someone's life.

She needed a distraction. Something to keep her mind off the past and keep her moving toward the future. But she couldn't think straight without enough oxygen getting to her brain, and she was running out of time. Bear would be too far ahead of her for her to figure out what he was up to.

Mandy squeezed her hands into fists and took a deep breath, holding for a count of ten. Then she let it out slowly, fighting the urge to take another gulp of fresh air. Tears gathered at the corners of her eyes, but she kept them at bay. When all the air had exited her lungs, she took another long, slow breath and held it. Another count of ten. Exhale. Repeat.

After a solid minute, Mandy felt her heart rate decrease and her panic subsided into something more manageable. She stood and began walking, hoping no one had thought it strange she'd been kneeling on the sidewalk for a few minutes without moving. It was still early enough that the streets were quiet.

Mandy took in her surroundings, noticing who was opening up shop and who was driving. Bear had taught her to keep a mental list of the last ten vehicles she'd encountered, updating it as new ones passed by. The point was to see if anyone drove by a second or third time, indicating she was being watched or followed. But it seemed as though no one in Boonesville was all that interested in what a fifteen-year-old girl was doing walking down the street at seven in the morning dressed in floral patterns, despite the fact that school was out and all the other teenagers in town were probably still in bed.

Bear had headed out that morning to get their belongings from the bed-and-breakfast, so she had some idea of his first destination. But the look in his eyes told her that he was up to something else. Mandy racked her brain for what it could be and came up with several possibilities.

The least likely on the list was that Bear would go confront Luke straightaway and get that over with. They still didn't know much about the man or how dangerous he was. It was best to gather intel before they made that move.

But where could Bear get that information? Mandy's first instinct was the diner or the bar. Bette knew everyone in town, and while Mandy didn't think she was a gossip, per se, she did think the woman would be more than willing to chat with Bear and answer any of his questions. Mandy didn't know much about the old man who owned the bar, but someone in there would probably be willing to talk for a free drink.

Mandy cut down a side street as soon as the bed-and-breakfast came into view. She couldn't let Bear catch her. He'd be furious that she was out on her own, let alone that she wasn't carrying out the mission he gave her to keep an eye on Iris. Not for the first time, Mandy wondered if she'd made the right choice abandoning her duty to follow Bear. Sure, they needed to learn more about Iris, but Mandy had a feeling the woman wouldn't let anything slip. Iris' mask had been too good when they'd first met.

With renewed determination, Mandy picked up her pace until she could see the bed-and-breakfast from her vantage point between two houses. Bear had just left the building, their belongings in hand, but had stopped short of pulling out of the parking lot. Squinting, Mandy caught sight of Sheriff Woodard leaning against the hood of the truck. A shiver snaked down her spine. It wasn't that she disliked the man, but the memories of last night's events made her stomach churn.

It was too bad she didn't have a listening device to hear their exchange. A small smile crept across her lips as she imagined Bear's sarcastic comments. He couldn't help but poke people, searching for their triggers and weaknesses. That went double for people with authority. Quadruple for cops.

Even though she couldn't hear what they were saying, Mandy could read their body language. Woodard looked angry and suspicious with the way he had his arms crossed over his chest. Bear looked more relaxed, but he was always ready to make his first move. There was no way he'd get into it with the sheriff if he could help it, but it was best to be prepared. Woodard seemed like a decent cop, but he also didn't seem to be the kind of person who wouldn't stop until someone was held responsible. Guilty or not.

Only a minute or two went by before Bear got back into the truck and drove away. Woodard watched him go, then climbed into his cruiser and drove off in the opposite direction. Whatever words had been exchanged weren't enough to make the sheriff follow Bear. That was a good sign.

Mandy took a deep breath and jogged after Bear's truck. Luckily for her, the speed limit in town was only twenty miles per hour, and Bear was doing his best to keep to it. If she were following the road like he was, she'd fall behind. But she had the advantage of being able to cross through people's yards and hop fences. She only got yelled at once, by an old man reading his newspaper on his back porch, wearing nothing but his boxers. She waved her apology and kept moving. She had to find out where Bear was going.

At first, all he did was drive a little way, then backtrack. He'd cut down one street only to turn around and drive in the opposite direction a minute or so later. Mandy knew he was making sure Woodard didn't follow him, but she couldn't help her annoyance. If he didn't stop soon, she'd collapse to the ground.

When he hit a road leading to the farms outside town, Mandy was worried she'd lose him for good. But there was only so much she could do, and she was trying to avoid another panic attack. With that in mind, she set a pace for herself and let her thoughts drift away. She didn't think about anything but putting one foot in front of the other. It was a beautiful day out already, and she let the sun warm her shoulders and the breeze cool the sweat on her brow.

She forgot how much she'd missed this.

Mandy only came out of her trance when she spotted Amos's truck parked in front of a barn on someone's property. Bear hadn't told her he'd spoken to anyone else in town, and she wasn't sure whether Amos was aware of what Bear was getting up to. Still, it was strange to see him parked there, with the barn door open, and no one else around. Was he sneaking around, or had he been invited to stop by?

The sound of another truck's engine made her ears perk up, and on pure instinct alone, she dove into the high grass along the road. It was itchy and hot and made her nose tingle, but she didn't dare move from her spot. Crouched this low to the ground, she doubted anyone would be able to spot her. But from her vantage point, she would be able to see the truck's driver. Was it someone else meeting Bear, or just a random passerby?

As the truck drew nearer, cresting the hill she'd just run up, the engine grew louder. It was much newer than the hunk of junk Bear had been driving, but it was by no means quiet. She wondered if Bear could hear it from the barn and whether he was worried about getting caught or someone showing up unannounced.

Mandy crouched lower as the truck came into view. It slowed down, giving her an extra second or two to see inside the driver's side window. It was only a brief glimpse, but there was no mistaking the man in the front seat. The man was bald and wore a white button-up shirt with a tie. There was another figure in the passenger seat, and while she hadn't been able to see his face, she would've bet money he had light brown hair and wore a similar outfit. From the expression on the first man's face, he didn't look friendly. And considering they'd been the men to push Rhonda around, Mandy was all but certain they were up to no good.

Were they here for Bear, or whoever owned the house? They couldn't have been following Bear, or Mandy would've noticed them. Showing up at the same time as Bear was a coincidence, though that didn't put her at ease either. They looked like the shoot-first ask-questions-later kind of guys.

Mandy's relief when they passed by the house was momentary as she heard them come to a stop a few hundred feet down the road and then cut the engine. They would only do that if they were planning on sneaking up on Bear.

Gritting her teeth and clenching her fists, Mandy only had one thought in her head.

Not if I can help it.

30

BEAR WASN'T SURE HOW MUCH TIME HE HAD BEFORE SOMEONE CAME HOME and spotted him, but he needed to know what he was getting himself into.

The meth lab was crude. Homemade items and leftover milk bottles seemed to support most of the operation. As organized as it was, Bear could tell that whoever had set this up had done so through trial and error. The pile of trash and broken bottles in the corner spoke to that.

But *who* had set it up? Bear didn't know anything about Garrett Cohen, but there was no way he didn't know this was run inside his own barn. Odds were, he'd been the one to expand the building and set up the hidden door. But was Garrett just the person who allowed them to work in his barn, or was he the one working? Considering the rest of the barn had been practically abandoned, Bear had a hunch Garrett was a part of the daily crew.

But what about Luke? Was this his idea, or Garrett's? And how far up was Garrett in the food chain? Maybe that was part of the reason Amos didn't want to talk about the man. Any indication that the old farmer had been talking to Bear might cause Garrett to snitch to Luke.

Bear no longer wanted to be trapped in this tiny room with such highly flammable materials. Meth lab explosions weren't an uncommon occurrence, and while it looked like whoever was making it knew what they were doing, accidents happened. And he didn't want to be caught in the middle of one.

Yet, there was no better time than the present to look for a clue about Garrett or Luke. Or the operation, Luke ran. It seemed like there was more at play here than he knew, but he had no evidence to support that hunch.

Bear walked a circuit around the room, looking at all the bottles and beakers, tubes and trivets. Most everything looked like it had come out of someone's kitchen or the local hardware store. A few items looked a little more high-tech, and he had to wonder if Luke was investing more into the operation as he made more money. That meant Luke had bigger plans, and Bear had bigger problems.

As Bear made his way around the room, he kept an eye out for any random slips of paper with notes scratched on them. Notebooks. Napkins. Anything to give him insight into whatever was going on. But there was nothing. Either Garrett didn't keep notes, or he kept them on him at all times. It was smart, in case someone did discover the lab.

Near the door was a box with the flaps folded together. Closed but not sealed. Bear stuck a couple of fingers in the opening and tugged. The flaps blossomed, and it took a moment for Bear to realize what he was looking at.

About a hundred bags sat stacked on top of each other, all sealed and organized. There were no labels, but the evidence was all around him. Whatever Luke was into, he was out to make a fast profit. And he didn't care how many people died along the way.

The scuff of a boot was the only indication Bear was no longer alone. Instinct set in, and he flattened himself against the wall next to the door, propped open only a couple of inches. Whoever was on the other side would either have to stick their head into the opening or pull it open wider to see what was on the other side. Either way, Bear would have the element of surprise.

A few seconds passed while adrenaline flooded Bear's body. His heart was steady due to years of experience and conditioning. The rest of his body was poised for action, coiled and ready to strike. Whoever was on the other side would have no idea what hit them, and that would give Bear the best advantage.

A hand curled around the opening to the door, pulling it wider. It revealed a man's arm, then his shoulder and torso, then his face. The man was bald, wearing a white button-down shirt, and black slacks with a matching tie. It didn't take much for Bear to put two and two together. This was one of the men that had attacked Rhonda. But if he was here, where was his partner?

Bear no longer liked his odds. If the other man pulled a gun and started shooting, they'd both go up in flame. Not to mention Bear was quite literally backed into a corner. The man could lock Bear in the room and set something against the door so he couldn't escape. Would they leave him there to rot? Maybe. There was a lot of product inside, but keeping him contained would allow them the upper hand.

No, Bear had to make his move now.

Before the bald man even knew Bear was there, he stepped forward and rammed his shoulder into the door, making the other guy stumble backwards in shock. Bear slipped out of the room and squared up with his opponent, not wanting to throw the first punch if he didn't have to. While Bear knew this guy and his partner had no problem pushing people around, he wanted to give them the benefit of the doubt. He was here for information, not a fight.

Unfortunately, the other guy didn't feel the same way. As soon as he regained his footing, the man pulled a knife from a leather hip sheath. Bear kicked himself for missing that, but at least it wasn't a gun. Bear would've been able to match him with his own pistol but firing shots around a meth lab was dangerous.

Just because the guy had gone for the knife didn't mean he had no other weapons on him.

Bear didn't let the man get close. He danced to the right and picked up a pitchfork from against the wall outside the hidden room. Now *he* had the upper hand.

"Who the fuck are you?" the guy spat.

"No one," Bear said. "Just stopped by to visit a friend."

The other man's face stretched into a grin. "Good, then you can give Mr. Salazar a message for me."

"I'm not really the messenger type," Bear said. "Bad memory."

"I think you'll remember this one." Baldy tossed his knife to the other hand. "All you have to say is Mr. Reagan sends his regards. Your face will do the rest of the talking."

"My face usually does all the talking," Bear said, giving the man a condescending look. "That's where my mouth is."

Baldy scowled. "When I'm done with you, your mouth won't be doing any talking."

"Then how am I supposed to give anyone your message?"

The bald-headed man roared in anger and charged Bear, which was not the smartest move, but it did take him by surprise for a split second. Bear lifted his pitchfork like a jousting stick, but at the last second, the other guy spun to the right and got inside Bear's reach. Bear had been expecting this. As sharp as the guy's knife was, it was still small, and Bear used the handle of the pitchfork to knock his hand away. At the same time, he stepped forward and headbutted the guy in the nose. He didn't hear the satisfactory crunch he was looking for, but blood began to pour down the man's face, which was still a win in his book.

The man stepped back and checked his nose, his eyes narrowing in anger as he looked back up at Bear. "I'm going to kill you."

"Again, how am I supposed to deliver this message for you?" Bear asked. "I think you need to work on your pitch a bit more. I can give you some pointers if you want."

Baldy was apparently done with Bear's shit. He charged again, attempting to get in close with the same move. But Bear had already decided this guy wasn't smart and was ready for him this time. Instead of using the sharp end of the instrument in his hand, Bear stepped back and slammed the handle against the side of the man's temple. He crumpled to the ground.

Bear didn't waste any time. He wasn't interested in this fight, and he now had the information he needed. Garrett was operating a meth lab for Luke, and these goons were here on behalf of someone named Mr. Reagan. And this Mr. Reagan wanted to send Luke a message, confirming

Bear's hunch that they didn't work for Luke. There were still plenty of puzzle pieces Bear was missing, but he had a few more now.

Bear grabbed a length of rope from the wall and wrapped it around the man's wrists, then tied it off to one of the support posts for the barn. It wouldn't take the guy long to wake up or undo his restraints, even after Bear tossed the knife away, but he didn't need to keep him at bay for long. He just needed enough time to get to the truck and get out of there. Hopefully, the guy hadn't taken note of the license plate to be able to connect it to Amos. If he did, it'd only be a matter of time before they showed up on the old farmer's doorstep.

But Bear had bigger issues. As soon as he stepped outside the door, he saw that all four tires on the truck had been slashed.

The man inside the barn shouted in anger, and Bear knew it was time to go. With the other man still out here somewhere, Bear didn't want to risk being out in the open. His best bet was to make for the cornfields and run back to town under the crops' cover. They weren't quite tall enough yet to conceal his full height, but if he stayed crouched and moved erratically, it'd be hard to keep track of him.

Bear grabbed the bags from the truck and slung him over his shoulders, grateful that Mandy had packed as light as he had. Another shout from the barn sent him running up the driveway before making a hard left into the cornfield. The stalks were difficult to run through without jostling them, especially with a pair of duffel bags slung over his shoulders. But he tried to stay between a row for a good fifty feet before cutting over and running down the next one. Maybe they'd mistake all the movement for the breeze.

With sweat forming on his brow from sun exposure and exertion, Bear couldn't get to the road fast enough. He'd be able to cross there, then follow the fields back into town. At some point, he'd leave the farmland behind and be exposed again, but by that time, he hoped to have lost his pursuers.

As soon as the thought occurred to him, he heard the revving of a truck engine. It was coming straight for him, so he did the only thing he could think of—cut a hard right and began running in the opposite direction. This would send him deeper into farm country, but also give him the best chance to escape. If he had to, he'd dump the bags and come back for them later.

The truck remained behind him, not as loud as Amos's vehicle, but enough that he could follow its movement. It occurred to him that even though he was crouched, the person in the truck had a vantage point that allowed them to see the top of Bear's head. The only way he'd be able to disappear would be to lie flat and crawl across the ground. He'd have to toss the bags. And it'd be much slower going.

Before he could decide, the truck veered from the road and barreled through the corn. It bounced haphazardly across the uneven ground, and just as Bear considered staying still and jumping out of the way at the last possible second, the vehicle took a sharp left and the driver slammed on the brakes, coming to a full stop a couple feet away.

Bear could barely process what he was seeing. The driver leaned across the front seat and pushed open the passenger door. Her hair was wild, and there was a light in her eyes that he hadn't seen in days.

"Well, don't just stand there," Mandy said, a mischievous grin on her face. "Get in!"

31

BEAR WENT AROUND TO THE DRIVER'S SIDE DOOR AND SCOOTED MANDY over so he could get behind the wheel, much to Mandy's chagrin. While he was grateful that she'd been the one behind the wheel, he wasn't about to let her be in charge of their getaway.

"What the hell are you doing here?" He didn't bother controlling his frustration. "I told you to stay at the house and keep an eye on Iris."

"Aren't you glad I came?" Mandy asked, innocence lacing her words.

"That's beside the point," Bear said. "You abandoned your mission."

"We both know you only gave me that mission to keep me occupied while you did who knows what."

"Doesn't mean it wasn't important. We need to find out more about Iris." Bear turned the truck around and headed back toward town. "I trusted you to do that."

Mandy hung her head. "Sorry." Sounding like she meant it. Mostly. "But Iris can wait. I got pictures of the guys who were following you. I think they're the same guys who beat up Rhonda."

"Let me see," Bear said, taking the phone Mandy offered him. He recognized Baldy immediately. The other guy had brown hair and was dressed the same, just like Rhonda had described. "Met the bald guy in the barn. You see where the other one went?"

Mandy took the phone back. "Think he went up to the house. I kept watch from the end of the driveway. As soon as the bald guy went inside the barn, I took the truck. I was gonna cause a distraction, but then I saw you run out through the fields, so I figured I'd give you a lift."

Bear shook his head, but he ruffled Mandy's hair, anyway. "Thanks, kid. Would've been better if you'd listened to me in the first place, but I appreciate the assist."

Mandy beamed, then remembered she was supposed to look chastised. Dropping her smile, she nodded solemnly, folding her hands in her lap. Bear chuckled. She never could take anything seriously. Wonder where she got that from.

"What's next?" Mandy asked.

"Search the truck," he told her. "Glove box, center console, backseat. I want to know who these guys are. Sounds like they work for a guy named Mr. Reagan, who's apparently not happy with Luke."

Mandy opened the glove box. "Maybe Luke works for Reagan too. Could be why these guys are in town. Checking up on things."

"My thoughts exactly." Bear couldn't help the burst of pride that went through his chest. "Did you find anything?"

"Napkins from a couple fast-food places. Sauce packets. Nothing important."

"Everything's important," Bear reminded her.

Mandy sighed. "Fast food means they've been traveling. Probably trying to keep a low profile. They're from out of town. But we already knew that."

"It's good to confirm. Could be important later."

"In case they want us to get them lunch?" Mandy asked.

Bear suppressed his chuckle this time. It would only encourage her. "What else did you find?"

Mandy opened the center console. "Bingo. Receipt for a car rental. They've had this truck for about a week. Looks like they got it in Reno. Why didn't they just fly?"

"Maybe they had more stops to make along the way. More distributors to check up on." Bear checked to make sure his rearview was still clear before he continued. "More than likely, it was so they could transport drugs or weapons. Anything back there?"

Mandy climbed over the back seat to look, but she came up a few minutes later with empty hands. "Either they didn't have anything, or they took it somewhere else. They've got to have a homebase to go back to, right?"

"Right. Joyce's is the only place in town, unless they're staying with someone else they know. But I think someone would've noticed and said something. Means they're staying elsewhere and coming back each day. Thinking about it, that makes the most sense."

Mandy settled into the front seat and buckled up again. "Where to now?"

Bear cut her a glance. "I was gonna retrieve those wallets we tossed yesterday. Want me to drop you off at the diner?"

Mandy went still at the mention of the wallets, then took a deep breath and blew it back out, forcing herself to relax. She didn't meet Bear's gaze, but her voice remained steady. "I'd like to go with you."

"Are you sure?"

Mandy nodded, still looking straight ahead. "I don't want to be afraid."

Bear threw an arm around Mandy's tiny frame and gave her a squeeze. He didn't know what to say, and even if he did, it would come out thick with emotion. He was proud of her—not just because of her strength, but because of her vulnerability. He wanted her to know she could talk to him about anything, even the hard stuff. Although they weren't always the best at communicating their feelings, as Mandy got older, he felt like they were making progress. He hoped that never went away.

Bear drove past the field with the wallets until coming to a dirt road. Pulling onto it, he parked about fifty feet down, making it difficult to spot the truck. It'd take a while for the goons to walk back to town or call someone to pick them up. By that time, Bear hoped to be well on his way out of town. Since the truck was a rental, he wasn't too concerned about it having a tracking device for them to follow, but he'd need to ditch it sooner or later.

Bear got out of the truck and walked around to Mandy's door, opening it for her and helping her hop down to the ground. He could see the panic on her face, and he noticed her muttering under her breath.

"You don't have to do this," Bear reminded her. "If at any point you want to go back to the truck, just say the word."

Mandy stopped muttering and looked up at him, taking a deep breath and setting her mouth in a determined line. "I can do it."

"I know you can." He ruffled her hair again and chuckled at the glare she shot him. "Come on, let's make this quick."

Bear walked back toward the road but stopped short of walking along the shoulder. He didn't want to be spotted on private property. There were no cops around, but if one drove by, he'd look even more suspicious.

With that in mind, Bear cut through the field a couple feet shy of the road. Once they walked down far enough to Mandy's spot from the day before, he turned away from the road and gauged the distance he'd thrown the wallets. If he could get close enough to where they'd landed, there was no doubt he and Mandy would find them again.

"Stay there," Bear said, putting a hand up to stop Mandy from walking any farther. He walked another couple of feet to her right before stopping. "If we walk straight about fifty feet, then fan out in a circle, we should come across them."

"Okay." Mandy's voice came out a little breathier now, but her expression stayed determined.

Bear gave her an encouraging nod, and then the two of them walked forward at a steady pace. Unlikely as it was they'd find anything this close to the road, Bear kept his eyes peeled. Maybe the guy threw something incriminating into the field before attacking the woman. Most likely, the police would've found something this close to the road, but they had a small force, and something told Bear they didn't have a lot of experience with the legwork involved in a murder investigation.

"I thought she was Iris," Mandy said, her voice quiet but clear. "That's why I followed her."

"You wanted to know why she left."

"And why she left me that note. Why she didn't want me to tell you about it." Mandy looked over at him. "I hadn't decided whether I would. I'm sorry."

"It's okay." Bear meant it, knowing she wouldn't keep anything vital from him. She was doing what she thought was right. "I understand."

"I followed her like you taught me, staying out of sight. I thought she was up to something, and I wanted to know what it was before I confronted her. Then that guy came out of nowhere."

Bear didn't interrupt. Letting her gather her courage and find the right words. His only job was to listen.

"At first, I thought he was sneaking up on her, but then he shouted something. I was too far away to hear it. They looked like they were arguing after that. I tried to get closer, and that's when he brought out the knife."

Mandy choked back a sob, and for a few minutes, all they did was walk forward at a snail's pace, looking at the ground for any evidence that might give them a clue as to who these people were and what they were doing out here yesterday.

"I didn't think. I just ran forward. I didn't have a plan, I reacted. It was stupid."

"You were going on instinct," Bear said. He'd wanted to remain quiet, but he couldn't listen to her beat herself up like this. "It's the same thing I would've done. See someone in trouble, and you want to help. You get that from me."

Mandy smiled weakly. "I was too late, though. When I got there, he'd already stabbed her. She was bleeding so much. That's when I realized it wasn't Iris."

Bear had been wondering about this, too. The woman had looked a lot like Iris—same build, same hair color. But they looked different enough that they couldn't have been twins or even sisters. That didn't mean they weren't related, though. Was that what Iris was hiding from them? Was that why she was so interested in what had happened to them?

"I was quiet when I snuck up on him." Mandy stopped walking, and all Bear wanted to do was wrap her in his arms, but he didn't want to break the spell. Wanted her to keep talking, to get it all off her chest. "He had no idea I was there. But I must've made a sound because he whirled on me with the knife out. I reacted without thinking. Ducked, rolled. Came up with my knife in my hand. He lunged again, but he was sloppy. I saw the opening, and I took it. It was easy. The knife slid right in, like he was made of butter." She was sobbing now. "It didn't even shock me. I did it, and then jumped back, out of the way. I saw him fall. Saw blood fill his mouth. Heard him choke on it. And I didn't care. Just felt relief that he was no longer a threat. That's when I went over to the woman. Held her. She was still alive. She looked at me and tried to say something, but it came out garbled. I heard her take her last breath. Saw her eyes go vacant."

Bear unstuck his feet from the ground and moved over to her. Mandy resisted when he put his arms around her, but he didn't let go. He knew what she felt right now—horrible guilt over taking another person's life. She would always question whether that had been the right choice, whether there could've been another solution. This little girl of his would carry that burden for the rest of her life, and there was nothing he could do to carry it for her. Tears formed as he considered how much his daughter had changed in the last twenty-four hours.

Mandy finally stopped fighting and sank into Bear's hug. He was holding her whole weight in his arms as she sobbed. Five whole minutes passed before she settled and was able to stand up again. When she pushed away from him this time, he let her go.

Bear knelt in front of her so he could look her in the eyes. She didn't look away, even though he could tell she wanted to. "You didn't do anything wrong. You tried to save someone. That's a good thing." Waiting until she nodded, he continued. "We don't always get to save people. I've been where you are before, plenty of times. I know how this feels. And it's not good."

"Does it ever get any easier?" Mandy asked, her voice watery and still full of emotion.

"It depends." Bear thought of Sasha, and of how much pain her memory still caused him. "I'm not gonna lie to you. It's tough. It'll always be tough. But you'll learn to handle it. It makes you work harder, be more vigilant. It's a tough lesson to learn, but in the end, it'll make you stronger."

Mandy nodded and stepped away. "I think this is the spot. Should we fan out?"

Bear wanted to keep her talking, but he knew most of the work had to be done on her own time, in her own mind. All he could do was be there when she needed him most. And right now, she needed the distraction.

"Go for it," Bear said, moving back to his own spot. "Last one to find a wallet has to buy dinner."

"Guess you owe me dinner then," Mandy said, picking something up off the ground. She waved it at Bear with a grin on her face. "Too slow, old man."

Bear groaned theatrically. "Fine, you win. Whose is it?"

"Raymond Adderman. It's the guy's wallet." Staring at it for a moment before shaking herself clear of her thoughts, she opened it up. "Couple bucks. Credit card. Not much else."

"Is the address local?" Bear asked, still searching the ground. The woman's couldn't be too far away.

"Boonesville, yeah," she said. "Out on Peach Street. You know where that is?"

"Not too far from the bar. A street or two over." Bear spotted a splash of red against the stalks of corn. "Got the woman's."

Mandy joined him as he bent down to pick it up. "What's her name?"

"Lily," Bear said. He froze at the familiar last name and levied a look at Mandy. "Lily Duvall."

32

Bear's first instinct was to go back to Amos' farmhouse and confront Iris. How did either of them expect him to help them if they didn't tell Bear the whole truth? When he'd first met Iris, he thought she was just a tourist, someone heading to St. Louis for one reason or another. She'd played her cards right, acting overly friendly and chatty. But in the short time he'd been around her since finding her again, Iris was a different person.

Not to mention she had been related to the dead woman. And somehow, she was tied to both Amos and whatever was going on with Luke Salazar. But if every move she'd made so far had been intentional, did that mean she'd meant to drag him and Mandy into this mess?

Despite the havoc this situation had caused, Bear didn't think Iris would do that to Mandy. She was just a child, after all. Bear could come up with a couple of reasons why Iris might've dragged him into this but bringing Mandy in didn't make any sense.

That still left a lot of questions. All of which would have to wait.

Needing to cool down before talking to Iris, Bear decided to show up at Raymond Adderman's house. If the man had lived alone or the house was locked, Bear wouldn't find anything. He could break in, but there was too high a chance of getting caught, and that wasn't worth the trouble. He didn't even know what he was looking for. All Bear knew was that Iris was connected to Luke, Amos, and Lily, who was connected to Raymond, but Bear couldn't even begin to guess the full picture here. He needed more information.

It wasn't hard to find the man's house sandwiched between two similar looking homes, all of which looked too small for the average American family. The paint on Raymond's front porch was peeling, and the concrete steps leading to the front door were cracked and uneven. A couple of shingles from the roof were scattered around the front yard, and it looked like the man had been in the middle of fixing the siding on one end of the house.

Now, that project would never be finished.

Bear would've felt sympathy for the man's death if he hadn't killed Lily Duvall and tried to do the same to Mandy. Bear never reveled in another person's death, but he found he didn't feel bad about what had happened.

Bear pulled the truck as far up the driveway as he could, hoping the two goons wouldn't come across it any time soon.

Mandy followed him out of the truck and around to the front of the house. They both looked up at its sorry state, wondering if they could even walk across the front porch without it falling through. But before either could make a move, the screen door to the house next door squeaked opened and fell shut again. A boy about Mandy's age emerged, walked down the front steps, and climbed onto the bike he'd left haphazardly in the front yard, not noticing either of them.

But Bear recognized him.

"Benji?" Bear asked.

Benji's head snapped up, and his eyes widened as he took in Bear's hulking form. Before Bear could get another word out, the kid straightened his bike, and got ready to take off without a moment's hesitation.

Mandy moved before Bear could. "Wait!" she yelled, darting out from behind Bear and jumping directly in Benji's path forward. Instead of swerving around her, the kid slammed on his brakes and almost toppled over. Bear stayed put, so he didn't spook the kid again.

Benji looked Mandy up and down. "Who are you? I don't recognize you from school."

164

"I don't go to school here," Mandy said, making her voice light and more girlish. "My name is Mandy. Yours is Benji, right?"

Benji nodded. "Are you new in town?"

"We're not staying." Mandy gestured to Bear. "My dad and I are just visiting."

Benji's eyes somehow widened even more. They were at risk of popping out of his head now. "Your *dad*?" he squeaked.

Mandy laughed. "Yeah, my dad. We were hoping we could ask you about something."

Benji tossed a look at Bear that made it clear he had no interest in interacting with them any more than necessary.

Mandy also saw the look and changed her approach. "Please? It'll only take a minute, and it's really important. Don't be afraid of my dad. He's a teddy bear."

Benji straightened up at that. "I'm not afraid." He looked at Bear defiantly. "But I don't have to answer any of your questions. You're not the cops."

"Whatever Luke is paying you," Bear said, "I'll double it."

Benji's mouth dropped open in shock. Bear had a feeling it had more to do with the fact that he even knew who Luke was, let alone that Benji was working for him, than it was about the money. But no matter the reason, it seemed to work. Benji leaned back on his bike, steadying himself with both legs, and crossed his arms over his chest. "What do you want to know?"

"Raymond Adderman lived here, right?" Bear asked, pointing to the house next door.

Benji's face hardened. "Yeah. He was always nice to me. Still can't believe he's gone. Hope they catch whoever did that to him."

Mandy took a menacing step forward. "He killed someone. He wasn't a good person."

"You don't know that," the kid said. "It could've been a setup. Someone probably lied to the cops about it. I bet—"

"I was there," Mandy hissed. "I saw it happen."

Benji's mouth snapped shut, and his face softened in response to the emotion on her face. "I'm sorry."

"It's okay." Mandy pushed some hair out of her face, and Bear could see her rearrange her expression into something more aloof. "I guess we don't always know who's living next to us, do we?"

Benji looked a little shaken up now. "No, I guess not."

"Do you work for Luke Salazar," Mandy asked.

"Not by choice," Benji said, looking away in embarrassment now. "We needed the money. I didn't know what else to do. Jake, his brother, introduced me to him. Said all I had to do was deliver some packages around town. I thought it was, like, stolen electronics or something. I didn't know what I was getting into, and by the time I figured it out—"

"It was too late," Bear finished. Benji nodded, and Bear was grateful to see some of the posturing leave his expression. "Is that how you knew Raymond?" When Benji nodded again, Bear asked, "How did Raymond and Luke know each other?"

"I think they were friends when they were kids," Benji said. "It seemed like they'd known each other for a long time. But I don't think Raymond liked Luke very much. I heard that Ray went to jail. But it should've been Luke."

"Then why was Raymond working with Luke?" Mandy asked.

Benji shrugged. "Beats me. I never asked."

"What's your impression of Luke?" Bear asked.

Benji looked surprised that anyone wanted to know his opinion. "He has anger issues. Serious ones. That's where Jake gets it from. Or they both get it from their dad."

"How many guys does he have working for him?" Bear asked.

"Not sure." Benji looked a lot more comfortable talking to them now, resting his forearms on the handlebars of his bike and the nervousness leaving his voice. "Raymond was always with him. I know he's got a few other guys that he sends out to push people around. Luke doesn't like to get his hands dirty."

"Any idea where he's getting his product?"

Benji shook his head. "He doesn't tell us that stuff. I don't think even Jake knows."

"Ever heard of a guy named Mr. Reagan?"

Benji shook his head again. "Sorry."

Bear pulled a wad of cash out of his wallet and handed it to the kid. "This is for your mom." He pulled a couple more bills out. "This is for you. Buy something good with it."

Benji looked down at the money in wonder. He'd never seen so much in one place before, let alone held it and called it his own. When he looked up at Bear, it was in awe. "Are you sure?"

"Stay out of trouble. You don't need friends like Jake. Your mom loves you a lot, and she's worried about you. Don't get mixed up with people like Luke. And if you are, get out. Got it?"

Benji nodded his head, and Bear thought maybe his words had gotten to him. Or maybe it was just the money. Then Benji looked away, conflict written across his face. Bear gave him a few seconds, and in that moment, Benji came to some sort of conclusion. When he looked up again, there was determination in his eyes.

"I was about to go meet someone. To drop money off to one of Luke's guys." Pulling a rumpled paper bag out of his pocket, he gave it to Bear. "What if he gets mad at me?"

"I won't mention you talked to me. If someone asks, tell them I took it from you. Jake and the others already met me once. It won't be hard for them to believe."

Benji still looked nervous, but he nodded his head. Before he could say anything in return, however, the screen door squeaked open again, and his mother stepped out onto the front porch in her bathrobe and slippers.

"Ma'am," Bear said, inclining his head toward her.

"Everything okay out here?" she asked.

"Just having a chat with Benji," Bear said, putting a comforting hand on the kid's shoulder. "He was just gonna go back inside."

Cindy picked up the hint. Even from his vantage point, Bear could see the tears forming in her eyes. "Thank you," she said. When her voice was steadier, she continued. "Can I make you breakfast? Coffee?"

Bear's gaze slid to the minivan sitting in the driveway.

"Actually, there is one thing."

33

CINDY HAD LOOKED DUBIOUS WHEN BEAR ASKED TO BORROW HER CAR, BUT after Benji told her Bear was doing him a favor, she was more than willing to hand over the car keys. Mandy, on the other hand, was much less understanding about being left behind. But it was for her own good.

Benji had given the bag of cash to Bear, who stuffed it into his pocket. Bear already had a low opinion of Luke, but what kind of scumbag used kids to do their dirty work? Without a doubt, Luke was taking advantage of Benji's poverty, using it as leverage. From Bear's previous observations, he knew the other kid, Brent, was in a similar situation.

Benji had told Bear one of two people would show up at the drop point. The first was a man named Caleb, who the kid described as tall and gangly. He apparently wasn't much of a fighter, but he was smart and found a way to talk himself into—or out of—whatever he wanted. After Raymond, this guy was probably Luke's closest confidant. At the very least, the Boonesville Kingpin was just using Caleb for his brains.

The other guy who could show up to the drop point was the opposite —big, dumb, and always ready to throw a punch. Benji described him as a hulking guy who had at least twenty to thirty pounds on Bear but stood a good four or five inches shorter. He had a military haircut and a sharp widow's peak. He also always wore a leather jacket and the same pair of dark-wash jeans. His name was Big Tony.

And because Bear didn't know which he would get, he had decided Mandy couldn't come along for the ride. She'd whined and pleaded, but Bear gave her one of his patented looks and she'd huffed, crossed her arms, and looked away. That was as good as it would get. He'd felt guilty seeing the tears in her eyes at being left behind, but it wasn't worth the risk. Clearly, these people didn't mind leveraging kids to their advantage, and he wasn't about to let them lay a hand on his daughter.

Mandy stayed back with Benji and Cindy, who promised to feed her lunch and keep her entertained. Bear had only hesitated for a second, wondering if the woman would be capable of looking after two kids, but her eyes seemed brighter than they had the other night. Maybe he'd given her some hope for the future. Besides, Mandy was more than capable of taking care of herself.

The truck stayed behind in Raymond's driveway. It was far enough back that it wouldn't be visible from the street. Bear figured the two guys he'd met at Garrett's barn would look for their vehicle eventually, but by the time they found it, if ever, he'd be far enough away. He'd already warned Cindy to keep the doors locked, and if she saw the men, pretend they weren't home. Aside from giving her his number in case of emergency, there wasn't much else Bear could do for them. There were no relatives she could stay with, so it was all about hunkering down until this all blew over.

As Bear neared his destination, he went through his mental checklist to prepare for what was coming next. His body was feeling pretty good—the soreness from earlier in the morning had faded away. He was still tired from his restless night's sleep. If he'd been smart, he would've stuck around for lunch to let his aching muscles soak up some calories, but he'd wanted to get to the drop point before the other man. He needed a few extra minutes to observe.

The drop point was the local playground. The day was beautiful and sunny, but that didn't do it any favors. The whole thing was in rough shape, like it hadn't been updated since the eighties. The colors had once been bright yellow, red, and blue, now they were faded and rusted. Bear parked along the street, not surprised at the lack of kids playing on the equipment. The slide was made of metal, and probably well over a hundred degrees from the last few hours of bright sun. There was a jungle gym and some monkey bars, along with a set of swings, though it looked like two of them had been ripped down at some point. Even the ground was covered in wooden mulch instead of rubber chunks. There was no doubt in Bear's mind that the injuries here wouldn't be worth the cheap thrills.

Bear stayed in the minivan, cracking the window, and leaning the seat back a few inches, so the bulk of his frame was out of view. The guy meeting Benji would expect a kid on a bike, not a grown man in a vehicle. It'd give Bear a minute or two to observe who he was meeting and decide his best course of action.

Luckily, he didn't have to wait long. A beat-up silver Corolla sped past Bear and swerved into a parking space a few spaces down. The figure emerged from the car, slamming the door shut and walking casually toward the playground. It was Big Tony.

Of course, it was.

Benji had done the man a few favors. He was definitely shorter than Bear, but it looked like he had a good fifty pounds on him. Even from a distance, Bear could tell the man's hands were massive. Getting punched in the face by those things would pack a wallop. The man's thighs were like tree trunks but moving all that muscle would take time. Chances were, he wouldn't be all that quick. Bear was big, but he'd learned to move quick.

"Might not even come to that," Bear muttered to himself. He wasn't looking for a fight, but thinking about this guy pushing Benji around made his blood boil. The kid on the bike who looked like Brent's little brother had been even younger than the others, and he'd seemed terrified to be out there with them. That was no life for a kid. Who did Luke think he was?

The man did a circuit around the playground, as though Benji might be hiding behind something, ready to jump out at any second. When Tony was satisfied he was alone, he picked a bench and sat down, stuffing his hands in his jacket pockets and keeping his head on a swivel. He must not have been anticipating much trouble though, because his gaze passed right over the minivan at least half a dozen times.

One unknown factor was whether the guy was armed. There was a decent chance he wasn't, considering he thought he was meeting a kid. But these types of guys usually carried. If it wasn't a gun, it was a knife. Sometimes both.

"Only one way to find out," Bear said, realizing that talking out loud to himself wasn't a good sign. Having Mandy as a lookout would've been nice, but she wouldn't be able to stay in the van. All that worry wasn't worth the extra set of eyes.

Bear pushed his door open and let it fall shut as quietly as possible. Big Tony hadn't noticed him yet, and Bear wanted to keep it that way. Instead of making straight for the playground, Bear took the long way around, walking down the sidewalk like he had a destination in mind. He could see Big Tony clock him from his bench, but after a few seconds, he looked away again. Either this guy had no idea who Bear was yet, or he was too stupid to remember. Or too arrogant to think Bear posed a threat.

It worked out for Bear. He hooked right and walked along the sidewalk until he was directly behind Big Tony, then he veered off the path and trudged through the grass, dry and crunchy under his shoes. Big Tony still didn't turn around, and only appeared to notice Bear when he plopped onto the bench next to him.

The big man's head snapped to the right to stare at Bear, and Bear could see the gears working in the man's brain, wondering what this guy was up to. Tony looked around the park, as though a kid or a dog would materialize out of thin air to explain Bear's presence there. But when nothing appeared, he turned to glare at Bear again.

"Hey man," Bear said, a wide grin on his face. He needed to blow off a little steam. "Got a light?"

"No." Big Tony's voice was higher than Bear would've expected, but it was loud enough to carry. "Get outta here."

Bear blinked his eyes innocently. "Why?"

"I got business. Go. Before I make you go."

"It's a free country," Bear said. "Is your name on the park? Do you own it?"

Big Tony was quick to anger. He pulled his massive fists out of his jacket and clenched them on his legs. At least he wasn't holding a weapon. "You've got five seconds," he said. "You don't want to make me angry."

"I think I do." Bear couldn't help but laugh. This guy was a caricature of a goon. At least the man he encountered at Garrett's barn had fashion sense. "Here, I thought you were the guy I was supposed to deliver to, but I guess not." Bear pulled out the bag of money. "I'll just keep this for myself, then."

Big Tony snatched for the bag, but Bear had been right about the man's reaction times—slow as hell. Bear had plenty of time to move it far out of the man's reach and then stuff it back into his coat. "Hey, you told me to get lost. I don't want to make you angry."

"Hand it over," Big Tony growled. He got to his feet, so he was towering over Bear. "Now."

"I have a few questions first." Bear stayed seated, throwing one arm over the back of the bench and balancing one ankle on top of the opposite knee. It made Big Tony even angrier. "Does pushing around little kids make you feel tough and powerful?" Bear didn't wait for an answer. "I think it makes you pathetic."

Big Tony clenched his fists at his sides. He looked like a kid about to throw a temper tantrum. "You have five seconds to hand it over."

"Can you even count that high, big man?"

Tony lunged, but Bear was ready for it. He leaned to the side and kicked a foot out, aiming for the man's right knee. It buckled. Tony went down howling, grabbing at his leg. Bear stood, planting his feet.

"Look man." Bear dropped the congenial attitude. "This isn't going to end well for you. Give me some information about Luke, and I'll let you walk away."

Tony didn't bother answering. He stood and tested his weight. When he was sure it would hold, he glared at Bear and pulled out a hunting knife. The thing was long and sharp. Serrated on one side. And though it looked like there was a spot of rust near the handle, Bear was almost certain it was blood. Whether it was human was another question.

A knife was better than a gun, however, and Bear was happy to know all the cards were on the table. Big Tony would use brute force, not speed or skill, so it wouldn't take long for Bear to disarm him. But what would he do with the guy after that?

"You're really not going to answer my questions?" Bear asked. "I promise I'll make it as easy on you as possible. I know you're slow, but you gotta know something."

"I'm not telling you shit," Tony spat. "You either give me that money now—or later. Either way, I'm gonna kill you."

Bear furrowed his brow. "That's not much incentive to hand over the cash, now, is it?"

Tony slashed the knife through the air, mostly for show. Bear was still a few inches out of reach, but he jumped back and put the bench between them. He had to make one final attempt at getting some information, or this whole thing would be a bust.

"Just tell me one thing," Bear said. "Who's Mr. Reagan?"

That made Tony pause. He cocked his head to one side, but Bear couldn't tell if he was digesting the question or confused as to how Bear knew that name. After a few seconds, the big man finally spoke. "You work for Mr. Reagan?"

"What if I do?"

Tony lowered the knife an inch or two. "What do you want?"

"Information. Like I said."

Tony squinted his eyes. "You checking up on us?"

"Mr. Reagan isn't too pleased." Bear thought back to what Baldy had said in the barn. He'd wanted to send Luke a message. "You have any idea why that might be?"

Tony's eyes darted back and forth, but before he could answer, his gaze shifted somewhere over Bear's shoulder. Then his eyes grew wide. He threw up a hand and yelled, "Wait!"

Bear spun to his left just as a baseball bat whistled through the air past his head. When he turned to meet his second attacker, he was surprised to find Caleb, the tall, gangly guy Benji had warned him about. Caleb's description had been way more accurate. He was a couple inches taller than Bear, but rail-thin to the point where his joints stuck out like sharp corners on a table. It was discomforting to witness.

"He works for Mr. Reagan," Big Tony told his companion.

Caleb sneered at his partner. "Do you know that for sure?" As Tony computed that question, Caleb turned to Bear. "Who are you? What do you want?"

"Came here to deliver a package." Bear patted the pocket holding the bag full of money. "Wanted some intel in exchange for it. Your friend here isn't too bright."

"You're the guy who's been causing trouble around town. You're a lot uglier than Jake made you out to be."

"A lot meaner, too." Bear wasn't going to let this guy get a rise out of him. But he wasn't going to get anything out of Caleb either. "You're not going to tell me what I want to know, are you?"

"Unless it's directions to the highway, not a chance."

"Then I guess you can give Luke a message." Bear shifted his weight, ready for what came next. "Tell him I have his money. If he wants it, he can come get it from me. Tomorrow. Noon. In the center of town. We can negotiate his resignation. If he knows what's good for him, he'll put this town in his rearview."

Caleb threw his head back and laughed. "Luke isn't afraid of you. You're gonna regret threatening him."

Bear shrugged. "I've done a lot of regrettable things in my life. Threatening douchebags who push kids around isn't one of them. What'll it be? Deliver the message, or get your asses handed to you?"

"I'll take option C," Caleb said. "Bash your head in and call it a day."

As Caleb raised the bat to swing, Big Tony caught the shift in conversation and raised his knife. The pair of them circled in opposite directions, coming at Bear from two different angles. As threatening as their weapons were, these guys were amateurs. They were used to roughing up kids and elderly farmers. They had no idea who Bear was or what he was capable of.

Caleb swung first but telegraphed the move, allowing Bear enough time to raise his hand and catch the bat in his grasp. The swing would've hurt if it had landed against his temple, but the slap only made Bear's hand sting. Caleb was too skinny to put any real power behind it and let go when Bear tugged on the bat.

Bear used the momentum to swing at Big Tony who was charging him with the knife out in front. Swinging the bat in a perfect arch, Bear knocked the weapon out of the other man's hands and potentially broke a couple of fingers as he did so. Now the two of them were down two weapons, and Bear was up one.

He didn't wait for Tony to recover. Bear swung the bat hard enough to knock the big man out without killing him. He doubted either of these guys would risk a police investigation by filing assault charges. But Bear did want to teach him a lesson. Maybe take him out of the game for a few days.

As soon as Tony's unconscious body hit the ground, Caleb realized the tide was turning and spun to run away. Bear swung the bat like a golf club and watched as the beanpole took a tumble of his own, landing face first in the pile of woodchips next to the bench. Caleb groaned, then flipped over onto his back, throwing a handful of the chips at Bear's face. Bear whacked them away with an open palm and brought the bat down on the man's shin. Caleb cried out in shock and pain.

Bear bent over the guy. "I'm gonna make sure you remember this." He brought the bat down on his other shin. Not enough to break the leg, but enough to leave a nasty bruise. Walking would be painful for a few hours. "Tell Luke. Tomorrow at noon. Town center. Either he puts an end to his operation, or I do it for him."

Caleb had enough energy left to spit out a few more words. "You're gonna regret this."

"Not as much as I'm gonna enjoy it," Bear said, bringing the bat down once more, this time against the side of Caleb's knee. There was a loud pop, and the guy screamed. Dislocated, not broken. It'd be painful, but he figured the guy should be grateful Bear left him conscious. Brain damage would make it hard for Caleb to deliver his message.

Bear dropped the bat and let the sound of Caleb's screams fade away as he made it back to the minivan, pulling out into the street and driving away with the sun at his back. It really was a beautiful day.

34

"Start from the beginning. And don't lie to me this time."

Luke pointed his gun at Big Tony's head. The oaf was sitting on the couch in his basement, gripping the armrests like they were the only thing tethering him to the earth. The big idiot was stupid, but Luke was dead serious. Something had been missing from his story the first time around. It was better just to tell the truth and get it over with.

"Went to go meet the kid in the park," Tony said. "Benny."

"Benji," Luke ground out. "Only the kid didn't show up, did he?"

Big Tony shook his head, then licked his lips. His eyes were moving back and forth like he was searching for the answer that would get Luke to lower his gun. "Then the guy showed up. The one who's been sticking his nose in our business."

Our business. Luke scoffed. But he could tell those weren't Big Tony's words. They were Caleb's. He didn't know where Tony's better half was, but they'd get to that, eventually. "Just the one guy? Or were there more of them?"

"M-more of them," Tony stammered. "Three or four."

"I thought you said there was five?" Luke's arm was getting tired, but he kept the gun steady.

Big Tony hung his head. "I don't remember."

"How many were there, Tony?" Luke waved the gun in front of his face. "Tell me the truth."

"Just the one." Tony swallowed. "Just the one guy."

Now they were getting somewhere. "What happened?"

"He showed up. Wanted information. Said he'd give me the money if I answered his questions. But I didn't! I swear I didn't."

Luke believed him, if only because he trusted Caleb to keep Tony's mouth shut for him. "What kind of questions? What did he want to know?"

"He asked about you. Wanted to know where you were. Then he asked about Mr. Reagan."

That raised Luke's hackles. Who was this guy, and how could he know about Mr. Reagan? Only a select few knew the identity of their benefactor. Raymond and Caleb. Garrett. And Tony, but he was worthless. Telling Tony anything was like telling a cardboard box.

"What else?"

"That's it," Tony said. "Caleb snuck up behind him, tried to knock him down. We went to jump him, but he was fast. And strong. Ain't never seen someone move like that."

Luke lowered the gun, and Tony relaxed his shoulders. "Caleb have any idea who this guy was?"

The oaf shook his head, spittle flying in all directions. "Said he fought like someone with training, though."

"And where is Caleb now?"

"Hospital," Tony said. "Hurt his knee. Couldn't walk. Told me to come back here and tell you that he'd be back as soon as he had it checked out."

"He tell you anything else?" Luke asked.

"The guy had a message for you."

Luke waited for Big Tony to continue, and when it became clear that he was waiting for a follow-up question, Luke asked it through gritted teeth. "What was the message?"

Tony sat up a little straighter, concern still flooding his eyes. He might've been big, but he was terrified of Luke. "If you want your money back, meet him in town center tomorrow at noon."

The doorbell interrupted whatever Luke was about to say next. Big Tony appeared relieved that the spotlight was off him now.

Trudging up the stairs, Luke yanked open the front door. He wasn't expecting anyone, which didn't mean much. He always had people coming and going, picking up product and dropping off money. Hell, maybe this new guy had come to apologize and hand over the cash he'd stolen.

But the person on the other side of the door was one of his runners, a woman named Rhonda who ran her own farm. She'd been one of the easiest to blackmail. After a few days of observing her, Luke had figured out she had a gambling problem. Owed lots of people, lots of money. In exchange for some extra cash, she'd help deliver some of his product to the city. A few trips turned into a few dozen. Luke would have liked to believe his charisma had kept her working for him, but they both knew it was her own greed that kept her going.

"What the hell are you doing here?" Luke asked. The runners were, under no circumstance, ever to show up at his home.

"I-I have news," Rhonda said. "I figured you'd want to know."

Luke pulled her inside and slammed the door after her. "And you thought you'd show up at my doorstep instead of leaving me a message?"

Rhonda shook. It was a good thing she was only responsible for dropping off shipments. She was useless otherwise. It was a wonder she could tend to her own farm. Her eyes grew wide when she saw the pistol still in Luke's hand. When Big Tony trudged up the stairs to see who had arrived, she pressed herself into the wall, her hand searching for the doorknob.

Luke waggled a finger at her. "No, no. You had balls enough to come here, you better finish the job. What did you want to tell me?"

"I-I can come b-back," she said. "At a better time?"

Luke gripped the gun tighter in his hand and took a menacing step forward. "You have ten seconds to spit it out. I'm not responsible for what happens next."

"Two guys were snooping around Garrett's farm. They pushed me around." She pointed to her cheek, which looked a little purple under her eye. Luke had just thought it was bad makeup at first. "I didn't recognize them."

"Was one of them big with a beard?" Luke asked.

Rhonda shook her head. "N-no, but I've seen him t-too."

"Where? When?"

"At Amos'," she said. "He was staying at Amos' place."

Luke froze. That was news to him. He turned to Big Tony. "Did you know about this?"

The oaf shook his head again, sending more spittle flying. Luke saw a drop land on the wall and grimaced. Disgusting.

Luke turned back to Rhonda. "What else? Why is he staying there?"

"I-I don't know. I didn't ask." Rhonda must've realized that was a mistake, because she hurried forward. "But there was someone else there, too. A woman. She looked like Lily."

That caught Luke off-guard. How did he not know? This town had been under his thumb for over a year, and now everything was falling to pieces. And it had all started when that guy showed up and started getting involved. Who the hell was he, and why did he care so much about what was going on around here?

Luke was about to order Rhonda to go back to Amos' house and learn whatever she could about the new guy when another knock sounded on the door. He swore loudly, not caring if the person on the other side could hear him. "Am I running a motel around here? Why the fuck is everyone showing up at my goddamn house?"

He yanked the door open, sending Rhonda stumbling back, ready to chew the head off of whoever had decided to disturb him. But when he saw the men on the other side, he froze. He didn't have to recognize the other men to know who they were. Two guys, both dressed in black slacks, button-down shirts, and black ties. They were either Feds or Mr. Reagan's men. Luke's gut pointed to the latter. Everything else was going wrong today, so why not this?

Luke's stomach tightened, but he'd never admit it was from anxiety. There weren't many people in this world he was afraid of, but Mr. Reagan was one. Not only was he rich and powerful, but he also had the means of taking away all of Luke's dreams with the snap of his fingers. Luke had already lost his best friend and ex-girlfriend. He wasn't about to lose this.

"Can I help you, gentlemen?"

The bald man stepped into Luke's house without invitation, his partner on his heels. "Mr. Reagan sends his regards. He'd like an update on the shipping schedule."

"I'm a little busy right now," Luke said, gesturing to Big Tony and Rhonda, as if they were guests. "Let me get back to you."

The bald man eyed the gun in Luke's hand, unconcerned. His partner, however, made a subtle move to show Luke he was packing, too. "Mr. Reagan doesn't like to be kept waiting."

Luke ground his teeth together. "Well, Mr. Reagan isn't here right now, is he?" For a second, Luke wondered if he was. He was curious to meet his mysterious benefactor. But Mr. Reagan's presence would mean the beginning of the end for Luke.

The man with the brown hair didn't bother arguing their case. He pulled his gun, pointed it at Big Tony, and pulled the trigger. He tumbled down the steps, back into the basement at such a speed that it cracked the wall at the bottom of the stairs. Luke had turned just in time to see the bullet land between the man's eyeballs. There was no chance he'd recover from that.

Rhonda started screaming, clutching her face and pressing herself back into the wall. The guy in the suit turned his gun on her but didn't pull the trigger. Either she couldn't see him through her tears, or she couldn't stop herself from screaming. Luke didn't have much empathy for the woman, but more dead bodies would draw attention, and that was the last thing he needed right now.

Gripping the barrel of his own gun in his hand, Luke slapped her across the face with the butt of his pistol, sending her tumbling to the ground and knocking her out cold. If she were smart, she'd stay down until they left. He was just happy she'd finally shut up.

"Right." Luke grabbed his jacket off the wall as though he hadn't just witnessed a murder. "Let me give you the grand tour."

35

BEAR FELT CONFIDENT AFTER HIS CONFRONTATION IN THE PARK. BETWEEN Caleb and Tony, Bear's message would undoubtedly get back to Luke. He probably wouldn't care about Bear beating up his goons, but he would care about Bear taking the money. Guys like Luke Salazar always cared more about money than their employees.

When Bear arrived back at Cindy's, the truck still sat in Raymond's driveway. It'd only be a matter of time until the goons found it. And now that Bear had pissed off Luke, they'd all be gunning for him, hurting others along the way. Benji would be the first.

With that in mind, Bear loaded Cindy, Benji, and Mandy into the van and drove them to Amos' house. Even if the old farmer wasn't too happy about the unexpected guests, he doubted he'd turn the mother and son away. With any luck, it'd only be for a few days, and Benji might have more information against Luke.

Besides, he and Mandy seemed to be getting along. Maybe well enough for her to stay out of trouble, at least for a little while.

Bear knocked before entering and found Amos and Iris sitting at the dinner table, deep in conversation. When Bear stepped inside they broke off. Amos got to his feet when he realized Cindy and Benji were in tow. The old man looked to Bear with questions in his eyes.

"Sorry to do this to you," Bear said, "but do you have an extra room for these two?"

"Of course." Amos didn't even bat an eye. "Is everyone okay?" Spotting Mandy, he pursed his lips. "Young lady, you were supposed to be in your room."

Mandy had the wherewithal to appear ashamed, but Bear could see right through it. "Sorry."

"Don't feel too bad. She's a sneaky one." Bear watched as Mandy fought to keep the pride off her face. "But if it wasn't for her, I might not be here right now."

"Why is that?" Amos asked.

"The two men Rhonda described followed me somehow. They found me at Garrett's farm."

Amos blanched. "You went to Garrett's farm?" He exchanged a look with Iris, then turned back to Bear, shaking his head. "You shouldn't have done that."

"You haven't been straight with me. Figured I needed to find my own answers." When Amos stayed quiet, Bear asked. "Why is it such a big deal?"

"Garrett is not what we call a trustworthy person. He'll talk to anyone with a dollar. Did he see you?"

"No. Far as I could tell, he wasn't home."

"You're lucky. The first thing he'd do is tell Luke you were snooping around."

"They slashed the tires on the old truck." Now Bear felt a little bad. "Couldn't drive it, so I took theirs. I'll make sure you get a new set before I leave town."

Amos hung his head, but he looked resigned. "Are you hurt?"

"Nah." Bear led Cindy and Benji over to the table before he continued. "They tried, but this one kept an eye on me." He ruffled Mandy's hair. Trying to scowl, she was fighting a smile at the same time. "Went back to the field from yesterday. Found the man's wallet. Name was Raymond Adderman. Ring a bell?"

Amos nodded, but didn't seem surprised. Then his eyes drifted over to Cindy. "Lived next door to you."

"Saw Benji out in the yard," Bear explained. "He was running an errand for Luke. I went instead, met a couple of Luke's guys."

"Caleb and Tony?" Amos asked. "They're usually the ones doing the enforcing."

"This time, they'll be delivering a message to Luke for me. Maybe Garrett will leave you out of it."

"Doubt it." For what it was worth, Amos looked more concerned for Bear than himself. "Did you—"

"They're fine. Caleb might end up with a limp, but it'll be a good reminder not to mess with strangers." Bear looked down at Benji, who was avoiding eye contact. "Seems like Luke works for a man named Mr. Reagan. Ever heard of him?"

"Can't say that I have." Amos scratched at his head. "Doesn't ring a bell, anyway."

Bear believed him. But he also saw the way Iris' lips had pressed together in a tight line. "Found another wallet while we were there, too. The woman who died was named Lily Duvall." Bear waited until Iris met his gaze. "Why didn't you tell me?"

"Didn't seem like you needed to know."

Bear quelled the anger bubbling in his stomach. It was difficult to keep his voice even, but he did so for the sake of Cindy and Benji. He didn't want to scare them. "I can't help you if I don't know the whole truth."

"I'm not convinced we can trust you." Iris sat back in her chair, crossing her arms over her chest.

"Likewise," Bear said. "Neither of us will get anywhere unless we come to a truce."

Iris blew out a breath and looked at Amos. They both remained silent, but something passed between them. An understanding. A resignation.

Amos was the first to break their gaze. "I'll get these two settled in upstairs." He led the way into the living room and over to the staircase. "Come on, Mandy. I could use an extra hand."

Mandy hesitated, torn between helping and wanting to know what Iris was going to disclose. Bear gave her a little push in the other direction. "Go on. I'll fill you in later."

Iris waited until the floorboards upstairs were creaking under everyone's weight. "You ever worry you treat her too much like an adult?"

The question had no venom behind it, and Bear tried his best not to bristle. "Kid's been through a lot. It'd be a disservice to treat her like a child." Bear wasn't used to being vulnerable, especially with someone he knew was keeping secrets from him. "Wish she could have a normal childhood. Thought about it a million times. But life didn't offer us that option. I'm doing the best I can."

"She's a good kid," Iris said. Her voice was quiet now. Contemplative. "She looks up to you."

He chuckled quietly. "She doesn't know any better."

Iris nodded. Then bit her lip. "My cousin was like that."

"Lily?"

She nodded again. "I was two years older, but we were close. Like sisters." Iris looked like she wanted to cry, but she was able to keep the tears at bay. "I went off to college. Wanted to—" She stumbled here. Only for a fraction of a second, but Bear could tell she wanted to say one thing, then chose another. "Wanted to do something bigger with my life. Lily always struggled in school. Couldn't quite get the hang of it. We went our separate ways. Lost touch for a while. Tracked her down a few years ago. She wasn't doing too well. Got mixed up with some bad people."

"Raymond?" Bear asked. "Luke?"

"Yeah. Lily started doing drugs. But I knew she didn't want that life. She was just depressed and broke and lonely. We started talking once a week. Then every day. She told me what was going on here, and I wanted to get her out."

"That's why you came." Bear tried to remove any trace of blame from his voice. "The bus. That was you, wasn't it? When it broke down. How? How'd you do it?"

Iris looked up at him with sorrow in her eyes. "I wanted to come up with a cover story. Make it less obvious. Never meant to get you involved. I hope you believe that."

"I do." Bear scratched at his beard as he let the *how* of it all go. "I'm sorry about Lily. If Luke knew she wanted out—"

"Luke killed her." Iris' face hardened. "Raymond might've been the one to do it, but Luke told him to. They'd been dating on and off for a few years. He wasn't good to her. Or when he was, it was just long enough to make her fall in love again."

"Manipulative."

Iris' jaw was set. "She wanted out. And she didn't want him to hurt anyone else. She was gonna go to the cops. I was gonna be here to make sure nothing happened to her. And I was too late."

"That's not your fault," Bear began.

"I'll deal with my own demons when this is all over," she said. "For now, I just want to nail Luke to the wall."

Bear nodded, deciding to switch the subject. "How'd you meet Amos?"

"Lily. They'd been working together, exchanging information, trying to work out the best time to shut Luke down. But this goes higher than him. It's bigger. Much bigger."

"Mr. Reagan," Bear offered. "You recognized the name."

Iris looked like she was at war with herself, trying to figure out what to say, how much to reveal now. Bear wondered who she really was and how she'd gotten mixed up in this mess.

Iris opened her mouth to answer, but before she could, there was a pounding on the door.

36

AMOS CAME DOWNSTAIRS, FOLLOWED CLOSELY BY DAISY AND MANDY. CINDY and Benji remained upstairs. When she entered the kitchen, Mandy threw Bear a questioning look, but he just shrugged and shook his head. At the rate this day was going, there was no telling who was on the other side.

When Amos opened the door, the worst-case scenario appeared. Two police officers stood on the front porch, one of whom was Sheriff Woodard, who Daisy sniffed excitedly. Amos let the two men in without asking why they were there. Bear thought it strange that Amos would give the men the chance to snoop around, considering what he was involved in.

Then again, it'd be more of a red flag if he'd kept them waiting on the porch.

"What brings you over here, Chuck?" Amos asked.

It took Bear a moment to realize the old farmer was talking to Sheriff Woodard. The sheriff and his deputy stood in the kitchen, each giving it a glance before landing on the group of people in front of them. The deputy didn't let his eyes wander far from Bear. Even though he hadn't done anything wrong—for the most part—Bear had a sinking feeling.

"We'd like to question Mr. Logan."

Bear bristled. "About what?"

The deputy took a more aggressive stance, but Woodard held up a hand. "Can we speak in private?"

"This isn't my home," Bear said. "You'll have to ask Amos."

"What's this about?" Amos asked. "The man's been here with me all night. What's going on?"

"Do you know anyone by the name of Anthony Abbott?" Woodard asked Bear.

Bear had to force back a laugh. "Everyone I know in this town is in this house right now, save for Joyce and Bette. I guess Locke. Man makes a mean burger."

"Answer the damn question," the deputy barked.

Bear crossed his arms over his chest. "Your listening comprehension ain't too great, is it? Let me spell it out for you then. No, I don't know anyone named Anthony Abbott."

Amos stepped in before the deputy could do anything. "Why? What happened?"

"The man's dead," Woodard said. "Considering Mr. Logan is still a suspect in our previous investigation, I'd like to have a chat with him. I saw him at Joyce's earlier this morning. His best bet is for us to clear his name. I'm doing you both the honor of showing up here to talk about this, but we can go down to the station if you'd like." Woodard looked past Bear to Mandy.

Bear looked over his shoulder at Mandy, too. The last thing he wanted to do was answer their questions, but the truth of the matter was he had nothing to hide. And the last thing he wanted to do was leave Mandy by herself.

He turned back to Amos. "It's all right. I'll answer best I can."

Amos looked resigned. "Can I get you gentlemen anything? Water? Lemonade?"

"You know I'll never turn down a glass of your lemonade, Amos." Woodard pulled out a chair at the head of the table and motioned for Bear to sit in the one next to him. Then he looked up at his deputy. "You're here to take notes, Mason. You understand?"

Deputy Mason didn't look too happy about it, but he pulled out his notepad and sat at the opposite end of the table while Amos got their drinks.

At the same time, Iris stood and herded Mandy to the living room. "Come on," she said. "Let's give them some privacy."

Mandy tried to protest. "But—"

"Go." Bear gave her a look. "I'll be done soon. We can talk later. Spend some time with Iris."

Mandy didn't look happy about that either, but she must've caught the implication in Bear's voice because she didn't argue. With one more look over her shoulder, she allowed Iris to push her through the living room and upstairs. Only when their footsteps stopped creaking through the house did Woodard turn back to Bear.

"Where did you go after I saw you leave Joyce's this morning?" Woodard asked.

Bear didn't hesitate. "Out to Garrett's place. Amos mentioned he might be able to help me get out to the city before the weekend, so I figured I'd go ask him in person. More personal than a phone call, you know?"

Amos shot Bear a look from behind the officer's backs but didn't contradict Bear's story.

"Garrett will be able to confirm this?"

"Doubt it," Bear said. "Couldn't find him. Don't think he was home."

"Where'd you go after that?"

Woodard would go out to Garret's anyway, and they'd find Amos' truck. It would corroborate Bear's story, but it'd raise another set of questions. It would be best to tell the truth at this point. At least in part. "Barn door was open." Bear ignored another sharp look from Amos. "Went inside to see if Garrett was there. Then went up to the house. By the time I got back, my tires had been slashed."

Both Woodard and Mason looked up. "Your tires were slashed?" Woodard asked. "Who would do that?"

"Beats me." Bear kept his voice casual. "Figured it was some kids. Doubt I ran over something that popped all four tires, but I guess it's possible. Ended up having to walk back into town. That was a pain in the ass."

"You weren't concerned about the truck? Or that you might be attacked by whoever had slashed your tires?"

"Didn't see or hear anyone. Told Amos I'd replace the tires before I head out of here. Nothing else I could really do, you know?"

"Fair enough," Woodard said, sounding only half convinced. When Amos set a glass of lemonade down in front of him, Woodard nodded at the man.

"You need anymore, just let me know," Amos said, placing glasses in front of Bear and Mason, then sitting down with one himself.

"Did you come straight back here after that?" Woodard asked. "That's quite a hike."

"No, I went to Cindy's house." There was no point in mentioning his trip into the cornfield for Raymond and Lily's wallets. That wouldn't do him any favors. "Don't know her last name. Kid's name is Benji."

"How do you know them?" Woodard asked.

"Met her at the bar." Woodard raised an eye, and Bear waved off the silent question. "She asked me for some help with her kid. You can ask Locke about that. Benji had gotten in with the wrong crowd, she wanted me to talk to him. Her house was closer than Amos', so I figured I'd stop by there. She let me borrow her van."

Woodard's eyebrow stayed raised. "Just like that? You only met her, what, yesterday?"

Bear shrugged. "Guess I made an impression. I talked to Benji. Straightened him out. And he listened. She was grateful."

"Guess so," Woodard said. Silence fell over the table, except for Mason's scribbling on the notepad in front of him. "Then what?"

This is where Bear had to decide. Leaving out the part where he'd gone into the cornfield wasn't too much of a risk. Only Mandy knew about that. But Bear had left Cindy, Benji, and Mandy at the house while he took the van out himself. If he lied now and Woodard questioned the kid or his mother, there was a good chance the sheriff would know Bear hadn't been truthful. Then they'd be back to square one, with Bear as the number one suspect.

Then again, if Woodard knew Bear had gotten into a scuffle with

Caleb and Big Tony—Bear froze, realization hitting him like a freight train. "Anthony Abbott," Bear repeated. "Does he go by Big Tony?"

Woodard eyed him. Even the deputy looked up from his notepad. "He does," Woodard said. "So, you do know him?"

Bear shook his head. "Didn't put two and two together. Only knew him as Big Tony. That was an honest mistake."

"I'm trying to give you the benefit of the doubt here, Mr. Logan," Woodard said, "but it's getting harder and harder. How did you know him?"

"Benji had said the guy was bullying him. Trying to blackmail him into doing something he didn't want to because his family needed the money. They were supposed to meet in the park a couple blocks over. I went instead."

"So, you saw him an hour or so before he was killed?" Woodard asked. "You can see why this is suspicious."

Bear remained calm, though it was hard to ignore the smirk on Mason's face. "I went to the park to talk to him. He swung on me. I defended myself. His buddy Caleb came up behind me. I knocked them both out, busted the other guy's knee. Then I left. That's the last time I saw them."

"You don't look like you have any injuries," Mason said, pausing in the middle of his notetaking.

"It wasn't a fair fight," Bear said. "I'm used to the odds against me, and they weren't very good. Even with a knife and a bat."

Woodard chewed at the inside of his cheek. "Do you own a gun, Mr. Logan?"

"I do." They'd be able to find that out one way or another. "But I don't have one on me."

"Is there one in this house?" Woodard asked.

"You know damn well there is," Amos said. "And it's mine."

Woodard ignored the farmer. "Do you have a gun in this house, Mr. Logan?"

"No." That was a lie. He'd hidden it last night. Bear doubted they'd be able to find it. "It's at home, back East."

"You can see why this turn of events is concerning, can't you?" Woodard asked.

Even Bear had to admit it didn't look good.

"After the park, I went back to Cindy's house and picked them up. Then we all came here. You can ask them what happened. I wasn't gone for more than ten, maybe fifteen minutes."

Woodard glanced up at the ceiling. "Cindy's here? Now?"

"Yes sir," Bear answered.

Woodard rubbed a hand down his face. "Mason, go talk to her. See if her story matches."

"Hope you don't mind, Chuck," Amos said, "but I'm gonna accompany the deputy here. Make sure he doesn't get lost."

Mason scowled, but Woodard nodded his head. When the pair of them left the room, the sheriff turned back to Bear. "Okay, Mr. Logan. We're gonna run through this again. Let's start from the top."

37

Mandy was so annoyed. Yet again, the adults—not just Bear—were making decisions for her. Three years away from being a legal adult, yet she felt as though she wasn't allowed to share her input. Now the police were questioning Bear about another murder, and a woman she hardly knew was dragging her away. A woman she thought had been her friend, who'd lied to Mandy about everything.

When they reached the top of the stairs, Mandy pulled her arm from Iris' grasp and walked into the room she shared with Bear. At first, Mandy thought Iris would walk away and go to her own room. At least that would give Mandy a chance to sneak downstairs and listen. But Iris stood in the doorway, hovering, looking concerned and apologetic.

It was hard not to snap at her. "What?" Mandy asked.

"Look, I know you're mad at me," Iris said, leaning against the door-jamb. "I'm sorry for hurting your feelings."

"You didn't hurt my feelings," Mandy said. "But you got my dad in trouble." When Iris opened her mouth, Mandy shook her head to stop her. "I know you didn't do it on purpose, and I know you had a good reason. I'm sorry about your cousin, but you didn't stop to think about how this could affect us. And now look where we are."

Iris stared at Mandy, a small smile creeping up on her face. "When I first met you, I thought you were just a normal kid."

"Gross."

Iris laughed. "But you're a lot more than that, Mandy. Your dad is so proud of you. I can see it in his eyes every time he looks at you. You're his pride and joy. And he'd do anything to protect you."

"Yeah, well, sometimes I think someone needs to protect him."

"Did you enjoy *A Wrinkle in Time?*"

Mandy twisted her mouth to one side. She had loved it, but she didn't want to admit that to Iris. "Never got to finish it." It was hard to keep the bitterness from her voice. "But I liked the different creatures and stuff."

"And the part about Meg saving her father?"

Mandy shrugged. Then rolled her eyes. "You got me. Yeah, I liked it. So what?"

"You remind me a lot of Meg. I thought that as soon as I met you."

The bitter taste intensified. "Were you planning on screwing us over from the minute we met you?"

Iris frowned, and looked hurt. "No, of course not, but I didn't know you guys would come this way when the bus broke down."

"The bus *you* caused to break down."

"I didn't plan on anyone getting hurt, and they didn't. Then you came to Boonesville, and I followed."

"Because it was your plan all along."

She nodded. "I sent the bus away because I wanted a logical excuse for why I'd been stuck here. It was unfortunate that you had to get caught in it. I didn't want my cousin to die, and I didn't want you to be involved in that either."

Mandy looked at the floor, trying not to think about what had happened to Lily and what she'd done to Raymond the day before, but it was hard. Iris' intentions had been flawed, but not malicious. And she'd lost someone she used to feel close to. Like a sister.

"I'm sorry about Lily." It was hard for Mandy to say her name aloud. "My dad is doing the best he can, but you're keeping something from us. He can't help if he doesn't know the whole picture."

"I'm still not sure if I can trust him."

"It's not like he wanted to be here," Mandy said. "We'd be halfway to California by now if we'd been able to catch that bus. He wanted nothing to do with this town or whatever is going on here, but now the police are questioning him for a second time, and he hasn't turned on Amos. Or you. What don't you trust about him?"

Iris tried to search for the right words, but she couldn't find them. Resigned, she shrugged. "You're right. I don't have a good reason."

"Do you trust me?" Mandy asked.

There was no hesitation in Iris' voice. "Yes."

"That's a start." Mandy sat down on the bed and patted a spot next to her. Iris walked over and climbed up, leaning back against the wall and hugging her knees to her chest. "So, what are you keeping from us? You said this is bigger than just what's going on in town."

"I don't know everything," Iris admitted, "but whoever Luke is getting his supply from is a bad guy. A crime lord with pull in a lot of cities, and no one knows his real identity. He's been a big problem for a while, and the authorities haven't gotten at all close to finding him."

"How do you know that?"

Iris looked away. "I have my sources."

"Are you a journalist?" Mandy asked.

"No."

"A cop?"

Iris laughed. "Definitely not." Sighing, she looked at Mandy. "This isn't about trust, it's about protection, and I'm not ready to give myself away yet."

Mandy debated whether she should push it. For now, it didn't matter how Iris knew all of this. "Do you know his name?"

"Mr. Reagan. Probably fake. A codename or something."

"And he's supplying Luke," Mandy continued.

"Who's skimming from him, making his own product, and selling it. And he's blackmailing half the townspeople in order to do it."

"What's he got, on Amos?" Mandy asked.

Iris shook her head. "That's not for me to say." She sighed again and rested her chin on her knees. "Luke isn't a complete idiot. He's not afraid to shake someone down. And if he's that volatile—"

"It's only a matter of time before he reaches his boiling point and comes after us."

"Exactly." There was true despair in Iris' eyes. "Lily died trying to bring his operation down. I don't want that to be in vain. But I don't want anyone else to get hurt."

"And if we take down Luke's operation, we'll be on Mr. Reagan's radar."

"He has money. Men. Influence. Power. He could wipe us off the face of the planet, and no one would miss us."

Mandy shrugged. "It's not anything my dad hasn't dealt with before."

It was Iris' turn to be the interrogator now. Her eyes narrowed and her face steeled. "Who is he? Really?"

Mandy felt immense pleasure in getting to hold something over Iris' head now. "That's not for me to say."

38

BEAR DIDN'T STAND AS AMOS SHOWED SHERIFF WOODARD AND DEPUTY Mason to the door. A few quiet words were exchanged between the men. Woodard looked over his shoulder at Bear, as though resigning himself to leaving the house without putting him in cuffs. Until they found the murder weapon, it was all just conjecture.

Cindy and Benji had corroborated Bear's story, and even the officers had to admit that ten or fifteen minutes wouldn't have been enough time to put a bullet in the guy's head and dump his body along the back road where a couple of kids had stumbled upon it. Besides, there had been no gunshots reported from the park, and no evidence in the van. Deputy Mason had checked himself.

Amos closed the door and turned back around, dragging a hand down his face and looking years older than he had the day Bear met him. "Hope you're at least as much help as you are trouble," the old farmer said. "Not sure I can handle much more than this."

"It's usually about half and half," Bear offered. He was tired, too.

"You're either a mass murderer, an unlucky son of a bitch, or someone's out to get you."

"Definitely not option A," Bear said. "Maybe C. Most likely B."

"What are we gonna do?" Amos asked.

"Stop Luke. Then make sure no one else fills the void in his absence."

"Easy as that?"

"Easy as that," Bear said. Silence entered the room and sat with them for a few minutes. "It would help to know why Big Tony was murdered in the first place. My guess is because he didn't get the money from Benji, but it was only about a thousand dollars."

"Not much in the grand scheme of things," Amos agreed.

"Maybe Luke needs every penny because he's worried about paying someone off, but why shoot the guy? Why not send him out again to go collect debts?"

"Luke's volatile. He's smart, but he's got anger issues. Maybe he just snapped."

"And if that's the case," Bear said, "then he just got a lot more dangerous."

Daisy, who had wandered in from lounging in front of the fireplace in the living room, sat at Amos' feet and stared at the front door. Seconds later, they heard tires on the dirt driveway and a car door slam shut. Footsteps up the stairs and across the front porch, and then frantic pounding on the door.

"Amos! Amos, open up!"

"Rhonda?" Amos asked, jumping to his feet and striding over to the door. When he opened it, she stumbled inside, nearly tripping over her feet. Amos caught sight of her face, and his eyes went wide. "My God, what happened?"

Rhonda was unsteady as she sat down at the table in one of the kitchen chairs. Amos poured her a glass of water, and she took a shaky sip before looking up. Bear could see a deep purple bruise blossoming across her face. It was much larger than what she'd sported the other day.

"What happened?" Bear repeated. "Was it the men from the other day? Did they find you again?"

Footsteps sounded above, and soon two sets of feet were running down the stairs. Mandy came skidding into the kitchen with Iris close on her tail.

"What happened?" Mandy asked, first looking at Bear.

Iris noticed their new guest a second later. "Rhonda, what happened? Who hurt you?"

Rhonda was sobbing so hard, she couldn't speak. Amos gently made her take another sip of her water. A few moments later, she was breathing normally, tears still streaming down her face.

"Gotta admit, you're scarin' me a little, Rhon," Amos said. "What in the blazes is goin' on?"

Rhonda looked up at him, her eyes shining and pleading. "I did a terrible thing."

"What terrible thing?"

Rhonda glanced at Bear, and then away again. It didn't take a genius to put the two together, and before she spoke again, Bear had already figured out what was happening.

"She went to Luke," Bear said. He tried to keep the accusation out of his voice, but it was difficult. "Didn't you?"

Rhonda nodded. "I was scared. I knew he was looking for you. I thought maybe if I told him, he would—" She gulped and started crying again.

"You thought he would leave you alone. That he might not hurt anyone else if he had me out of the picture," Bear supplied.

"Who hurt you?" Amos asked, his voice still gentle.

"Luke hit me across the face with his gun. Kn-knocked me out. I woke up, and everyone was gone. And—and—" She hiccupped. "And he was dead."

"Luke is dead?" Iris asked. Bear had almost forgotten she and Mandy were standing there.

Rhonda shook her head. "Tony Abbott. One of the men shot him, point blank. Just shot him in the head. Fell down the stairs. That's when Luke knocked me out. The body was still there when I woke up. I ran. I just ran. Didn't realize where I was until I walked through my front door. Couldn't stand the sight of myself, and I just threw up everywhere. Then I realized what I'd done. I had to come here and warn you."

Bear turned to the old farmer. "Luke knows we're working together."

Amos shrugged. "It was only a matter of time. A risk I was willing to take." Turning to Rhonda, though his eyes were sympathetic, there was no hiding the anger in them. "You betrayed us. All of us. We're trying to help you."

"I-I was scared," Rhonda said. Her eyes were puffy and red. "I was going to ask him not to hurt you, but I didn't get the chance."

"You should've known better." Amos sounded more disappointed than anything. He took a deep breath, and Bear could tell he was trying to forgive the woman. "But you can make up for it by telling Sheriff Woodard what you saw. It'll exonerate Riley here."

Rhonda was distraught. "He'll ask questions. He'll find out about everything. My involvement. *Our* involvement."

"It had to end sooner or later," Amos admitted. "I'd rather come out the other side with my conscience as clear as possible. Wouldn't you?"

Rhonda didn't say anything, but after a moment, she nodded her head.

Amos turned to Bear. "We need a new game plan."

"We need to know Luke's plan," Iris added. "Otherwise, we're sitting ducks."

As the group sat in silence, the rotary phone hanging on the wall rang. When Bear had first seen it, he thought it was just a relic of the past, a non-functioning decoration.

Amos squeezed by Rhonda, pulled the phone off the hook, and held it to his ear. He looked like he was about to say hello when he snapped his mouth shut and his eyes narrowed. Bear counted the seconds as they passed. Before he got to ten, Amos hung up and turned back to the group.

"It was Luke," Amos said to Bear. "He said my services are no longer needed."

39

THE ROOM WAS SILENT. DAISY STOOD FROM HER SPOT AT AMOS' FEET AND walked over to the door. She tilted her head, first to one side, then the next. A low growl escaped her mouth as she raised her hackles.

"Someone's here," Amos said. "And they're not friends."

"She can tell that?" Rhonda asked.

"She can. It's gotta be Luke."

"He wouldn't come out here by himself," Bear said. "I doubt he'd come at all. He'd send his men."

"Coward," Iris spat.

Bear looked around the room. Iris looked ready for a fight, and Bear had to admit he was, too. Amos was tough, but he couldn't take on a guy forty years younger than him. Rhonda and Cindy didn't seem like the type, and Mandy and Benji were just kids. He had no idea how many were out there, and he wondered if he and Iris could take them on alone.

Daisy barked twice, low and angry, sounding much bigger than she was. That got Bear moving. He pointed to Iris. "You're with me. The rest of you, turn off all the lights. Close all the blinds. Stay away from the windows. Amos, I'd get that gun of yours."

"What about you?" he asked. "What are you gonna do?"

"Stop them before they get started." Turning to Iris, Bear steadied her with a look. "I'm not lookin' to add more bodies to my conscience."

"If it comes down to me or them, I'm choosing me," she said.

Amos shuffled out of the room, then returned with his shotgun and a handful of zip ties, which he split between the two of them. "Got these to secure some of the packages for transport." Guilt made way for resignation. "Don't think I'll need them anymore."

"This'll do," Bear said. Amos nodded.

Bear ran upstairs to retrieve his gun and met Iris back in the kitchen. She had tucked her own weapon into her waistband. "Just in case," she said.

Bear nodded.

"Dad?" Mandy tugged on his arm. "What about me?"

Bear kept his voice low so the others wouldn't hear. "I need you to keep an eye on Rhonda, Cindy, and Benji. Make sure they don't run. Or do anything stupid."

For once, Mandy didn't argue. Maybe she thought it was a mission worth her time. Or maybe she knew Bear wouldn't budge at a time like this. "Okay," she said. "Be careful."

"Always," he replied, kissing the top of her hair. Turning to Amos, he said, "Let's go."

Amos led Bear and Iris into a room they hadn't been in before. With the lights off, it was hard to see, but it looked small and warm. Daisy stayed close, no longer growling, but her fur still standing on end. The old farmer pointed to a door. "Leads out back. Got about fifty yards before you hit the fields. There's a shed halfway between."

"Lights?" Bear asked.

"No. Moon's close to full, though. Gonna be bright out there."

"Thanks Amos."

"Suppose I should be the one thanking you," Amos said, clapping him on the back and looking between Bear and Iris. "just hope we can stop Luke before things get worse. Before more people get hurt." The pain on his face indicated he was thinking of someone specific.

"You're worried about your daughter," Bear said. "And your granddaughter."

"Should've known you'd be able to put that together." Amos shook his head. "I'm ashamed of what I've done, but I'm not sorry about trying to protect my family." He took a deep breath, and Bear could see his knuckles turn white around the barrel of his shotgun, even in the dark of the room. "But enough is enough. This is no way to live. If something happens to my daughter. If that piece-of-shit ex-husband of hers tries something—"

"We won't give them the chance." Iris squeezed Amos' shoulder. "First, we stop Luke. Then we figure out how to help Gracie."

Amos nodded, his voice too thick with emotion to speak.

After exchanging a nod with Iris, Bear pulled open the back door. Checked if the coast was clear. Gauged the distance to the shed. And then to the field.

"Plan?" Iris whispered at his shoulder.

"You go right. I go left. Meet in the middle. Take down and zip tie anyone we find. Defend the house."

"Simple. To the point." There was a smile in Iris' voice. "I like it."

Bear looked over his shoulder at her and saw the anticipation on her face. He felt the same. There was no more time to waste. Crouching low, he slipped out of the house, took one more glance at his surroundings, and darted for the shed. It was bright enough from the moon that the small structure cast a shadow on the ground. That's what Bear aimed for.

When he made it to the shed, he looked back, signaling the all-clear for Iris to follow him. She did, making it a fraction quicker than he had. They waited for a moment, listening to the sounds around them. But all Bear could hear were crickets singing nearby and coyotes howling in the distance.

Turning toward the field, Bear took off again, moving just as fast. When he made it to the corn, he slipped between the stalks, doing his best not to rustle them. His bulk was going to be an issue, but Luke's men would just think it was the breeze. Iris would have less trouble.

Bear signaled her, and she sprinted forward, making it to the target destination in less time than him. She made her way through the field in silence. He waited until she was out of sight before heading toward the front of the house.

It had occurred to Bear that Luke's men could be using the same strategy, but they'd have to come out eventually. He assumed their main target was the farmhouse and the people inside. But he still paused every twenty feet to listen for anyone sneaking up on him.

Luke's men didn't seem too smart, though. As Bear rounded the front of the house, he saw a guy standing off to the side, maybe a dozen feet from where Bear hid. It looked like the man was fiddling with something in his hands. From behind, Bear couldn't tell what it was.

The man didn't hear Bear's approach. In a moment, Bear had an arm locked around the man's neck. No matter how much the guy struggled and tried to rip at Bear's forearm, he kept it in place. After a moment, the man went limp and fell to the ground. Something bounced from his hand and rolled away. Bear put the zip ties around his wrists and ankles, then dragged him deep into the field.

Bear sprinted through the stalks, knowing it was only a matter of time before the man regained his senses. He wouldn't be going anywhere fast, but he'd be able to cause problems sooner or later. Bear had to make sure to subdue the rest of the guys.

Near the front of the house, Bear spotted another man. He was closer to the line separating Amos' lawn from the cornfield. Bear was about to sprint out from his cover when he noticed this guy was looking down at something in his hands. It had a subtle glow, but Bear realized it wasn't a phone. The moonlight was just bouncing off the glass. As the guy turned, the moonlight hit it at just the right angle so Bear could make it out.

A Molotov cocktail.

Panic swept through Bear's body, and he bolted from his cover. He heard the flick of a lighter right before Bear tackled the guy to the ground. The bottle flew from the man's hands and smashed into pieces, spraying Bear's arm with liquid. The lighter went flying in the opposite direction, the flame extinguished.

The man on the ground groaned under Bear's weight. He bucked Bear off and rolled, yelling out in pain when his arm hit the shards of glass. While he was distracted, Bear got to his feet, not letting the other man do the same. In one quick motion, he kicked up a leg and landed the sole of his boot against the other man's temple. The guy crumpled and Bear tied his wrists and ankles, hauling him into the field just like his friend.

A shout alerted Bear to Iris' presence. He watched as she darted out from the field on the opposite side of the house. She didn't have the advantage of being taller or heavier than her opponent like Bear did, but she was faster. In no time, Bear witnessed her take out the man's legs and send him crashing to the ground.

Bear darted toward her, not bothering to keep to his cover. He saw a side of Iris he hadn't expected. If he had any doubts, she wasn't who she said she was, they were gone now. The way she moved was that of a trained fighter. It was almost elegant, the way she sparred with her opponent.

As he neared, Iris blocked a punch to the gut, but gave the guy an opening to knock her on the chin. Her head snapped to the side, but she didn't cry out or even stumble. She turned back toward the man, her eyes as wild as her hair, and faked a jab before throwing a right hook. It caught the man off guard enough that she was able to kick out with her right leg and take out his knee. As he buckled over, she spun and landed a round-house kick to the side of his head. He collapsed to the ground, unmoving.

Bear made it to her just as she began to zip tie her adversary. "You good?" Bear asked.

"Yeah." She barely sounded winded. "You?"

Bear searched the ground for the guy's Molotov cocktail. He was relieved when he found it about two feet away. "They're trying to burn the house down."

"Saw that. I stopped two guys. You?"

"Same."

"Think there's more?" she asked.

Bear was about to answer when his ears pricked up at a new sound.

Fire alarms blared, and he could already see flames licking up the walls inside the darkened house.

40

MANDY DIDN'T LIKE WATCHING BEAR SLIP OUT INTO THE NIGHT, KNOWING he would probably be outnumbered when he went up against Luke's men. Iris was more than she'd let on, and if Bear trusted her to fight by his side, Mandy had to accept that. While it still bothered her that the woman had lied to them, they had connected upstairs in Mandy's room. Sure, Iris still hadn't told Mandy everything—like who she really was—but she had opened up about what she knew of Mr. Reagan. That was a start. If they'd had more time, maybe Mandy would've gotten more out of her.

Then everything had gone to hell.

Rhonda was freaking out, and if she didn't calm down soon, Mandy would have to do something about it. The woman needed a sedative. Since that wasn't an option, she considered maybe knocking her out cold. Amos would probably frown upon that, but Mandy decided to keep it in her back pocket as an option. Just in case.

"We need to leave," Rhonda said, going for the door.

Mandy cut her off before she made it two steps. "My dad told us to stay here. It's safer."

"Yeah? What does he know?"

"More than you," Mandy snapped.

Amos stepped up to the two of them. "Rhonda, we have to trust them. Don't got another choice."

Rhonda shook her head, her frizzy hair threatening to whip Mandy in the face, but she back away from the door. "He's got us trapped here."

"And whose fault is that?" Mandy couldn't help it. Rhonda was the reason Luke knew anything, after all.

The woman looked like Mandy had slapped her in the face. Tears ran down her face. "I thought I was protecting Amos."

"You thought you were protecting yourself," Mandy said. She kept the heat out of her voice. There was no point in wasting energy on this woman. "But that doesn't matter now. We need to turn off all the lights and close the blinds. Will you help me?"

Shocked, Rhonda nodded and followed Mandy into the living room, closing curtains as she went. The last thing Mandy wanted was to be around Rhonda, but she didn't trust the woman not to sneak past Amos. He wasn't as quick. If Rhonda managed to escape, there was no telling what would happen. Maybe one of Luke's men would shoot her, or maybe she'd go back to Luke and tell him some other part of their plan.

Cindy came down from the second floor, Benji close behind. "What's happening?"

"Luke's men are here," Mandy said. She tugged on one of the curtains, but it wouldn't close. She was too short to get the right angle. Amos helped her. "We need to make sure the house is dark. Make it harder for them to see inside. Can you close the second floor curtains?"

Cindy looked terrified, but Benji nodded his head and dragged his mom back up the stairs. There wasn't enough Mandy to micromanage everyone. Amos was the only one inside the house she could trust. Well, maybe Benji too. He had proven to be somewhat useful.

When they finished in the living room, Amos went to the kitchen to close the blinds. Mandy took Rhonda by the arm, dragging her up the stairs. For her part, Rhonda didn't fight. She allowed Mandy to pull her into a bedroom, and she began closing windows and tugging on curtains.

It was hard not to take her time to look out the window and search for Bear, but she couldn't risk it. Still, she couldn't help but wonder what was going on out there.

A crash of glass from below made Mandy freeze. They were in the last room on the second floor, and she hurried to finish closing all the curtains. Who knew one house could have so many windows? Shutting off the lights proved to make moving around more difficult, and she ran into Rhonda on her way through the door and out into the hall. It almost sent her tumbling to the floor.

Regaining her feet, Mandy dashed over to the staircase, nearly running into Benji too. She could see better here, and it took her a split-second to realize why. Her brain couldn't process what her eyes were seeing, and it was only when the fire alarm went off that she understood.

The breeze from outside blew through the broken window, making the curtains flutter. Flames slithered across the floor, spreading out from the shattered bottle that had landed in the center of the room.

It had only taken seconds for the rug to catch fire. From there, tendrils of flames spread in every direction until the curtains were blazing. Mandy knew they had minutes before the inferno would be totally out of their control.

Someone grabbed Mandy by the shoulders and hauled her back. Fighting out of the grasp, Mandy jabbed an elbow back and felt it connect. Rhonda grunted in response, letting go and stumbling back. Before she had fully recovered, she was already trying to reach for Mandy again.

"Get back! It's too dangerous," she wheezed.

Mandy ignored her and bounded down the stairs before the fire could work its way closer. The smoke would become a problem first, but they had to put out the flames. Amos had the same idea. He charged in with a fire extinguisher, working his way from the fire's origin, up to the curtains and everything in between.

"This isn't enough," he shouted at Mandy.

"Is there a second one?"

Through the roaring flames, Mandy only heard the man say, "Basement. I don't know where it is."

"I'll search with you," Mandy said. She turned to Benji and shouted, "Help! Find a bucket to hold water and put out the fire."

Benji nodded and dashed toward the bathroom. Mandy hoped he'd find something up there. If not, he'd have to cross the flames, inching closer to the stairs to get down to the kitchen. There was no guarantee Cindy—or Rhonda, for that matter—would let him do that.

But that wasn't Mandy's problem right now. As Amos' fire extinguisher ran dry, he tossed it away and ran as fast as he could for the door to the basement. Mandy followed, tripping over herself in her haste.

When they got to the bottom of the stairs, they both stumbled to a stop.

The space was mostly unfinished, at least from what Mandy could tell. Boxes and random piles of furniture and books and clothes and *things* were scattered everywhere, with just a few pathways to the back of the room. From that direction, smoke billowed forward, black, heavy, and clawing at their throats.

"There's storm cellar doors on the other end here," Amos said. "They must've gotten in that way."

Mandy stepped forward and could feel the increase in heat. The fire crackled, and with every passing second, the smoke thickened. But she could still make out the wooden support beams just beyond the haze. It wouldn't take long for the rest of the house to go up in flames.

"Gotta make sure those support beams don't go down," Amos said.

"We'll need more than that fire extinguisher." She called out for Benji, and he came running down the stairs a minute later. "Form an assembly line. Cindy works the sink and fills up whatever she can find. Rhonda takes half and works on the living room. You grab the rest and pass it down to me."

Cindy came into view, coughing into her shirt. "That's never going to work. The fire's too big already."

"You have a better idea?" Mandy snapped.

Amos looked up to the top of the stairs. "My whole life is down here. So many memories of Annabelle. Please, I can't lose her again."

Cindy looked torn, and even Mandy knew it wasn't the best idea. If they were smart, they would just get out. But she also couldn't blame Amos for wanting to try. "We do what we can," Mandy said. "When it gets too dangerous, we get out."

"What about the men outside?" Benji asked.

"We hope my dad's taken care of them by then."

Something popped, and Mandy whipped around in time to see a pile of old books shift and fall over. Within seconds, they were all alight, and now she had a better view into the back of the basement. All she could see was flames.

"Blankets against the far wall." Amos pointed off to the right. "Smother the flames."

Mandy didn't hesitate. Sprinting to the far wall, she grabbed a pile of comforters that smelled like they'd been down here for several decades. There was a chance they'd catch fire if she wasn't careful, but it was worth the risk.

She had a vision of the fire reaching the wood steps, and her and Amos being stuck down here while the house crumbled around them. Bear would dig and dig and dig, and he might never find her.

"Mandy!" Amos called, his voice cracking from fear and smoke inhalation. "Come on!"

Mandy shook herself, running back the way she'd come. She almost collided with Benji, who had the first bucket of water ready. Tossing the blankets down, she grabbed the bucket from him and pointed back toward the stairs. "Keep them coming. Whatever you do, don't let the flames reach the steps."

Benji turned on his heel and ran, charging up the stairs in time for his mom to return with another bucket. Where they had found them, Mandy didn't know. There was only one thing on her mind now.

Put out the flames.

Charging forward, Mandy dumped the bucket of water on the books, dousing as wide an area as she could. The water evaporated, and the flames found a newer, dryer avenue. Benji replaced the bucket in her hand and ran the other back up the stairs. Mandy rinsed and repeated, then went back to grab the blankets, tossing half to Amos and they began smothering what they could.

But while they saved the book pile, the flames were licking at other area of the basement. There was too much stuff and not enough hands to put out what was needed. Mandy was sweating and coughing, and Amos sounded worse than her.

There was a pop and a crack, and a support beam at the back of the basement shifted to one side. The floor above was starting to warp with the heat.

Mandy tried to imagine what that would be like for Amos, losing his lifelong home. She had never called a place home for longer than a few months. She'd never felt tied to a particular place. But if she'd lived in the same house for most of her life, had built the number of memories Amos had, she could only imagine he'd feel like he was losing a part of himself. Amos' wife stayed alive in the photographs on these walls.

Rushing forward, Amos started slapping at the flames with a blanket, snuffing them out as quickly as new ones rose. A pile of boxes filled with who-knew-what toppled over, singeing his arm and causing him to cry out loud. But he didn't stop.

Benji came back with another bucket, and Mandy ran forward, shoulder to shoulder with Amos, working toward the back of the basement and the cracked support beam. When the bucket was empty, Benji replaced it with the next and ran back upstairs. Mandy kept working, trusting that the ceiling would hold for a few minutes longer. Hoping Bear was having better luck than they were.

As Mandy's arms grew heavier and her eyes became blurrier with soot and tears, she heard the sound of hope in the air. Sirens. Distant but distinct. Firetrucks. Had someone called the fire department, or had they seen the smoke?

She turned to tell Amos they only had to hold out hope for another minute or so, but as soon as she turned around, the support beam gave a final ear-splitting crack, and the ceiling above caved in on the old man. Mandy barely had a chance to jump out of the way of the debris before watching Amos get crushed beneath it.

41

Bear had told Iris to call the firefighters and wait at the end of the driveway. The words were barely out of his mouth before he sprinted across the lawn and through the front door.

Cindy, Benji, and Rhonda were frantic, arguing amongst themselves. Benji was the only one with his head on his shoulders, and he knew to sum up the situation for Bear.

"The fire collapsed living room floor." He was taking in huge gulps of air and choking on the smoke. "Amos and Mandy are in the basement."

Bear didn't need to know more than that. Time was precious. "Get yourselves out."

"Are you sure?" Benji asked, resisting as his mother tugged on his arm.

Bear's only answer was to dart to the top of the basement stairs. The smoke was thick and black. It stung his eyes and burned his lungs. The best he could do to combat that was pull his shirt up over his nose and mouth. It would work until he needed both hands.

He tore down the stairs. There were piles of junk everywhere—all of it flammable. The haze made it difficult to see, but it wasn't hard to guess what some of the items were. A table here, a pile of books there, all at risk of going up in flame.

Through the smoke, Bear heard Mandy calling out for Amos. The anguish in her voice made his heart seize. Was she hurt, or was Amos in trouble? He couldn't tell, and before he could think better of it, he charged forward through the smoke and fire to get to his daughter.

Mandy was at the far end, as flames licked closer and closer to her body. She dug through a pile of debris. It took Bear a fraction of a second to understand. Amos had been buried alive.

Bear charged forward, pushing mountains of boxes out of his way. The fire wouldn't have been half as bad if there hadn't been so much stuff down here, but he couldn't blame Amos for that. No one anticipated someone setting fire to the place.

Mandy was on her knees, hauling chunks of the fallen ceiling out of the way. An arm stuck out from the pile, curled into a loose fist and unmoving. Had Amos been killed by the crash, or just knocked unconscious? He'd get him out either way. The old man deserved that.

But he wasn't about to risk Mandy's life, too.

"Go." Bear moved her away from the pile. "I got this. Get out."

"But Amos—"

"I'll get him." Bear knelt to her level and began digging. "Go help the others. Find the dog. Make sure no one's hurt."

Mandy hesitated, but Bear could tell she was exhausted. Every few seconds, she coughed, trying to expel the smoke from her lungs. Sweat dripped down her face, and her shirt was dirty and soaked. She wouldn't be able to help for much longer, anyway. She'd only risk hurting herself.

Mandy pushed up from her knees, laid an encouraging hand on Bear's shoulder, then ran for the stairs. Bear watched her jog up and hit the landing, turn to catch a glimpse of him one more time, then disappear.

Bear's muscles were fatigued from the fighting, but the adrenaline kept him moving. There was a chance the debris could suffocate the old man. A love seat had fallen through the hole above, and he wouldn't be able to crawl out from under it by himself.

Following Amos' hand, Bear uncovered his arm, then his shoulder, and finally his head. The man was unconscious but breathing. It felt like hours had passed since Bear had first heard the sirens, and yet there was still no sign of the firemen. Mandy would've directed them to the basement, so what was taking so long?

He couldn't worry about that now. Bear drove his shoulder into the love seat and pushed it off the old man, uncovering more of his chest and torso. Some of the chunks of ceiling were large, and in less than a minute, Bear had Amos completely uncovered. Just in time for the old farmer to come around, groaning and twisting his head away from the dust and smoke. Every time he coughed, he groaned louder.

"Need you to get up, old man," Bear said. "We gotta move."

"Who you callin' old, son? Got plenty of life left in me."

"Can you stand?"

"Need some help." Another groan. "I think my arm's broken."

"Gonna have to grin and bear it till we get out of here." Bear helped Amos sit up, and from this angle, he could see Amo's forearm split in two. The bone hadn't gone through the skin, but there was an unnatural bump in the middle where his radius had broken. Not ideal, but it looked like a clean break.

"Guess I'm not bailin' hay for a while," Amos said, getting to his feet.

"We'll get that part figured out." Bear let Amos lean on him while they stumbled forward. "After all this is over, there's gonna be a lot of people who'll be grateful for what you've done."

"We'll see," Amos said. "Can't count on such things."

Bear dragged Amos forward, not bothering to look behind him as more debris crashed down. It drove a cloud of smoke forward, and Bear wished he had something covering his face. He coughed, feeling phlegm building in the back of his throat. His lungs would be angry at him for a while.

Finally, as they reached the bottom of the stairs, two men appeared on the landing above, dressed in firefighter garb.

"Anyone else down there?" one asked.

"No," Bear answered, allowing the second to come down the stairs and grab Amos. "Careful. He's got a broken arm. Maybe a concussion. Didn't get a chance to look him over for any other bleeding."

"You injured?" the first man asked.

"I'm good." Bear coughed his way up the stairs. "Just need some air."

"EMT on standby," the second firefighter said. "We'll get everyone checked out."

"The fire started on the other side," Amos said. "The storm doors—"

"We're working on it. We'll do what we can, Amos."

"Thank you, George." Amos coughed again, his knees buckling under the strain.

Bear allowed himself to be led out of the house and over to the paramedics, who were treating Mandy for a few small scrapes on her hands. Benji was breathing through an oxygen mask, but otherwise looked fine. He sat up a little straighter when Amos and Bear emerged, and both Cindy and Rhonda looked relieved. Iris stood off to the side, talking to Sheriff Woodard. The one silver lining was that Deputy Mason was nowhere to be found.

As soon as Woodard saw Amos, he tilted his head back in relief. Then he caught sight of Bear and motioned him over. With one more quick glance to make sure Mandy was okay, Bear ambled over to the pair, hoping the sheriff wouldn't find some way to blame him for the housefire.

"You injured?" Woodard asked.

"Nothing I can't handle."

"Good." Woodard took a deep breath, then looked Bear in the eye as though trying to read his thoughts. He could feel the sheriff sizing him up and waited until the man found what he wanted to say. "Seems as though I owe you an apology."

Bear scratched his head in mock confusion. "Can I get that in writing?"

Woodard chuckled, but after a moment, his face grew serious again. "I apologize, Mr. Logan. I think we got off on the wrong foot, and I've spent a lot of time chasing you down when I should've been lookin' elsewhere."

"Not that I'm complaining," Bear said, "but why the change of heart?"

Woodard hooked his thumbs through his belt loops and blew out a big breath. "Evidence doesn't match up, for one. And everyone I talk to vouches for your character. Either you're a good guy, Mr. Logan, or you've got half the town fooled."

"I'm not that good of an actor," Bear said.

"Maybe not. Rhonda told me she witnessed someone else kill Tony Abbot, and that she was afraid to come forward before now. We've got a description of the man, and we'll be on the lookout. And Iris told me you were protecting this lot while the house was attacked. I appreciate you doin' what we couldn't. Not easy for me to admit that, but I'm not above thankin' someone who deserves it."

"Appreciate that," Bear said.

"Now comes the big question," Woodard said. "You have any idea who did this?"

Bear looked at Iris, who met his gaze with a steady one of her own. They hadn't discussed it, but it wasn't hard to figure out that Iris and the others weren't going to turn on Luke. Rhonda had named one of Reagan's men as the killer, and Bear assumed she hadn't mentioned Luke at all. If he had half the town blackmailed, what good would it do to go after him? He'd have to come up with some alibi, or force one of the others to take the fall.

No, they had to do this on their own. He wouldn't name Luke.

"I can do you one better. Got a couple of guys tied up in the cornfield. Figured you'd want to talk to them."

"Are you serious?" Woodard asked.

"Dead."

Woodard called in backup on the radio pinned to his shoulder. Iris volunteered to show the deputies where the men were located.

When Woodard was done giving orders, he nodded in Amos' direction. "He doing all right?"

"Broken arm. Maybe a concussion. He'll have to go to the hospital."

Woodard looked up at the old farmhouse, still smoking, but it no longer seemed to be burning. "Where will you go?"

"Not sure yet," Bear said.

But that was a lie. He was tired of playing defense. It was time to take the fight to Luke's doorstep.

42

BEAR HADN'T GONE TO LUKE BECAUSE HE WASN'T READY TO START something he couldn't finish. But Luke had pushed the envelope by striking first, and Bear regretted the decisions he'd made that led him to this point. If he'd come face to face with Luke earlier, maybe Amos wouldn't have been hurt and perhaps his home might still be intact.

But if Bear had done anything differently, he might be dead by now, with only Mandy left to mourn him.

There was no point in looking back. Luke had made his move, and it was time for Bear to retaliate. Mandy hadn't wanted him to go alone, but Bear wasn't looking to do more than talk to the guy. Luke deserved more of Bear's wrath than that, even before he'd had his men set fire to Amos' home, but Bear was trying to get the rest of the townspeople out of this situation unscathed.

After Woodard left with Amos in the ambulance, Cindy said she'd stay behind with Mandy to watch the house. Once the place cleared and was in no immediate danger of going up again, she'd take the kids back to her house. It was the best they could do for now, and Bear hoped he wouldn't be gone long anyway.

He'd found the keys to Amos' newer truck on the kitchen table and driven to the address Cindy had provided. Apparently, this had been

Luke's grandmother's house, and Bear wondered how long ago she'd died and whether she'd known the path he'd gone down. Not for the first time, Bear wondered how his own actions would impact Mandy's future and whether he was doing right by her.

Shaking himself from those thoughts, Bear pulled into the driveway, unconcerned about staying concealed. Luke wouldn't expect him to make such a direct response, and it was better to go in unannounced. Not that his chances of getting shot were zero this way.

But after no one answered Luke's door, Bear realized he wasn't home. Considering he had no idea where else the guy would be, Bear did the next best thing he could think of.

He broke into Luke's house.

In terms of trying to stay out of trouble with the law, this wasn't the best way to go about it, but Woodard was busy, and his deputies were more concerned about arson and murder than a little B&E from a citizen that Woodard had just apologized to an hour earlier.

If anything, now was the best time for Bear to do some law breaking.

The front door was locked, but Bear had grabbed his lockpick kit on the way out. Sure, he could break a window and get in just fine, but there was no point in leaving evidence or alerting Luke to the idea that someone had snooped around his house. Bear's plan was to get in, see if Luke left any incriminating evidence around, then get out. Simple as that.

Closing the door behind him with a soft click, Bear stood still and listened to the sounds of the house. Though it did creak and groan in a few places, he didn't hear footsteps of a human or an animal. He was safe now. But for how long?

Treading lightly, Bear made his way through the kitchen, looking for receipts or notes or messages of any kind. There were none in there or the living room, and Bear once again wondered how long Luke had been living in this house. It was still decorated like an elderly woman's home, but was that because his grandmother's death had been recent, or because Luke was too lazy to make it his own?

Bear moved into the back, going from the spare bedroom to the bathroom to the master bedroom. This looked more like Luke's room, with posters of bands and half-naked women hanging on the wall, interspersed with his grandmother's knick-knacks and doilies.

Bear found a couple of prescription pill bottles and a few empty cigarette cartons, but nothing incriminating. Or even interesting, for that matter. There was no doubt in Bear's mind that Luke was the mastermind here, but did he keep his home and business separate?

There was only one place left to check. The basement. Keeping the light off, Bear made his way down the creaky steps, pausing every third step or so to listen for movement. Hearing none, he hit the landing and noticed a huge crack in the wall, like someone had fallen down the stairs and landed against it. Hard.

Luke had moved a half-dead plant to cover the space, but it wasn't hard to figure out what had happened. Especially because Rhonda had told Bear she'd witnessed one of the other goons shoot Big Tony in the head. His dead body had made that impact against the wall, and though there was no blood, Bear was sure he could find some hair fibers or other evidence to prove what had happened.

Taking out his phone, Bear snapped a picture of the wall with his flash on. He used the momentary brightness to survey the room, but in that quick snap, nothing jumped out at him. And no one seemed to be hiding in the shadows.

Bear pulled a small flashlight out of his pocket and turned it on the rest of the room. It was a risk if someone was down here. If he could get out of the house sooner rather than later—preferably with evidence in hand—then the other man would be none the wiser. It was a win-win scenario.

The light illuminated the room, casting a glow across the equipment strewn around the floor. There were a couple of couches and a TV down here, but most of the room was covered in boxes and metal parts for machines Bear wasn't familiar with. It didn't quite look like Garrett's setup, though, which ruled out a meth lab.

Bear took a step closer, snapping pictures left and right. Something itched at the back of his neck. He didn't like backing himself into a corner like this. He could figure out what the equipment was for later, when he reviewed the pictures. For now, he knew he had Luke on something. It was just determining what exactly it was.

As Bear turned to cross the room and head back up the stairs, the front door opened, and he heard light footsteps on the floor above him. It didn't take long for Bear to figure out who it was.

"Luke?" Jake called. Something thumped against the floor, like a heavy bag. "You home?"

Bear crept across the room and tucked himself into a corner. By the time Jake saw him, it would be too late to run away. He didn't want to give the kid a heart attack, but it was clear that Jake knew plenty about Luke's operation. If Bear could get the kid to talk, it could go a long way.

"Luke?" Jake called out again. "Is that your new truck in the driveway? It's pretty sweet." It sounded like Jake went to the fridge and grabbed a snack. When he spoke again, his mouth was full. "When can I drive it? You know, I'll be sixteen in three months. I'll even just stick to parking lots. Come on, man."

Bear pressed himself against the wall as Jake descended the steps. From his vantage point, Bear could see he was eating an apple. He waited until the kid had swallowed before lunging forward and grabbing him by the arm. Jake screamed and covered his head, a far cry from the tough guy act he had put on yesterday. Bear couldn't help but laugh.

When Jake heard the deep baritone rumble of Bear's chuckle, he looked up in alarm, realizing it wasn't his brother playing a prank on him. Jake's eyes went wide, and he struggled to free himself from Bear's iron-clad grip.

"What are you doing here?" Jake screamed at him. "When my brother gets home—"

"He won't do shit," Bear said, letting go of the kid and stepping in front of the staircase, the only exit from the basement. "Relax. I'm not going to hurt you."

Jake stood defiantly, but Bear noted that his knees were shaking. "Luke's gonna beat the shit out of you, old man."

"Watch your mouth," Bear roared. Jake's mouth snapped shut. "I may be an asshole, but I don't hurt kids. You know your brother tried to burn Amos' house down an hour ago? Benji was there. He almost died."

Jake's eyes went even wider.

"By the look on your face, you didn't know. Luke doesn't share much with you, does he?"

"He trusts me, if that's what you're trying to say," Jake said.

"Does he? Good." Bear let a devilish grin spread over his face. "Then you won't mind if I ask you some questions."

43

"I'M NOT TELLING YOU SHIT," JAKE SAID.

Bear grabbed the kid by the shoulder and pushed him back into the chair behind him. "Look, you can either answer to me, or Sheriff Woodard." He pointed at the equipment behind him. "This is pretty damning evidence. You want to be caught in the middle of that?"

"You broke into the house." Jake crossed his arms over his chest. "It won't count."

Bear chuckled. "You don't know much about the real world, kid. Or what I'm capable of. Best advice I can give you is to tell me what you know."

Jake's eyes searched for an escape, but Bear was still blocking the stairs. His gaze must've landed on the crack in the wall because they went wide, and then he blanched. "You broke the wall! This was my grandma's house. Luke is gonna be pissed."

"Luke already knows about it. The guy who did that is no longer among the living." Bear leaned in close. He wanted to scare the kid enough to get him to talk, but not enough to traumatize Jake for the rest of his life. "Do you really know what your brother gets up to in his spare time? Do you know what he's capable of?"

"He wouldn't do that," Jake said, but he didn't sound convinced.

"Look, all I want is some information on Mr. Reagan. That's who your brother works for, right?"

Jake snorted. "Yeah, sure."

"He's been skimming off the top, hasn't he? Trying to make his own fortune."

"Trying to make his own *name*. He's gonna make sure we have everything we need for the rest of our lives."

Bear furrowed his eyebrows together. "Where are your parents?"

Jake looked away. "Dead."

"I'm sorry to hear that."

"No, you're not."

"I am, but you don't need to believe me." Bear took a second to recenter himself. "How did Luke and Mr. Reagan start working together?"

"No idea." The words were flippant, but the undercurrent of fear told Bear it was the truth, and Jake was afraid he'd punish him for it. "One day, he just came home and said he got a new job. Had a bunch of cash. We went out to dinner that night. It was awesome. I'd never had seafood before."

Bear couldn't help feeling bad for Jake. He might've been fifteen, but he was still just a kid. Didn't understand the scope of what Luke was involved in or the danger it presented to the entire town. He just knew they had more money than they ever had before, and people respected his brother. Or, at least, they were afraid of him.

"When did Luke get the idea of starting his own business?"

Jake shrugged. "Don't know. But he's been talking about it forever. Thought he had a good chance with Mr. Reagan since he's not from around here."

"Your brother's not afraid of Mr. Reagan, then?"

"Hell no. He says that if Reagan ever shows up here, he'll take him out and replace him. Then we'll move to the city and get out of this place."

The statement sounded arrogant. Bear had seen and dealt with plenty of guys like Luke. Sure, he was ruthless and intelligent, but he was also impulsive and quick to anger. That was a dangerous combination, and those kinds of people combusted sooner or later. Bear just hoped Jake wouldn't get caught in the crossfire.

"What else do you know about Reagan?"

"That you shouldn't mess with him." Jake sat up a little straighter in his chair, as though invoking Reagan's name was like wearing a bulletproof vest. "He's a powerful guy. That's why he uses a fake name. Why he won't come out here himself. He stays in the shadows."

Bear kept his face impassive, but he chewed over this information. At first, he thought Reagan might just be someone from the city who used rural towns as distribution centers. It was a real last name, after all. But if it was a codename, could that imply Reagan worked for the government? He'd be a lot more dangerous than Luke could handle, and Bear wasn't sure he wanted to kick that hornet's nest.

If Reagan found out Bear took out Luke, knowing the man had been stealing from him, Reagan might not get further involved with Bear or this town. But even knowing of Mr. Reagan's existence could be enough for Bear to stay on the guy's radar. Not to mention Reagan was running a drug operation that affected thousands if not tens of thousands of people. Could Bear really turn a blind eye to that in good conscience?

"Where's your brother now?" Bear asked. Ready to end this, he'd figure out the rest later.

"If he's not here, then he's probably at his other place."

"You know the way?"

Jake nodded. "I can draw you a map. Or write down—"

"Nah," Bear said. "You're coming with me."

Jake protested all the way to the truck, but Bear kept an iron-clad grip on his arm, throwing him inside and making sure he didn't try to make a run for it. Bear knew something was off. After all that, there was no way Jake would just give up Luke's location without more poking and prodding. Maybe he was scared and not showing it, but this reeked of something else.

Jake led him back out to the fields beyond town, this time in the opposite direction of Garrett's farm. The kid said he had no idea what was out here and maybe he was telling the truth.

Jake was antsy the whole way. He kept tugging on his seatbelt and shifting in his seat and pressing his face close to the window. Bear could see the worried expression in his eyes reflected in the glass. But the silence seemed to disturb the kid more than Bear's interrogation, so he let Jake stew.

Sure enough, as they turned onto a long dirt road, Jake threw his arms out. "Stop. Stop!" He was breathing heavily. "It's a setup."

Bear slammed on his brakes, causing dirt and stones to fly everywhere. The two of them nearly hit the dash, and Jake's eyes were now the widest they'd ever been.

"Come again?" Bear asked.

"It's a setup. Luke's out here, but he has cameras at the end of the lane."

"I didn't see any cameras."

"They're hidden in the trees."

"And if he sees me strolling up the lane, what's going to happen?"

"I don't know." Jake was panicked now. "He's got guns. Some of his guys shoot first and ask questions later."

"And you were willing to send me out here to die?" Bear asked, an unimpressed look on his face.

Jake bowed his head. "I didn't want you to die. I-I just. My brother would be so mad at me." When the kid looked up, Bear thought he saw the real Jake. "I have to live with him. You have no idea what he's like. If I sent you to him, maybe he would trust me more. Maybe he would treat me better."

For the second time that night, Bear was reminded that Jake was just a kid. There was no telling how long ago his parents had died, but it seemed obvious that Luke had been the one raising him. The kid had a skewed sense of right and wrong. Could Bear blame him for that, when it was Luke's influence?

Movement through the passenger side window caught Bear's attention, and he looked beyond Jake to the tree line in the distance. There was more cover out here with the trees and the unmaintained brush. Luke and his men had been able to sneak up on them undetected. And now they stood there, in the open, with several rifles pointed in their direction.

Luke's expression was devilish. His eyes were dark and hooded, and the stubble on his face gave him a wild look. A grin spread across his lips, and even though Bear was certain it was just his imagination, his teeth looked pointed. Jake might still have some good left in him, but Luke had lost all sense of humanity.

Jake saw the surprise in Bear's eyes and turned. He gasped when he saw Luke with a gun pointed at him, and then frantically started waving and shouting. He went to push open the door, but Bear leaned over and slammed it shut. He could already see what would happen next.

Luke raised the gun. His men followed suit.

"What is he doing?" Jake asked. "He sees me. He can see me."

Bear lifted his foot from the brake, hoping his reaction time was faster than a speeding bullet.

Luke's mouth moved, and even from a distance, Bear knew exactly what he'd said.

"Kill the son of a bitch."

After that, all Bear could hear was the rain of bullets against the side of the truck.

44

Jake didn't stop screaming until they made it back into town. Once they hit the main strip, he collapsed back into his seat with a whimper. Tears coated his face, and Bear was pretty sure the kid wet himself. It might've been funny in another context, but his older brother had tried to kill Bear and clearly hadn't cared that Jake was in the truck.

The smell wouldn't be hard to get out of the truck, but the bullet holes wouldn't buff out.

"He shot at me." Jake's voice held no emotion. "He tried to kill me."

Bear didn't know what to say. Luke tried to kill *him*. Jake was just in the way. That felt too much like splitting hairs. It wouldn't matter in a situation like this. As much as Bear didn't want to press him right now, he needed Jake to open his eyes.

"Your brother doesn't care about anyone but himself. And he doesn't give a shit about anything but making his next buck. Do you see that now?" Jake looked at Bear, still blinking back tears. "You gotta help us," Bear said. "Is there anything else you know?"

Jake swallowed. Taking so long to answer that Bear didn't think he would. "There are two guys in town. They wear suits. Luke's afraid of them. They're Reagan's men."

"Yeah, I had a run-in with them myself. Don't think they like me very much."

Jake gave a half-smile before letting it fall. "Luke always said if Reagan found out about what he was doing, Luke would torch the town before he laid down willingly."

That sounded like the Luke Bear had gotten to know over the last few days. After seeing how willing Luke was to gun down his brother, there was no doubt in Bear's mind that Luke would go to extreme lengths to protect his own ass.

"You think Reagan's men are on to him?" Bear asked.

Jake nodded. "Reagan wouldn't have sent them here if he wasn't suspicious. Luke was real worried when they showed up. He was acting different. Quiet. Like he was planning something."

That solidified it for Bear. It was now or never. As Bear pulled into Cindy's driveway, he held out his hand. Jake looked down at it in confusion.

"What?"

"I need your phone," Bear said. "I'm going to set up a meeting with Luke. We're going to end this."

Jake placed his phone in Bear's hand with an expression that told Bear he was at war with himself. "Are you going to kill him?"

"Wouldn't be my preference," Bear said. "But if it comes down to me or him, I'm choosing me."

Jake looked down at his hands folded in his lap. His voice was barely a whisper, but Bear caught the word all the same. "Good."

As much of a pain in the ass as this kid had been, Bear didn't wish this life on him. With his parents gone, his grandmother dead, and Luke either ending up in a cell or a grave, where would Jake go? Bear didn't want to take his future away from him, but the alternative had to be better than what he was living now.

Cindy met them at the door, Benji and Mandy not far behind. Mandy crushed Bear in a hug, then stood back to make sure he wasn't injured. When her eyes drifted to the truck and the bullet holes that riddled its side, she slapped a hand over her mouth and then looked up at him with questioning eyes.

"Luke," Bear said. "He'll stop at nothing."

Benji looked from the truck to Jake, who met no one's eyes. "Are you okay?"

It took Jake a minute to realize Benji was addressing him. Bear could see the barrage of emotions that flooded his face—from anger and defiance to fear and vulnerability. His expression finally settled on humility. Bear had to admit, it looked good on the kid.

"I'm sorry," Jake said. His voice broke, and he looked embarrassed, but he pushed through it. "For everything."

Benji looked astonished and wary, but after a moment he asked, "You hungry?"

Jake looked up, surprised, then nodded his head. Benji motioned for him to come inside, and the others let them through. Maybe this was the beginning of a genuine friendship between them. Or maybe it was the last time they'd ever see each other.

"He won't have anywhere to go after this," Bear said.

Cindy nodded. Her eyes seemed clearer than they had in days. Had she quit drinking? "We'll figure it out. He won't be alone."

Mandy looked up at Bear. "What now?"

He'd been wondering the same thing. But after his conversation with Jake, Bear could only think of one option. "Luke's got an army. We need our own."

Cindy blanched. "We should call the police."

"The police are bound by the law. They might be able to arrest Luke, but by the time they get a warrant, he could've torched half the town. I don't want to take that risk."

"These people have guns. They know how to fight."

"You'd be surprised what people can do with their backs against the wall." Bear thought of Amos, with his broken arm. If he were able, he'd fight, but he sat in a hospital right now, getting a cast fitted to his arm. "Iris and I will take care of Luke. And Reagan's men. Everyone else grew up here, just like you did. Could you get Benji and Jake to make a list of people Luke blackmailed? People who'd fight to get their lives back?"

"I guess," Cindy said, but she sounded hesitant. "And if they say no?"

"We'll jump that hurdle when we get to it. Make the list, call them, have everyone meet at Rhonda's place."

"What are you going to do?" Mandy asked.

"I'm gonna give Luke exactly what he wants."

Without further explanation, Bear stepped off the porch and pulled up Luke's name on Jake's phone. Holding the device to his ear, he only had to wait for two rings before the man picked up.

"Jake," Luke said, his voice casual. "You good?"

"I knew you were a piece of shit, Salazar," Bear said, "but that was pretty low, even for you."

Luke paused for the briefest of seconds, and when he spoke again, his voice was more rigid. "Where's Jake?"

"He's fine, no thanks to you. After you shot at him, he sang like a canary. Told me everything I needed to know."

"Bullshit. He wouldn't do that."

"That was before you tried to kill him, Luke. Actions have consequences. You'll learn that soon enough."

"So what? You're holding my little brother for ransom?"

Bear chuckled. "Don't need to. He wants nothing to do with you anymore."

"Then what?" Luke ground out. "If you're looking for a fight, I'll give you one."

"Looking forward to it."

"You're gonna leave this town in a casket, old man."

This time, Bear's laugh was loud enough to carry on the wind. "You have no idea who you're up against, kid. You're gonna wish Reagan was the only guy you had to worry about."

45

LUKE RESISTED THROWING HIS PHONE AGAINST THE WALL. THIS ONE WAS brand new, unlike the one he'd destroyed the other day. It wasn't like he couldn't afford a new one, but he had shit to do, and being without a phone, even for a few hours, would be a pain in the ass.

It was time to call in the cavalry.

He had discovered a few interesting pieces of information lately. That pain in the ass he'd just been talking to was named Riley Logan, and his kid—the one who'd killed Raymond—was named Mandy. The guy had been working with Amos to expose Luke's operation. And that was why Amos was now in the hospital with a broken arm. It should've put him in the morgue, but Luke was realizing most of his men were idiots. He'd change that once he cleaned up this mess.

It also turned out that Lily had a cousin just as nosy as she was. Iris Duvall. He'd had no idea she was in town until his guys tried torching Amos' house. They were unsuccessful in getting rid of those in his way, but what was done was done. The guys who had returned had been punished and sent out to redeem themselves. The rest could rot in jail for all Luke cared.

Logan had set out a challenge in front of Luke. Had told him he was bringing the fight to Luke's front doorstep. Metaphorically speaking, at least. Luke wouldn't stand down from a direct challenge like that, but if Logan thought he was getting a fair fight, he hadn't been doing his homework.

The only thing that gave Luke pause was Jake. Apparently, the kid didn't know how good he'd had it. Did Luke open fire on a truck while Jake was inside? Yes. But no one had aimed for him. It's not like he was going to kill his little brother, not when Luke wanted him to take over the operation. Had Luke gone too far? Maybe. But he was in too deep now.

A soft alarm sounded from Luke's computer in the corner of the cabin. He'd built this place on the bit of land his grandfather had purchased years ago. The plan had always been to build a new house, something to pass down through the family, but Grandpa had never gotten off his ass long enough to start it, let alone finish it. When Luke's parents died, the dream died too.

But Luke had inherited it when his grandmother had passed, and he'd had enough money at that point to build a cabin. It was nothing like his grandfather had dreamed, but he didn't plan on staying in Boonesville for the rest of his life. No, this was his backup, in case his house became compromised. And after Big Tony's death, Luke figured it would be better to lie low

"It's them," Garrett said from the computer. "They look pissed."

Garrett was just about the only competent person Luke had left. He looked like a meathead, but he was good with computers, and he'd been the only one willing to put in the work to help Luke get his business off the ground. That meant footing the bill to expand his barn and learning how to make meth. They'd had some delays while he figured it out, but in the end, Luke was glad to have Garrett at his side. Especially since no one else had proved their worth so far. Even Caleb had been useless against Logan.

Luke walked over to the monitors. The image on the screen was grainy, but there was no denying who was in the truck. Landis was driving, his bald head gleaming in the sun, while Rosenblatt surveyed the land around him. Their truck was kicking up dust and debris, and soon all Luke could see was a cloud of dirt.

Luke swore. "How the hell did they find us?"

Luke had last seen them at the meth lab. He'd tried to convince them he had no idea it was there and that if he ever ran into whoever owned it, he'd break their legs for trying to move in on his operation. The men hadn't been entirely convinced, and Luke had slipped away when their backs were turned. He didn't think anyone had known about his place out here, and now it'd been compromised twice in one day.

Maybe Logan had sent them. Or maybe it was a mole. Ever since Mr. Reagan's call, Luke had wondered if someone was feeding the guy information from the inside. There was no way he could've known about Luke's operation or Logan's arrival in town without someone snitching. But who would do that?

Ignoring the thought for now, Luke heard the truck pull up outside the door and went to greet his guests. His mind was already spinning the situation. If he could just manage to keep the men at bay for a little longer, Luke could deal with Logan and come back for these guys. If he was smart enough, Luke could maybe get Reagan's guys to work for *him*.

"Gentlemen." Luke greeted the men as soon as the guys jumped out of the truck. "I see you've found my—"

Landis stepped close and punched Luke in the face. One minute Luke was standing, and the next Landis was dragging him backwards into the cabin.

Luke tried to kick at Landis, but Rosenblatt aimed a gun at Luke's face. He stilled and watched as Landis turned to Garrett. "Looks like the address was correct. This is the second time your information has panned out in Mr. Reagan's favor."

Garrett stood, avoiding eye contact with Luke. "Like I said, I'm willing to do whatever it takes to—"

Landis pulled out his own gun and pointed it at Garrett. There was no warning. No hesitation. He pulled the trigger. Luke shut his eyes against the carnage, but he could hear the way Garrett's body hit the floor. Could smell the way his bowels let loose.

"That's your second warning," Landis told Luke. "Third bullet's for you."

A rush of emotion flooded through Luke. Fury at Garrett. Fear of Landis and Rosenblatt. Hope that he could worm his way out of this like he always did. "Look, I'm not sure what Reagan wants, but I promise you, I can—"

"*Mr.* Reagan wants what he's always wanted. For you to do your job."

"What do you think—"

Landis pistol-whipped him across the face. Luke heard a crack somewhere along his jaw and pain radiated upward, but he could still move it. Could still talk. Not that he was interested in risking a second beating.

Rosenblatt pulled Luke to his feet, then shoved him backward into the chair Garrett had occupied. Landis pulled a length of rope from his pocket and tied Luke's arms behind his back. The fibers cut into his wrists, but he couldn't help struggling against them. Unfortunately, Landis knew what he was doing. It would take a while to loosen them.

"Right," Landis said, stepping back to survey his work. "Let's try this again. Think you can tell the truth this time?"

"What do you think I've bee—"

Rosenblatt punched him in the eye, sending white light streaking through his vision. Luke's head snapped back, and his neck cracked, though it didn't feel like anything had been broken or fractured. This time, at least.

"That was a yes or no question," Landis said. "Let's try again. Do you think you can tell me the truth this time?"

Luke ground out the word. "Yes."

"Good dog," Landis sneered. "Next question. Did you really think you could get away with stealing from Mr. Reagan without him finding out?"

Luke's heart was pounding. This could be it for him. "I'm not. I swear, I wouldn't—"

Rosenblatt hit him again. This time, it was in the nose. Something crunched, and Luke could feel blood pouring down his face and down his throat, choking him. The fear and adrenaline in his bloodstream kept him from experiencing the true extent of the pain.

"Wrong. You're not as smart as you think you are. Mr. Reagan has eyes everywhere. People more loyal to him than to you, no matter how you try to line their pockets."

Luke bit back a curse. Fucking Garrett. And maybe others. Luke had done his best to cover his tracks, to pay off the people who might have a line back to Reagan. He'd been careful. Smart. Cautious, even. But it hadn't been enough.

"Mr. Reagan accepts the type of people he does business with. He knew what he was getting into when he struck a deal with you, Mr. Salazar." Landis polished his gun with the edge of his sleeve, enjoying the theatrics of this interaction. "He knew you couldn't resist taking a little from the top. It was part of the plan. What wasn't part of the plan, however, was stepping in on his territory. Did you really think he wouldn't notice?"

Luke was at a loss for words. They had him cornered. Pinned to the wall like a specimen, they were waiting to open up and dissect. He had known the risks all along, but part of him had believed he could get away with it. And if he hadn't been able to, he at least thought he could cut and run.

Rosenblatt reared back again, and Luke turned his head in time to catch the punch on his cheek rather than his eye socket. Pain radiated from the impact, but he'd narrowly avoided having his orbital bone ruptured. Silver linings.

Landis leaned in. "That was a question."

Luke had a limited number of options. If he denied it, there was a good chance Landis would blow his brains out. Neither he nor his partner had shown great restraint or patience, and Luke would be an idiot to think they'd start now.

He could admit to everything, but would Reagan show him mercy or kill him outright? There was less chance of death if he went this route, but the point still stood—Landis and Rosenblatt were hired guns. Reagan wouldn't have sent them out here unless they could clean up the mess Luke had made. And that began with pulling the thorn out of Reagan's side.

There was a third option, and though Luke had no idea if it would work, it gave him more than a slim chance of ending his night digging his own grave—if Landis would even give him that courtesy.

"I didn't want to," Luke said. The emotion in his voice was real, even if his words were a lie. "He made me. I didn't know what else to do."

That made Landis pause, at least. "Who made you?"

"Logan. Riley Logan. Big son of a bitch. He's been wreaking havoc all around town. Doesn't have a subtle bone in his body."

Landis and Rosenblatt exchanged a look, and that's how Luke knew he had them.

"He's the one that burned down the farmhouse," Luke said. "He's the one that set up the lab."

Landis looked down his nose at Luke. There was doubt in his eyes. But curiosity too. "What do you know about him?"

"Not much." Luke flinched when Rosenblatt shifted his weight. "But I know what his plans are tonight."

46

WHEN BEAR HAD CALLED LUKE, HE'D KNOWN THE OTHER MAN WOULDN'T
play by the rules. He'd gather as many of his men as he could, then attack
Bear the first chance he got. It'd be difficult for Bear to hide his plans as he
amassed his own army of farmers and shop owners, and so he didn't
bother being subtle about it. Sooner or later, Luke would show up.
Perhaps under the guise of darkness. If that was the case, they had a few
hours left to get their shit together.

Cindy had elected to stay at home with the boys, but she'd done her
part by calling at least a dozen people to Rhonda's house. Rhonda hadn't
been too happy that Bear had volunteered her place. At least until Bear
reminded her, Amos had a broken arm and had lost his house because of
her actions. She'd quieted down after that.

Bette and Sal showed up with sandwiches for everyone, and Locke
promised them all a beer on the house if they got through this unscathed.
Rhonda gathered farming equipment for weapons, and those who knew
how to shoot, which was most everyone in a place like this, had brought
their own guns. The objective wasn't to kill anyone, but to defend themselves. Bear had warned that Luke and his men would be armed. They'd
be shooting to kill.

There were a few others that Bear hadn't met, like the bookshop owner Mandy had met a few days ago. Introductions were made, names and handshakes exchanged. But they weren't there to be friends. They were there to finally stop Luke's reign of terror.

Joyce wasn't exactly a fighter, and once she found out about Amos' broken arm, she'd driven to the hospital to make sure he was well taken care of. While there, it seemed she'd informed the old farmer of Bear's plans.

Amos had few words for Bear given his current state, but they were full of encouragement. "Wish I could be there," he said. "Give 'em hell for me."

Bear promised he would. He apologized for the bullet holes in Amos' truck, too. The old farmer didn't seem concerned, but Bear made a mental note to pay the man back with interest. He'd been good to Bear and Mandy, had stood up for them when no one else had. The least Bear could do was leave him with a little something before they skipped town.

Mandy glanced up at Bear, looking the oldest she ever had. "What are you thinking about?"

"Wondering how we always get mixed up in this stuff," Bear said. "Is it me? Is it bad karma?"

"Karma isn't good or bad. It just is." Mandy turned back to the window. They were keeping watch out of the attic, hoping to spot Luke's approach. It was dark now, and clouds had obscured the moonlight. It'd be tough, but they had a good vantage point. "I actually think it's a good thing."

"How do you figure?"

Mandy shrugged, but Bear could tell she'd been thinking about this. "You're always there for those in trouble. Sure, sometimes you get shot at. But you've helped a lot more people than you've hurt."

"Huh." Bear couldn't argue with that logic, even though he would prefer to avoid getting shot at. "Maybe you've got a point there."

"You should definitely listen to me more often. I'm pretty smart."

Bear ruffled her hair. "Yeah, you are."

Mandy started tapping her fingers on the windowsill in a clear pattern. "Are you scared?"

"Concerned. Want to make sure everyone gets out of this unscathed." He pointed to her fingers. "What's that about?"

Mandy blushed, but she didn't stop. "Calms me down."

Bear let it go. He'd noticed the way she sometimes counted when she was under duress, but he had no experience dealing with someone who had OCD. Or compulsive tendencies, rather. Then again, he hadn't been around many kids who'd been through as much as Mandy had. Maybe it was time to see a doctor. She'd love that.

Mandy stood rigid against the window. She stopped tapping. "I see movement. No headlights. Three cars. No." She leaned closer. "Four. Two coming from the East, two from the West."

"Maybe fifteen or so guys, then." Bear moved her away from the window. It was dark up here, but he wasn't going to chance them shooting and hoping to hit someone. "About what we expected."

"Unless there's more on the other side," Mandy said. She resumed tapping.

"Prepare for the worst—"

"Hope for the best."

Bear kissed the top of her head. "Don't come down unless you have to. Keep calling out directions if you see anyone sneaking up on us. Stay low. If they start shooting at you, lay flat."

"I got it, Dad." Mandy looked up at him, the wise look in her eyes still firmly in place. It stood out in contrast to the innocence of her face. "Don't worry about me."

"It'll be a cold day in hell when that happens," he said, and against his better judgment, he descended the stairs.

The rest of the group was spread throughout the house, watching the front and the back. Those who had guns stood by the windows, and those who didn't were still preparing. At Bear's request, Rhonda had pulled out all of her cleaning supplies and a few specific household items, and he'd taught them how to make a couple of crude bombs. No one said it out loud, but they hoped the bombs would scare their enemies away more than they'd hurt them. After all, Luke's men lived in this town, too. Some of the people in Rhonda's house knew the others by name. Had sat next to them in church. Had invited them over for dinner, visited with them at the grocery store.

Madge from the bookshop was organizing their supplies. She'd known more than Bear expected and took to making the bombs quickly. The woman had chalked it up to reading a lot and watching plenty of television. Said 24 had been her favorite show ever. Maybe that was true, or maybe there was more to her than met the eye. She wouldn't be the only one in this town.

Iris stood by the front windows, crouched with her weapon at the ready. Bear hadn't figured out what her deal was yet, but she fought like someone who'd had training. He believed her story about coming to Boonesville for her cousin, but Mandy had filled him in on what she'd said about Mr. Reagan. If she wasn't in law enforcement, she had connections to someone who was. It made Bear want to distance himself from her, but he forced himself to walk over to her station. Soon enough, they'd be leaving, and whoever she was wouldn't matter.

Iris looked up when he approached. "You good?"

"Yeah. You?"

"Itching to get out there."

"They're on their way," Bear announced to the room. Everyone stood a little straighter at the news. "Be on guard. Let's minimalize causalities on both sides, but remember—if it's me or them, I'm choosing me. I suggest you all do the same."

"Great pep talk," Iris said, but there was no bite to her words. "You got a plan?"

"You know the plan."

"You seem like the kind of guy who has a plan within a plan. So, what is it?"

Bear chuckled. He might not have trusted her, but he had to admit, he kind of liked Iris. "I'm going for Luke. Tired of chasing him around town. Hope he'll go down without a fight, but I know better. You?"

"Reagan's men. I want answers." There was a glint in her eyes, and Bear could tell Iris didn't like the idea of giving up her chance to punch Luke in the face. "Make sure Luke regrets it."

Bear grinned. "I will."

47

BEAR HAD ANTICIPATED LUKE TRYING TO DO TO RHONDA'S HOUSE WHAT he'd done to Amos' and had several people on standby with buckets of water and fire extinguishers. Her house had storm cellar doors leading from the outside into the basement and up through the rest of the house. They could've locked them, but Bear had wanted to gain the element of surprise by catching that first line off guard. It would also give him a chance to sneak out of the house unnoticed.

As soon as the cellar doors opened, Bear dragged the first man down the steps and left him for Locke to take care of. The bartender had been more than happy to lend a hand and had told Bear he had a military background.

Two more men stood outside the doors, and Bear was on them in seconds. The first went down hard and fast while the second tried to take off into the cornfields. Bear's eyes had already adjusted to the night sky, so he could see well enough to catch the runaway and tackle him to the ground.

"Where's Luke," Bear growled into the man's ear.

The guy didn't even bother putting up a fight. "At the truck! At the truck. Please—"

Bear's punch silenced him. The man wouldn't be out for long, but he clearly wasn't a threat. He didn't want to be here at all. How many of Luke's men felt the same way? Was Luke blackmailing them, too? Maybe this fight would be over before it began.

Bear left Locke to deal with the two guys while he sprinted into the cornfield and veered to the right. He wondered if Mandy could see him right now. Was anyone coming for him? His phone was silenced in his pocket. He didn't risk pulling it out to check for messages. The light would be bright enough for anyone in the vicinity to notice his approach.

Bear came out the other side of the field at least a dozen yards from where two of the trucks were parked. Sure enough, Luke was arguing there with one of Reagan's goons, the bald one. Bear could hear them.

"I don't know how I can make this any clearer to you, Landis," Luke snarled. "Logan's the one running the operation. He's the one you want, not me."

Bear stood up a little straighter. So that was Luke's play. He was using Reagan's goons to take out Bear and the other townspeople. Bonus points if the goons died in the process. Then Luke could report back to Reagan, tell him Bear was out of the picture and everything could return to normal. Luke would still get his shipments, and he could still run his own business with his boss, none the wiser.

Bear couldn't have that, now, could he?

Stepping from the shadows, Bear cleared his throat and watched as the two men spun around to face him. "Hey fellas." Bear gave a little wave. "I hear this guy is slandering my name. I'd like to make a few corrections."

Luke apparently didn't want to give Bear the chance to clear his name. He pulled Landis's own pistol from the small of his back, lifted his arm, and shot Landis in the temple. Before the body even hit the ground, Luke was turning on Bear, taking aim, and pulling the trigger.

As soon as Luke aimed at Landis, Bear launched himself back into the field. If Luke went looking for him, he wouldn't be hard to find. Bear heard the engine of one of the trucks, roar to life. Then the tires peeled out on the gravel, and Luke sped away.

Bear wouldn't let him get far. Running over to the second truck, he hauled open the door and slipped into the front seat. When he reached for the ignition, he noticed the key was missing. Swearing, he searched the visor, the center console, even under the seat. Nothing.

Inspiration hit him. Landis. There was a fifty-fifty chance it was his truck. Hot-wiring it would be more time-consuming and less reliable. He could do it, but every second that ticked by meant Luke might slip from his grasp.

Reaching the body, Bear patted the man's pants pockets and found the fob in the left one. He bit back his cheer and sprinted to the truck. Revving the engine, Bear spun out in the same direction as Luke, pulling the seatbelt over his chest with one hand.

Luke had kept his headlights off, but Bear could still see the man's brake lights every so often. When Luke crested a hill and disappeared down the other side, Bear slammed his foot on the gas, pushing the truck far and fast.

There was no telling where Luke was headed, and Bear could come up with half a dozen possibilities off the top of his head. His first instinct was that Luke would try fleeing town and starting over elsewhere, but they weren't heading for the highway. Bear recognized this road even in the dark.

Garrett's farm came into view as Bear crested the next hill. Luke was already pulling into the driveway and jumping out a split-second after throwing the truck into park. He stumbled a little, then regained his footing, not bothering to shut the door behind him. A few seconds later, Luke ran into the barn.

Bear had two options. He could sneak up on Luke, catch him off guard, and overpower him. Woodard was just a phone call away, and after seeing what was in the barn and Luke's house, it wouldn't be hard to put two and two together. After that, it would just be a matter of rounding up the rest of Luke's men.

But that wasn't the option Bear was interested in. It had been a long, few days that had begun with Luke. It would end with him, too. Bear pulled into the driveway, not bothering to conceal his approach, skidding to a stop behind Luke's truck, blocking him in. It wouldn't be impossible to get out from his spot, but it would slow him down.

Bear waited a few seconds to see if Luke would emerge from the barn.

The only reason he was here would be to save some of the equipment. He might have thought his house was compromised, but with everyone distracted at Rhonda's, it was a good time to take what product he could, load up the truck, and head to the city. It'd be easier to disappear from there.

Bear ran at an angle toward the barn, hitting the outside wall and creeping along it until he came up to the door. He pulled out his gun and stopped long enough to listen to the sound of moving boxes and shuffling feet. The sound of bottles crashing to the ground and Luke cursing was enough to signal to Bear that he could slip into the barn without Luke knowing.

The inside of the barn looked the same as when Bear saw it last. It was unlikely Garrett still used it for more than storage at this point. The air was stuffy and most of the equipment and debris from the last time he was there was unmoved.

The door to the secret room was open, and as Bear watched, he saw a bottle fly across the room. It was empty, but the sound of glass smashing echoed around the building. Luke was tearing through the room for something.

Keeping his gun at the ready, Bear crept up to the door. He expected Luke's back to be turned, but the guy's head snapped up. He held a box under one arm and another bottle in his free hand. They stared at each other for the span of three seconds.

Then Luke threw the bottle at Bear's head.

Not knowing what was inside and whether it could hurt him, Bear spun away from the door and dodged the glass by a millimeter. It smashed to the ground, and yellow liquid erupted. The smell of ammonia intensified. Bear had just enough time to recover and face the door again before Luke threw a second bottle at him. Bear dodged again, and when he faced Luke for a third time, the other man had a gun trained on him.

"Don't move," Luke said. "Or I swear to God, I will end you."

Bear hesitated, but he didn't have many options. He'd lost his gun while dodging the bottles. "Is this what you wanted? All this destruction? All this death?"

Luke sneered at him. "Of course not. In my perfect world, you would've left town the day you got here, and I'd be running my business right under everyone's noses."

"You've hurt a lot of people, Luke."

"It's not like they ever did me any favors."

"What about your brother?" Bear asked. "What'd he ever do to you?"

Luke's face became a mask of fury. He stepped forward and jabbed his gun into the air, punctuating each word. "You don't know me. You don't know what I've been through."

"This is your last chance. Give it up. You can get help. Jake can still have a family."

The fury evaporated from Luke's face as quickly as it had arrived. "It's too late for me. This is all I've got."

"That's not true." Bear might not sympathize with Luke, but he was still young. Bear had seen plenty of people turn their lives around. It was never too late. "You've got plenty of time."

"More time than you, at least."

Bear saw the shift. Luke moved his gun and pointed at center mass. Bear didn't give him a chance to find his target. He dove to the side and rolled behind an unhitched tractor bucket. A shot rang out, whizzing past Bear and hitting the other side of the barn. A horrible feeling came over him. If Luke hit the bucket at the right angle, the bullet would ricochet. And if hit the lab behind him—Luke pulled the trigger again, the second shot hitting the ground where Bear had stood moments before. He wanted to tell Luke to stop and think about what he was doing, that it wasn't worth it, that he was going to get himself killed.

But then he pulled the trigger a third time. The rest of Bear's thoughts were drowned out by the explosion.

48

BEAR PACKED A RENTAL CAR FULL OF HIS AND MANDY'S BELONGINGS. NOT that there were many. A couple of bags, a cooler full of food from Amos, and a handful of books that Madge had gifted to Mandy, including her copy of *A Wrinkle in Time*. They'd keep her busy on the way to their next destination.

Where that was, Bear wasn't sure.

Sheriff Woodard had come to see him off. The man stepped up to Bear and reached out a hand. Bear shook it, surprised and grateful.

"I know you had a rough go of it here," Woodard said, "but if you ever find yourself around these parts again, you're welcome to stay whenever you like."

"Appreciate that," Bear said. "As long as you don't get any more urges to arrest me."

"Can't make any promises." Woodard winked, and it was good to see the man with a little levity on his face. "Grateful for what you've done for these people. For the town. You're a good man, Riley Logan."

Bear nodded his thanks, at a loss for words. After Luke's death, Woodard showed up and took control of the situation. Other than Landis, no one else had died. Luke's men hadn't been all that interested in waging an all-out war. They'd done their best to take over the house, but the town of Boonesville stepped up to the plate. You tend to reevaluate your life choices when you find yourself at the wrong end of a shotgun.

The sheriff and his deputies arrested Luke's men, and Bear's instinct had been right—many of them turned on each other, offering information for a get-out-of-jail-free card. Woodard had yet to decide if he would take anyone up on their offer, but those guys weren't exactly missed as they sat in the local jail, awaiting the verdict.

Woodard had wiped the slate clean with Bear. After talking to everyone and learning what lengths Bear had gone to in order to protect them, the sheriff couldn't in good conscience hold anything against him. Woodard made it clear he didn't approve of Bear's tactics, but there was only so much he could do.

Besides, Luke was out of the picture, and the rest of the town could get back to normal. Whatever blackmail Luke had held over their heads had died along with him.

The sheriff retreated when Iris approached, and Bear couldn't help but size her up one more time. He'd asked her who she really was, and she'd leveled him with a look that told him it wasn't worth asking a second time. But since Luke's death, she'd been more subdued, less quick to anger. Bear thought maybe this was the real Iris Duvall. Whoever that was.

"Heading out?" she asked, though she knew his answer.

"Yeah, just saying goodbyes." He looked over to Mandy, who was rubbing Daisy's stomach and laughing as the dog's tongue lolled out of her mouth. "Where are you gonna go now?"

"Not sure. Still have work to do."

Bear couldn't help himself. "What kind of work?"

Iris smiled. "Rosenblatt was a tough nut to crack, but I got one thing out of him before Woodard hauled him off."

This was news to Bear. "About Reagan?"

A look of concern washed over her face. "He knows who I am. Rosenblatt said Reagan would be in touch."

"That doesn't bode well."

"Exactly what I was thinking. But that wasn't the strange part."

Bear stayed silent. She'd tell him if she wanted to.

Iris looked up at him with wide eyes. "He told me I already know Reagan's real identity."

Bear felt as though an iron fist slammed into his gut, but he wasn't exactly sure why, and he couldn't escape the illogical feeling that he knew Reagan, too. "What are you going to do about it?"

She shrugged, her face all hard angles. "Find him. Simple as that."

Bear chuckled. "Yeah, simple."

"It'd be simpler if I had you at my back."

Bear raised an eyebrow. "That an invitation?"

"So, what if it is?"

Bear caught sight of Mandy standing and hugging Amos around the waist. "Back in the day, I'd already be gone looking for this guy. Someone needs to knock him down a peg or two."

"But not you," Iris said. "Not anymore."

"Not me," he agreed. "Not anymore. I've got *priorities*."

Mandy wandered over and hooked an arm around Bear's waist. She looked Iris up and down. There was no anger there, but there was more distrust than before. "You off to save the world?"

"One corner of it, at least," Iris said. "Trying to get your dad to come along for the ride."

Mandy looked up at him. "And you said no?"

"We're heading the other way."

"You don't even know where I'm going," Iris said, but there was laughter in her words.

"Maybe our paths will cross again," Bear said.

"Maybe." Iris twisted her lips in thought, chewing on the inside of her cheek. Then she pulled out a card from her back pocket and pressed it into Bear's hand. "If you change your mind, or ever need a favor, give me a call." She looked down at Mandy. "I'm sorry about all of this. But it was great getting to know you. Thank you for being so brave."

Mandy stood a little taller, and her cheeks turned pink. "You're welcome. See you around."

"I hope so," Iris said, a sad smile on her face.

Bear watched her walk back into Amos' house. She was helping him load up as many of his belongings as he could salvage so he could move in with Joyce until his house was livable again. Bear only looked down at the card in his hand when Iris had closed the door behind her. "Iris Duvall," Bear read aloud. "Federal Agent. Well, I'll be damned."

Amos walked up to Bear with a sheepish look on his face. "Sorry I didn't tell you, son. She wanted to keep it a secret."

"You got any idea who Mr. Reagan is and what he might be up to?"

"I don't. And I'm not sure I want to." Amos stuck out his hand, and Bear grasped it in a firm shake. "I know your time here has had its ups and downs, but I'm mighty grateful you got sent our way. Don't know what would've happened without you. Someone upstairs must be lookin' out for me."

Mandy jabbed Bear in his side with her elbow. "Karma."

Bear shook his head. "Sorry for the trouble I caused."

"Wasn't your fault. That's on Luke."

"Still. Wish things had been different."

Amos looked over his shoulder at the brand-new truck sitting in his driveway. Bear had gifted it to him since he'd totaled the last one. It sat next to the old truck that Bear had left at Garrett's. He'd had those tires replaced, too. Not to mention the check he'd mailed out that Amos had no idea about. It'd help cover the damage to his house and put his granddaughter through college.

When the old man turned back to Bear, his eyes were soft. "If things had been different, we might not be standing here now. You gave me my life back."

Bear was caught up in the emotion of the moment. When he found his voice again, he said, "You stay safe, old man. Heal fast. Don't push yourself."

"You sound like my daughter." Amos looked down at Mandy. "Keep an eye on him, will you?"

"Always," she said.

With that, Amos turned on his heel and followed Iris into the house. Bear and Mandy climbed into their car and turned it around in the driveway, watching all the familiar buildings of Main Street pass by in a blur. Before they knew it, they were on the highway, and the two of them had put Boonesville in their rearview mirror.

49

I̲ris̲ D̲uvall̲ ̲walked̲ ̲into̲ ̲the̲ ̲nondescript̲ ̲meeting̲ ̲room̲ ̲dressed̲ ̲in̲ ̲a̲ white button-down shirt, and navy slacks. Her hair was pulled back into a ponytail, and she'd kept her makeup clean and subtle. There was no doubt in her mind she was about to get chewed out, and she wanted to look as professional as possible. No reason to give them something else to latch on to.

Two minutes later, Richard Peake entered the room. Tall and fit, classically handsome, there was a bit of stubble on his face, and she could smell his cologne. Expensive.

Closing the door behind him, Peake stood at the head of the table opposite her. It could seat ten, but they were the only ones in there today. Why had he chosen a room so large? Maybe to intimidate her. Or maybe he'd wanted maximum distance between them.

"Agent Duvall," the man said, by way of greeting.

"Agent Peake," she said, imitating his formality.

He sighed. "Iris." It sounded like he'd already admitted defeat. With his thumb and forefinger, he pinched the bridge of his nose. Looked like he was in genuine pain. "What were you thinking?"

"Just doing my job, sir." She didn't let the formality in her voice go. It was for the best.

"You ignored direct orders."

"With all due respect, those orders were wrong, and you know it."

"You made this personal."

Iris tried to keep the emotion out of her voice and failed. "*He* made this personal."

Peake moved around the table and pulled out the chair next to her. Sat down. The look on his face wasn't quite pity, but she hated it all the same. "I'm sorry about Lily," he said. "Truly."

"Thank you." Iris kept her spine rigid, but her stomach churned.

"You know we can't let this go. *They* won't let this go."

She winced. "How bad?"

He shrugged. "A slap on the wrist. Desk duty for a couple months. I can probably get it down to one or two weeks. Some people wanted to see you get more time, but you've still got a couple friends around here."

Iris knew he was talking about himself. "Thank you," she said again, this time softer.

"But you're off the case."

Iris blanched. How could he do this to her? He knew how much time she'd put into this. How much she'd risked getting closer to Mr. Reagan's identity. Then, hearing that she already knows him, she couldn't give up now. "You can't—"

"I can't," he said, "but *they* can."

Something in his voice clued her in on the bigger picture. What she'd learned was the ace up her sleeve. And it wasn't time to play the card. "You found something on Mr. Reagan?"

"We found something better."

"What could be better?"

Peake slapped a picture down in front of her. It was the man she'd met in Indiana. Riley Logan. Only it looked like this had been taken a decade ago. Picking it up, she studied his face, looking into his eyes. They were darker than she remembered. More haunted. Maybe time and having something to live for did that to a person.

"Logan?" she asked, looking up at Peake. Ice filled her veins. Was *he* Reagan? "What about him? He's a nobody."

"He's far from a nobody. Come on." Peake looked at her in disbelief. "You've got better instincts than most. You're telling me you didn't think something was off about the guy?"

Iris had known there was more than met the eye with Riley Logan, but she didn't think something was *off*. He'd seemed like a devoted father and a loyal friend. Hell, he'd fought for a town full of people he'd just met and asked for nothing in return. Whoever he'd been to get on the Agency's radar back in the day, he seemed like a different person now.

"Who is he?" she asked.

Peake slipped the photo out of her grasp and put it back in his folder. "No one you need to concern yourself about."

"But—"

"It's above your paygrade." His tone left no room for argument. "I just wanted to say thank you for finding him. I mean, what are the chances?"

"Is he dangerous?"

"Very. But don't worry, we'll take care of him. You just have to lay low for now."

Iris knew what *taking care* of him meant. If she hadn't fought alongside the guy, maybe she would've been able to let it go. If she hadn't met his daughter and begun to care for her, maybe she could've forgotten him. But she was well past that point now.

One thing Iris Duvall didn't do was ignore her gut.

And she was terrible at lying low.

BEAR & MANDY'S story continues *Over the Edge*, coming in 2023. Click the link below to preorder now:
https://www.amazon.com/dp/B0BNQTQMYD

JOIN the LT Ryan reader family & receive a free copy of the Jack Noble story, *The Recruit*. Click the link below to get started:
https://ltryan.com/jack-noble-newsletter-signup-1

ALSO BY L.T. RYAN

Find All of L.T. Ryan's Books on Amazon Today!

The Jack Noble Series

The Recruit (free)

The First Deception (Prequel 1)

Noble Beginnings

A Deadly Distance

Ripple Effect (Bear Logan)

Thin Line

Noble Intentions

When Dead in Greece

Noble Retribution

Noble Betrayal

Never Go Home

Beyond Betrayal (Clarissa Abbot)

Tsunami

Fastrope (Coming Soon)

Mitch Tanner Series

The Depth of Darkness

Into The Darkness

Deliver Us From Darkness

Cassie Quinn Series

Path of Bones

Whisper of Bones

Symphony of Bones

Etched in Shadow

Concealed in Shadow

Betrayed in Shadow

Born from Ashes

Blake Brier Series

Unmasked

Unleashed

Uncharted

Drawpoint

Contrail

Detachment

Clear (Coming Soon)

Dalton Savage Series

Savage Grounds

Scorched Earth

Cold Sky (Coming Soon)

ABOUT THE AUTHOR

L.T. Ryan is a *USA Today* and international bestselling author. The new age of publishing offered L.T. the opportunity to blend his passions for creating, marketing, and technology to reach audiences with his popular Jack Noble series.

Living in central Virginia with his wife, the youngest of his three daughters, and their three dogs, L.T. enjoys staring out his window at the trees and mountains while he should be writing, as well as reading, hiking, running, and playing with gadgets. See what he's up to at http://ltryan.com.

Social Medial Links:

- Facebook (L.T. Ryan): https://www.facebook.com/LTRyanAuthor

- Facebook (Jack Noble Page): https://www.facebook.com/JackNobleBooks/

- Twitter: https://twitter.com/LTRyanWrites

- Goodreads: http://www.goodreads.com/author/show/6151659.L_T_Ryan

Made in the USA
Middletown, DE
03 July 2023

34550156R00156